THE IDLE HILL OF SUMMER

Julia Hamilton is thirty-one and lives in London with her two daughters, aged six and four. She has worked in publishing and is at present at work on her second novel. She is the daughter of Lord Belhaven and Stenton and was brought up in Scotland. The main character in *The Idle Hill of Summer*, Gerard Baillie, is based on her great-grandfather's first cousin who was killed during the defence of Amiens on Easter Day 1918. His war diaries were published by John Murray in 1924.

D0721872

JULIA HAMILTON

THE IDLE HILL OF SUMMER

Flamingo
Published by Fontana Paperbacks

First published by William Collins Sons & Co. Ltd 1988
First issued by Fontana Paperbacks 1989

Flamingo is an imprint of Fontana Paperbacks,
part of the Collins Publishing Group,
8 Grafton Street, London W1X 3LA

Copyright © Julia Hamilton 1988

Printed and bound in Great Britain by
William Collins Sons & Co. Ltd, Glasgow

For my brother, the Master of Belhaven, and in particular memory of Ralph Gerard Alexander Hamilton (1883–1918), another Master of Belhaven, who lies in the Catholic cemetery at the village of Rouvrel on the Somme.

With grateful thanks to Toby Buchan.

Amarae morti ne tradas nos
Do not deliver us to bitter death

On the idle hill of summer,
Sleepy with the flow of streams,
Far I hear the steady drummer
Drumming like a noise in dreams.

Far and near and low and louder
On the roads of earth go by
Dear to friends and food for powder
Soldiers marching, all to die.

East and West on fields forgotten
Bleach the bones of comrades slain,
Lovely lads and dead and rotten:
None that go return again.

A. E. Housman, *from* 'A Shropshire Lad'

Prologue

Gerard sat on in the dining-room after they had all gone to bed. Once or twice the butler put his head round the door, looking for a sign, wanting to clear away the glasses and tidy the dishes of sugared almonds and marrons glacés onto the sideboard, to get at the crumbs and ash on the table with his little dustpan and brush. The third time he appeared Gerard told him to go to bed, leave it. He would deal with Lady Baillie in the morning or get up early and do it himself, if necessary, although surely, surely, there was a housemaid who would have survived Hogmanay and be on duty?

But he wanted to be left alone in amongst the candles and the smell of his father's cigar smoke, the crumpled table-napkins, the decanters of wine and brandy and port. It was his last night and he wanted nothing disturbed, wanted to cross the bridge into the New Year on his own, slowly, sombrely, wanted to remember the dead: his friend Mahoney, killed in the beginnings of the battle at Ypres, whom he had knelt beside in a dirty cottage kitchen at Zonnebeke, until the blood had come out of his mouth and it was over. Mahoney, who came to him at night in his dreams.

He did not want to be hurried into 1915 and have the old year with its vital memories made all at once into history, Mahoney's death a statistic, his own struggles forgotten, but it was only possible to do this alone. In the company of others, even such company as it had been this evening – his wife Alice, his parents Lord and Lady

Baillie, Alex, a young cousin who was more like a brother to him – he had found the old year going slack in his hands, as if from one hour to the next, the hands moving upon the face of the clock, events which lived on in him were rendered lifeless, without efficacy. It was not like that. Hastening into 1915 with champagne, chit-chat about Asquith and his lack of moral fibre, the hope of an offensive somewhere – Flanders or the Eastern Front, it didn't much matter where, but a desire for something decisive, something crushing and final . . . How it made him sigh so . . . this: there could be no hope for any of them in a general way or for himself in particular if the bitter lessons of 1914, that long and single year, were to be forgotten or glossed over. We are our past: it lives in us, speaks through us, makes us act. Of all people he should know that. It was not events, past happenings, that could change, but the lessons drawn from them. There was the medicine, a medicine more like vaccination: too much could kill; not enough and one would still be sick.

And he thought of all the things, the crucial things out of the past year that had made him what he was now, that had brought him home to Scotland, to his family home here at Kildour, to this room, with its portraits of his Baillie ancestors with their plump Kneller faces and white necks, long, tapering hands clutching wraps of ridiculous gauze, the pair of Battonis done in Rome of the brothers Baillie, Alexander and William, one in a red waistcoat, one in a blue, hands clasped over pasta bellies, pleased with themselves and the ruins and the parasol pines.

A long table with candelabra and an epergne, decanters and grape scissors and fruit, all the lush disarray of a good dinner . . . glasses with wine still in them . . . and himself: Gerard Baillie, Capt. The Hon. G. A. Baillie, Master of Kildour, an only son of means, aged twenty-nine, a Catholic convert with a wife who was not, and, shortly, a child to be born. An officer in the artillery who had been wounded and returned home to convalesce. Wounded in hand-to-hand combat, in an incident, a mere fraction of a great battle that had begun to rage at that time; a battle some committee would no doubt later name and date, limiting the horrors and heroism to particular times and places with beginnings, ends, aims ... Whilst those who had been there would make their own histories out of experiences such as his. Little, scrappy, messy actions on the side; a street in an abandoned village, a house with a locked door and a German spy inside with a rifle, waiting, and the guns going hammer and tongs everywhere, shrapnel and bullets; actions which together made up a war and pushed the enemy back. Individual actions, individual incidents...

He leaned forward, clutching the table with both hands ... an incident in which he had killed a man with one straight shot through the heart, a man whose blood he had on his hands, a man he felt he had murdered. He looked at his hands, spreading the fingers on the table top; such good hands, strong and well made.

'Hands,' his mother had said to him once, 'are an infallible sign of a person's breeding.'

'Like horses, you mean?' (He was only ten at the time and had not yet learned how to express himself properly.)

'Well, not quite,' she had answered smilingly, nevertheless putting her tatting down and ringing the bell for the nursery girl.

Breeding or not, it made no difference. War was the great leveller, asking everything, promising nothing in return, rewarding perfect obedience by turning men into scraps of inert matter, handfuls of dust (Christian dust, in his case), collections of bones known only by a dog tag. War whose only proper object was itself. War which had thrown him into confusion of a kind he could never have imagined.

His deliberations about whether there could be such a thing as Just War seemed rather a bad joke now, so much

13

theological dust and ashes. Men liked killing each other and that was that. Men also liked to submit to death, to give themselves up to it, an army of year kings abandoning themselves to the Everlasting Arms, being ploughed into the soil. Of course, the early Church had known this, clever Augustine had known it, sitting at Hippo making up special rules about killing. When is a death not a death but an outburst of sanctified vitality? The answer: when Augustine says so.

But it was too late to turn back now, fifteen hundred years too late. Centuries had overlain the mistake, built gilded bridges of words over the abyss, creating the irresistible myth of the holy warrior, those upholders of Christendom, crusaders who lay in the graveyards and churches of Europe with their swords pressed to their stone bosoms. The men in the gathering mud at Flanders, the inheritors, altogether a less pretty memorial. Men like Mahoney... Too late, it was too late.

Now the primitive urge had become double-headed, wore the meek, downcast face of Duty. A duty indissolubly linked with killing, the sanctified tradition, the breaking of the commandment. But it was not his part to stand aside and, however you looked at it, the Germans had to be removed from foreign soil. There was no doubt about it. The fact that they were there in the first place was an evil, an absolute infringement, that could not now be dealt with in any other way but war – clobbering the swine, as his father would say. Killing as many of them as possible and hoping that when the carnage was over, the force, the blind urge of war could somehow be altered a little so that it became justice, justice in peace.

He sighed, sitting back in his chair, stretching his legs out in front of him, taking his glass into his hand. Did it make it any better knowing all this, attempting to trace the rot and probably muddling it absurdly? There were so many strands, so many different ends to unravel and reweave into an approximation of the truth. Only Alice

14

had some idea of what he was getting at; the rest of them – his father, Edmund, the priest who had come to see him in hospital – appeared to regard his attitude as an embarrassing aberration... 'One who owes a duty of obedience to the giver of the command does not himself "kill" – he is an instrument, a sword in its user's hand. For this reason the commandment forbidding killing was not broken by those who have waged wars on the authority of God...' He had unearthed a copy of *De Civitate Dei*, and puzzled over it. Such confidence! Augustine as divine interpreter, God's mouthpiece.

Sometimes he wondered how he had got himself into this bind, why it should have been his lot to have to quibble with revealed truth. Perhaps Mahoney was right: he was the typical, earnest convert, labouring over the small print, tedious and enquiring. Otherwise it would all have been so easy: 'One who owes a duty of obedience ... does not himself "kill"...' He knew the untruth of that.

Even so, he had chosen to go back. Something in him said this was the right thing to do, to give up to it, let it have its head. Lately, he had become aware of some certainty in himself, a dark circle of calm – words were inadequate for more than the sketchiest of outlines. It was no longer a question of mortality or immortality, more a question of knowledge and peace. This inner wholeness was more noticeable by its absence than its presence, but, even so, it sustained him in a negative sense by its lack, its poverty. He accepted his part, a part that had been ready and waiting for him since before his birth. A small part in a vast drama.

And he had killed a man, removed a life, only then, afterwards, realizing what it meant. Before that he had ranged guns in the artillery, seen men dropping like ninepins in the distance through the lenses of his Zeiss glasses. At a distance death was clean and clinical and detached, but face to face... Face to face one acted. It was quite simple really. Staring past a candle Gerard remembered the sound of blood in his ears, roaring, a sound like the falls at...

Face to face, he thought. I killed him, didn't want to, but I did. Had to. You learn to live with it or you go mad. Alice was right; one had to be prosaic, accepting. You couldn't be redeemed for something you hadn't done. In a sense he had been born with blood on his hands. Turning it round, though, one might imagine that the chap he had shot was probably all right. Sitting at God's right hand. In Paradise.

Paradise now seemed to him the world that had gone out with the summer. Paradise was a wife and some land and time to think. If only, he thought, one could reel in the past like a thread from a spool, if only time could be given back; and he remembered that hot and most beautiful of summers, remembered too the state of tremendous discontent he had been in, knowing even as he did so that the past could be made present by exactly this kind of desire, which was not desire so much as reflection upon a state of suffering – the kind of suffering, however, that made a pattern out of things, lending balance to misfortune.

And yet ... it had been Pascal's 'if'. If not that, then something else. His own folly as random and yet as perfectly mistimed as Princip's bungling: the Archduke dead, pretty, silly Sophie shot by mistake for the Governor of Bosnia and everything that followed. They were all waiting for it, the death of the 'King of Orstria' only a brilliant excuse. Why should life that was so easy have grown so difficult to bear? The moment when the Church should have unmuzzled itself but had not.

There had been indications, he supposed, warnings of a kind: the suffragettes, the frightful Futurist paintings Alice had been taken to see by Pamela, violence on the race course and in the Academy. Ireland's eternal flame. But war had been unthinkable. It was as if everyone had fallen asleep: the world ending and people yawning behind their hands and talking about the weather or

16

Lady Desborough's hat. Should these signs have been recognized as signs of a greater sickness? He did not know, knew nothing, and, anyway, it was too late now.

Tomorrow he would go by car and train from this place to London with Alice, and by another train the following day to the coast, Folkestone or Dover, he couldn't remember which. A boat to France, paddle-steamer, cattle-boat (like the first one). Then he would get up the line somehow, any means would do: a supply tender, a motor ambulance returning; there were plenty of unorthodox methods of finding his way into Ypres. He would spend the night there and go in search of his battery the following morning. All new men, different division, the lot.

Ypres ... how would it be now? The Cloth Hall, the cathedral half smashed, but the market going on, the inhabitants game, full of soldiers going up and down the line, full of wounded. He thought of the hospital where he had been in the Rue de Lille and of how his blighty had healed so mysteriously quickly, so much, in a way, against his wishes, and he thought of Edmund who had come to see him there.

Edmund.

Old friend, oldest friend, neighbour, childhood companion; weak-willed, handsome Edmund, who had taken a fancy to Alice in the summer and had – he might as well say it – an affair with her. An affair that had nearly ended in disaster. Edmund, who always took what he wanted and thought about it afterwards. Edmund, who thought Eros was God and Mars too; he was a pagan, really ... wasn't he? An Alaric of domestic sanctuaries, substituting charm for clemency. Or was he being unfair? Edmund's battalion had nearly been wiped out at Ypres in October and November – 'wearied out', he thought the expression was: how laconic and yet exact a description. Sometimes he felt wearied out himself thinking of it all: the public conflict, the war, and his own private troubles that seemed so mysteriously linked.

Edmund would have fought like hell and thought nothing of it.

He could not judge him.

Gerard took his feet off the table and poured more port. It must be very late although he did not want to look at his watch and think he must go upstairs simply because of the hour. He took a cigarette and lit it from a candle that had burned very low. It was quite silent in this room ... or was it? All at once, like the undamming of a stream, he seemed to hear the sound of so many voices talking out of the old year at him: family voices, his father and mother, Alice, Alex. Edmund. And the others who had not known the part of him that was rooted here, fixed and formed amongst the legends and traditions of this place ... Mahoney and his brother officers, the men at Suffolk, the young subaltern of the Queens whom he had talked to in the hospital at Ypres, rousing himself out of his own desolation to find words for someone at the edge of death, the wounded German farm-boy who had been with him at Ypres station, who had said, 'It is all lies ...' And the voice that had come out of nowhere to him in the Belgian château at the very beginning, with the words 'Made Whole Again'.

He closed his eyes and crossed into 1915.

CHAPTER ONE

Kildour. Kildour as it had always been . . . that last summer; life moving on its unchanging, stately way, the pattern of a hundred summers repeated.

A spare son had gone from there to Waterloo and been killed, going out on a wing and a song; he had been to the Duchess's Ball the night before, youth and beauty, dance and drink, then run for your swords, boys . . . Robert Baillie, that was – or no, perhaps it was John or Gerard, another Gerard. It didn't much matter: there were replacements.

The present Lord Baillie's father had been lost on an expedition searching for the source of the River Niger. A monument to him stood on the back hill, an ugly thing, but imposing, a granite obelisk known locally as Baillie's Cairn; he had left two sons and plenty of money.

Throughout this time there had been absences: the Crimea, someone had been about at the Mutiny, the Second Afghan War. Gerard's father had taken part in the famous march to Kandahar . . . Absences, yes, there had been absences, but the estate had gone on through good Factors and bad, sending its sons to man the colonial wars; peace had reigned there and in Europe (apart from that unfortunate scrap in 1870), and of course one didn't count the Balkans. Peace, long summers of it, reluctant springs, voluptuous autumns, winters . . . well, yes, winters. But there was always the shooting to make up for that.

*

19

It was the hottest summer in living memory. There were rumours of vegetables dug up in the tenants' back-gardens baked to a cinder in their skins. Odd this, a little sinister; but Edmund, whose story it was, only smiled when he heard others retelling it at dinner, and would not confirm or deny its authenticity. It amused him to make people guess, and he had had such a boring summer at Kincraig, his uncle's house that marched with Kildour, with only his aunt and uncle for company, until the season ended and the Baillies, the young Baillies, that is, arrived for the shooting at Kildour.

Edmund had fallen from his horse while with the Regiment at Gibraltar and had managed to injure himself quite badly during the course of a game of polo (perhaps he had been thinking of Hatty Rawdon at the wrong moment) and had been put to bed for the duration. At first he was too ill to care where he was or what became of him; concussion was succeeded by a brain fever of sorts, with accompanying deliriums and rantings, very melo-dramatic, rather in the manner of the best Victorian deathbed scenes. Only, of course, he did not die.

Later, when he was better, he had enjoyed teasing the nurses, demanding to know what he had raved about during the worst of it. One of them let on that he had called out the names of various women: Hetty, she said (Edmund sighed with relief, blessing the misplaced vowel; the CO's wife was game, but it had to be a secret), Cornelia somebody or other, a young thing, delicious, but whom Edmund pretended to know nothing about. The last part of his convalescence, here at Kincraig (which would one day be his), had been unutterably tedious. He missed the routine of the army and the hospital, the companionship and the jokes, and he missed pretty Mrs Rawdon whose ways had suited him so well: her contradictory nature, both passionate and cold, and the way she would withdraw from him after-wards as if he was repugnant to her, this little habit that kept him on fire, kept boredom at bay.

There would be a war, he was pretty sure of that. It was about the only thing that kept him going during the long, slow summer days at Kincraig; days in which he would watch the sun moving round his room in the morning, when it seemed to him a house of emptiness, a house of doors slamming in distant passages, always receding out of earshot, doors slammed by servants made grumpy at having to trail so far upstairs with trays in the unaccustomed heat, wearing their summer livery which smelt of moth. In the afternoons he was allowed onto the terrace to watch his uncle and aunt, Sir John and Lady Kerr, playing a game of croquet in which they both cheated; the clunk of the balls, the odd, strangled cry of the peacocks, the animal sounds from across the ha-ha, muffled by the afternoon haze, seemed to him death knells. At night he slept badly, not surprisingly, and would wake at intervals out of dreams in which consummation was always imminent, never achieved.

Quiet, Dr Farquhar said, extreme quiet, or the blow to the skull might flare up again, but anything, thought Edmund, anything at all would have been better than this.

He would lie in bed those hot mornings, too listless to read anything with attention longer than fifteen or so minutes (he had intended himself for Tolstoy, Thackeray, something improving), his eyes wandering the familiar room, listing its defects: the stain on the ceiling where a bath had overflowed upstairs, the damp by the fireplace, the bald patch in the corner by his bed, where, as a boy, he had systematically picked off one paper rose after another, and he would have in his mind the last item he had read out of the newspaper. By this means he had come to meditate upon a number of subjects that might otherwise have escaped him in Gibraltar. The death of the Habsburg heir had not seemed to him particularly significant; it lingered a day or two, only to be chased off the front pages by the death of Joe Chamberlain, and, of course, there was always Ireland and the frightful suffragettes, but, for all this, he knew enough to sense that Europe was a tinderbox. With the Austrian ultimatum to Serbia, a little excitement began to grow inside him, in spite of disclaimers from the Liberal press. There would be war.

Edmund had been too young for the war in South Africa although he had followed events with interest. Baden-Powell, in particular, had impressed him, hanging on like that at Mafeking. Real bravura there, and coolness; the man was a model of laconic disregard for hazards. And the rest of it ... skirmishing with the enemy against a perfect backdrop of veld and mountain, high, hot skies, and the knowledge, certainty really, of a victory in the end, bitter perhaps, but deserved. In his imagination a European war would be the same, tactically, and a good enemy, more of a challenge than the Boers, but not impossible. It would be a gentleman's war, an extension of the great tradition; above all, it would be something to do. Something to do in a world where, occasionally, it had seemed nothing would ever happen again.

Gerard's letter, received on the day war was declared, broke up his *ennui* a little. The world was edging its way into his bedroom again in major and minor ways, beginning with this: an invitation to the grouse at Kildour.

More and more he had begun to be curious about Gerard as the time drew near for them to meet again. They had not seen each other for five years, nearly one-sixth of their lives, really a very long time indeed. They had been more or less brought up together, after the death of Edmund's parents during a hunting expedition in some remote part of India; the baby (brought to England in the care of an elderly, female missionary) had been hurried back to his father's elder brother, John Kerr of Kincraig, and was brought up as the son of the house. Until the age of eight, he shared a governess with Gerard, going every day over the hill to Kildour, where he was treated as invisible unless Lord Baillie was in need of an object upon which to vent a rage, when Edmund had to share with Gerard the burden of parental displeasure.

At eight years old they were packed off to Temple Grove together, sharing canings and train journeys and the vicissitudes of English winters at Eastbourne where it was sometimes so cold the sea froze. At Eton they were drawn apart slightly by being in different houses, but they still went to and fro together as travelling companions, sharing sleepers and plum cake in the early journeys and later, at sixteen or so, illicit whisky and cigarettes, obtained from the friendly stewards who had been overseeing their travels for years. Then there was Sandhurst, after which Edmund departed for a Scottish regiment and service abroad.

They were companions, members of the same coterie, with a common aim of having as much fun as was humanly possible. The matrix of their friendship had always been, paradoxically, this lack of definition, this unconditional acceptance that although their friendship had been arranged by their families, it had appeared to work extremely well, because there had been no reason why it should do otherwise.

But now, Edmund thought, now things will be different. He felt, with Gerard becoming a Catholic, those shared perceptions of five years ago would have changed. Edmund felt considerable resentment that Gerard should voluntarily have left the old, charmed circle that was still perfectly good enough for him, choosing to become an RC, on account, it was said, of the backwash from a love-affair with a Nina somebody-or-other that had gone wrong. It was different to be born one, but this public flag-waving, this deliberate avowal seemed to him both embarrassing and unnecessary. Gerard's marriage had been acceptable enough: the girl, Alice Murray-Walker, was an only daughter of an insecure earl, Archie Carnegie, who had pot-hunted amongst the excesses and indulgences of the Marlborough House

Set, trying to keep up with men richer, less innocent and more able than he at securing the kingly favours. He had even waited politely until the old king was well in his grave before committing suicide. Some six months after this, Gerard had married Alice. His best man was a peer called O'Hallan, who had been with G. and perhaps still was, in the army. A Catholic, at any rate. It had rankled, however, not even to be asked, nor to receive a letter with his invitation saying sorry or explaining. Edmund had been glad not to go.

His aunt might cheat at croquet but she was not a willing gossip; to find out what was going on over the hill had required some rather tedious courtship in the form of accompanying her while she dead-headed the roses, holding her hat and the kneeling mat and spare secateurs.

'You know, of course, that Gerard has gone over to Rome,' she had said in tones of slight distaste, as if he was the victim of some unsocial but minor disease, 'in defiance of his poor father and mother. There were, I believe, ructions.'

'I can't imagine Lord Baillie liking it.'

'I can't imagine myself liking it,' said Aunt Maud, tartly. 'A most unnecessary step. Kath told me there was a girl who wouldn't have him, so he went off and became a Catholic instead.'

'Extraordinary. Wasn't her name Nina something?'

'Penn.' Aunt Maud straightened up and began to move along to the next bed. 'A fortune in ball-bearings. Now she's married to young William Carnegie and the cat is really amongst the pigeons.'

'So not a wife, but a sister-in-law?'

'Yes, and, furthermore, they'll all be there for the shoot, Kath tells me. She's the one I feel sorry for, really. Gerard and his father do nothing but scrap and the old boy's leg has been playing up again, so they've limited themselves to family and close friends for the twelfth.

Helena and David Few, Alex, Halliday's son, who must be sixteen now or seventeen, I can't remember, the Carnegies and you, staying. Your uncle will go over on the day. Give me the other pair, will you,' she went on, holding out a hand for the extra secateurs.

'What's Alice like?'

'Oh, sweet. Kath loves her. She looks exactly like – '

'Like . . . ?' Edmund watched the secateurs poised over a particularly plump dead-head.

'Darling, it's awfully hot. Don't you think you should go in?' Aunt Maud reached for her hat, avoiding his look.

'Like whom?' Edmund repeated, holding the hat high, out of reach.

'You're making me undignified,' she said, crossly. 'Go in or Farquhar will be after you.'

'Not until you tell me what you were going to say.' Edmund retreated a step, half amused by her fierceness. He put the hat behind his back.

'If you must know . . .' again, the uncharacteristic hesitation, 'she looks just like Kitty. There,' she said, turning back to her roses, 'now you'll be upset and blame me.'

'Kitty, indeed.' She was right. He would rather not have known that, or perhaps it was better to be prepared. Kitty was one of his Norfolk cousins who had fallen off her horse out hunting, banged her head and died. They would have been married some years by now.

'Do you want this?' he said, holding out the hat.

'No, thank you. I think we shall have tea; it must be about time, isn't it?'

'She's a dear girl,' Aunt Maud said as they walked across the lawn towards the house. 'You mustn't mind her being so alike.' Mind? Really, the old were quite dotty sometimes.

'There isn't much I could do about it, is there?'

'Suicide is so selfish,' she said, ignoring his tone. 'I always think they deserve unconsecrated ground.'

'Was he?'

'Of course not. He was an earl. You can't bury the laird outside the wall of the church.' She seemed not to notice the contradiction.

'I don't see why not.'

'Such a bad example. He would go on trying to compete with all those Jewish financiers, Bassoons and what not – '

'Sassoon, you mean.' Edmund waited for her at the top of the steps.

'I shall go and see about tea,' she said, giving him a look. 'For goodness' sake, keep out of the sun, or let me find you a hat.'

'All right.' Edmund went and sat down obediently. 'A hat. Thanks.'

When she was put out she liked to persecute him with small attentions. Go on, he thought, watching her hover, go and be busy. He didn't want her to apologize for mentioning Kitty. That would have been unbearable. Sometimes he wondered if he was still looking for Kitty in some way, bits of her, shards, fragments, in the characters and bodies of other women. Perhaps that was why ... he stared along the hot terrace at the bodies of dogs sleeping like princes in stuffed chairs, listening to his aunt's footsteps crossing the hall floor ... why he liked Hatty so much. She was nothing like Kitty; he knew he would not have to love her and be disappointed. She was calculating and very sexual, very ... Heat was sexual ... He would like no clothes, a dim room, and just some woman. He didn't know what he wanted, really. Activity? Shooting? New acquaintance? Some fun, now he was better, now old Farquhar had given permission for the grouse.

He closed his eyes and leaned into his chair, feeling hot and heavy and unsatisfied. Tomorrow he would go over the hill to Kildour and meet a girl who looked like Kitty. Gerry's wife who looked like Kitty. Gerry's wife ... Gerry. Tomorrow.

Edmund slept.

CHAPTER
TWO

He would motor himself. There had been ructions.

'You aren't well enough,' said his aunt.

'Well enough to shoot,' said his uncle, who was wearing a panama hat and looking somehow extraordinary, crumpled and summery. Frivolous, Edmund thought. The old shouldn't wear white. It is unbecoming.

'I'm perfectly all right.' Edmund climbed in again. They were all shouting.

'I still think ... ' Aunt Maud put a hand on her hat. There was a sort of hot gale coming from the car.

'Goodbye ... ' One hand on the wheel and waving. Glorious machine. Beast with wheels.

Edmund jerked out of sight, spinning up bits of gravel and dust, hearing something over the noise and power of the machine, his uncle's voice: 'Mind the narrow bridge at the burn ... '

And they fuss too, the old. Fuss, fuss, fuss. The bridge had been a cinch ... nearly a cinch; the wall had come at him rather, he had forgotten that curve, the way the wall bulged, but he had come out of it somehow and was off into the beyond, the hill road to Kildour. In a way he would have liked to stop at the burn and look: the water level had been low; hanging over the bridge looking for the handful of coins he had chucked in as a boy, pennies with Vicky's head on them, all ringlets and profile; only it would have been foolish to stop, the fear being that one might never get started again.

The hill road was heaven. He had done it on a bicycle, grinding up the endless hills as a boy, in a carriage, in a trap, on foot, but never like this in a motor car with the skyline flashing and dipping at him, the hot tarmacadam racing away in front and the sheep, silly, old, duchessy sheep in agonies of indecision about which way to turn with Progress bearing down on them.

Slower for the village, gently, gently past the manse, all Calvinistic gloom and heavy lace curtains, even on a day like this, slower still past the Baillie Arms. He was tempted to stop. The 'public hoos' had had a coat of whitewash, he noticed; a pole, more of a broom handle than anything else, hung out of a first-floor window over the entrance with a Union Jack attached to it, limp. Willy Duff and his patriotic duty. The old sot was probably charging extra already. He accelerated as people began to come out of their houses to look at the noise and the occupant of the motor and, although he wanted a drink, he did not want to be recognized and to have to be nice and talk about the war and why he was still here. He didn't look very ill. Medical board would sound to them like a business occupation of some kind, a nonsense, a prevarication.

At the park wall belonging to the house he began, for some reason, to feel nervous, as if he was crossing into another country with the wrong documents. It was a long time since he had been here; the wall looked high and unfriendly and immensely private, the gate-posts with their horses' heads almost insolent. Baillie. Baillie territory. He had, in fact, been in Baillie territory for some time, crossing the march line on the hill road without noticing. One bit of heather was very much like another, and of course the view was the same, up there.

Miles and miles of immaculate drive, the lodge, the kennels, the walled garden, then, at last, the house. Colossal house, ugly house, showing its worst face to visitors just arriving; a purist's nightmare, with the addenda of generations tacked onto a central block: old wing, new wing, tower, battlements. A village of a house.

Edmund brought the car to a halt outside the front steps, crashing the gears, and spraying gravel at a Chinese pheasant which ran away on absurdly elegant legs round the side of the house.

Nobody came out.

He climbed out of the Beast, unbuttoning the long coat his uncle had given him which made him feel like a veterinarian. Goggles he had disdained. Goggles made a chap feel just a little silly, he reckoned, although his uncle wore them, and his aunt. He had watched them going off to lunch the other day like a pair of elderly frogs on an outing. Sweet. And terribly silly.

Leaving his case he went inside. Still no one; a kind of mid-morning abandonment prevailed. He wondered if he was too early, whether they were all still in bed reading their letters and getting marmalade on the newspaper and having baths run for them. He felt like an intruder, a bore. The Man Who Arrived Too Early and Disturbed the Even Tenor of the Household. Was there an even tenor here? The place seemed the same, smelt the same. Where was everybody?

He picked up a copy of *Land and Water* and went and sat down on a sofa. A very ancient whippet in a dog basket by the fireplace opened one yellow eye and looked at him. He began to read an article about an improvement Alec Belhaven was making at Wishaw, the other side of the county. Land drainage or something, sounded rather technical. He knew Alec. Drank too much, but a good fellow, hadn't seen him for ages, of course ...

'Hello ... ' A very pretty girl in a white dress stood at the bottom of the stairs looking at him.

'Hello.' Edmund stood up, glad to be relieved of Alec and his drains.

'Have you been here ages? I thought I heard a motor. The others have all gone to look at something, ruins or a church. But no, it wouldn't be a church in this part of the world, would it? I'm afraid I'm not enough of an aesthete to remember. I'm Nina Carnegie and you must be Edmund. We've heard so much about you from Gerard,' she said, shaking his hand. 'You're rather an *enigma*.'

'I'm not at all sure I like the sound of that.'

'Oh, you mustn't worry . . . '

She had a way of emphasizing certain words which made him feel acutely uncomfortable. Then he remembered ball-bearings. He looked at her as she sat down, trying to find a flaw, some hint of her background: bad hands, short neck, some inelegance, but there was nothing. She was uncommonly pretty and graceful.

'You've been ill, Gerard said.'

'Yes. I had a fall in Gibraltar and wrecked my head. It meant a summer in bed, but I've been let off the hook to shoot, thank God.'

'Will you go back to bed afterwards?'

'No. I shall go to the war. I'm just waiting for red tape to unravel itself.'

'Like Gerard.'

He had a nasty feeling he was walking into a trap of some kind.

'Is Gerry . . . ?'

'You call him that, do you? It used to be my name for him, but of course he doesn't like it any more . . . '

'Oh.' Thin ice, thin ice, he thought; fascinating, but thin all the same. He was not sure he wanted these confidences, yet.

'You will find him very changed.' She looked up at him innocently. 'Do you mind my saying this?'

Edmund said nothing.

'Men are so loyal, but we're both friends of his, old friends. I thought I would fill you in a little, so that – '

'Yes?' The foundation of treachery was politeness. He felt doomed.

' . . . So that you might know what to expect. It would seem so *unfair* otherwise, for you, I mean, coming into a

31

little party like this, not knowing what to expect.'

'I expect to do some shooting,' he said, helplessly.

'My dear, such naivety!' she laughed, and sat back in her chair. 'I can't tell you what it's like here, a household of tensions . . . ' At this point Nina tried but failed to look careworn. 'Everyone brooding over some private sorrow. Gerard is immensely holy and goes about guarding the sacred flame. He argues with his father and isn't awfully nice to Alice most of the time, poor Alice... Of course you know about Archie?'

'Yes.'

'My sainted father-in-law . . . ' She closed her eyes a second, as if unable to contemplate it all. 'In the gun room, can you imagine? Bits of him everywhere. Of course, we're gutting the whole house. Were you ever there?'

'No.'

'It's beautiful. Much more beautiful than this.'

'I don't know it,' he said.

'I forget you haven't met Alice.'

'No.'

He looked at her and thought she was the kind of woman one would have to go to bed with to gain an advantage over. It surprised him to find that in spite of the perfectly enormous eyes, the thick, fair hair, the little *retroussé* nose that lent her profile exactly the right amount of aristocratic imperfection, the nipped waist, the ankles – or perhaps not. He looked. Scotch ankles, one flaw anyway . . . in spite of all this, he was surprised to find he did not want to.

'They're here.' She got up and looked over her shoulder at him, a gesture so winning he felt she must have practised it. 'It's been nice,' she said, 'having you to myself.'

Afterwards. Afterwards he found it was a scene that would keep muddling itself in his mind, the people getting in the wrong order and speaking out of turn. He would see Alex coming in and then remember he had not been there, had not arrived until the next day on the train from Lincolnshire. Snatches of later conversations would keep colouring those first impressions so that it seemed Alice looked as anxious and unhappy as he later knew her to be, and Gerard, who had really been quite brisk and pleased, seemed the Gerard of later on, angry and divided, at odds with everybody.

Sometimes he would have a dream of a dream of himself watching Kitty walk into the hall, risen from the dead out of the churchyard at Gt. Bicester, wondering how it was she had the wrong name and was married to Gerard.

But it had not been like that.

Here is Gerard in flannels and a white shirt with the sleeves rolled up, showing the dark hairs on his arms. Only the top button at his neck is undone. He is a little hot and flustered at not being here to greet Edmund, whom he can see has arrived. He pushes his hair off his forehead with one hand as he goes into the house. One part of him is overjoyed at having his old friend here again; the mere fact of his presence will, he supposes, subtly and without need for words, prove to Nina and to William and to Alice that there is a fun-loving part of him, a part of him that is like Edmund: handsome and at ease, debonair in a faintly self-deprecating way, a little uncaring perhaps, not so needful of approbation. But, at the same time, he knows this will be a false alliance, a kind of treachery to the minuscule but important part of him that is changed, that cannot go back; the part of him that operates most fully when he is alone in a state of half-meditation, half-prayer.

With Edmund's coming he foresees the collision of the old and the new, an encounter in which he does not trust himself to play the diplomat, wanting at the same time to be honest, but painfully aware, too, of his need for an ally at this trickiest of parties. There is no name that he is aware of for the state he is in but he thinks it might approximate to something like the dark night of the flesh, a variety of torture a thousand miles removed from the dark night of the soul, that point of blackness and confusion preceding union.

He hates the thought of Edmund laughing at him, or, worse still, being excessively polite in the way the British are when they think someone is a complete fool.

Mixed in with all this is the ever-present worry about Nina, and why, whenever he thinks of her, he still gets an erection. He cannot think how he should put this to Father Kinahan in language that is at once suitably euphemistic and yet explicit; always this dilemma confession throws him into of wanting to be exactly truthful and yet wanting ... wanting to put himself in a good light: the perfect convert, the man who goes forward without hesitation; the unpleasant feeling he has that he is still one of Ruysbroeck's 'hirelings', a man whose inner life is still the upward stirring exercise of lust, not love.

Behind Gerard comes Alice, dark-haired, pale, wearing a white dress much like Nina's with a broad band of ivory ribbon round her middle and white stockings, pretty kid shoes with buckles, and a hat. The inevitable hat. She is looking up at her brother William, the new earl, who has made a joke, rather a bad one actually, about Kerr's car.

William likes cars. Now he is married to Nina they have two, one each. He can hold his head up again at Coutts Bank in Lombard Street where the new Carnegie wealth is lodged, catalogued on series after series of documents in thick vellum with red ribbons tied round them and sealing wax. He is asked to luncheon by the Manager there; lots of courses in expensive, dark rooms with portraits of eighteenth-century Coots, Burdett Coutts, Money Coutts, Greater Crested ... asked to luncheon and made much of. The Manager's bland but pleased expression says much: You are rich. Ball-bearings will do well now there is a war. You have done everything expected of you. They drink Talbot and Cantenac-Brown and port bottled when Talleyrand was in long clothes. It is a sign of beatitude. Pin-striped Blessing.

Lady Baillie and Lady Few are in another conveyance (they have been sight-seeing), and have stopped at the walled garden to admire the peach trees on the south wall. Lady Baillie is sweating inside her layers of silk and cotton. One suspender has worked loose and is digging into the veined skin of her thigh.

The Fews are her friends, hers and Freddie's. David and Freddie sit side by side in the House together, dozing on the red-buttoned leather benches, coming awake only when there is a Division and most likely not properly even then. They are Lansdowne's men and both dislike Mr Asquith, saying it's only a matter of weeks now before he's bumped upstairs to doze quietly opposite them, away from the filibustering and bad manners of the Other Place. Helena Few is Gerard's godmother, or was. Lady B. understands he has new ones now that the Catholics have got him. She has not enquired who these people are. She sighs.

'Marvellous,' says Lord Few, who has heard the sigh but does not want to think of its implications. 'Really marvellous ... then we have had the weather for them this year ... ' He looks away skywards, fingering his moustache, which is white and important-looking. Perhaps he thinks Gerard should be horse-whipped. He does not like Catholics, thinks of them as insurrectionists. The lower orders, that is. He does not count the recusant aristocracy; there is, after all, a certain glamour attached to having ancestors who were willing to be tortured and hunted down for their religious principles. Gets a fellow into the history books, at any rate. He looks at his watch and then at his wife, who is eating a peach and dribbling juice down her front. He hopes Freddie

35

will be at luncheon. The society of women and the young all morning has tired him.

Lord Baillie is at the Estate Office going over the milk yields for the Home Farm, but onto the page in front of him, in between the columns of figures, comes his son's face; over, or somehow behind the drone of the Factor's voice, he hears Gerard shouting:

'You can't do that. You can't break the entail...'

'I shall write to Butters at D. & W. about it tomorrow.' Bloody boy. He was right, of course.

I am an old man with no weapons left, he thinks, quite enjoying feeling sorry for himself. An old man, past his prime, with a son who has disgraced the family name.

After an interval, he dismisses the Factor and thinks about luncheon. They are a party now. His wife tells him he is obliged to attend. Normally he has his meals and then goes off about his business. He hopes he will have Nina on his other side; Helena Few he is, of course, saddled with. He likes Nina, who allows him to put his hand on her knee. Sometimes he wishes Gerard could have married her, in spite of the fact she's a parvenue; perhaps the girl had the sense not to have him. But she would have stopped this nonsense. Alice is too meek and mild. He wonders how she puts up with all Gerard's carryings-on, the praying and reading out of that infernal breviary. Occasionally he has seen her look at Gerard in a way that is difficult to fathom. And no child either...

'And no child,' said Lady Baillie to Lady Few. They were walking up the drive towards the house with the sun in their faces.

'Well, it can't be the Papist influence there, can it? Children are encouraged. More souls to collar, I suppose.'

Helena thought of her own grandchildren, Ivo and Isobel, and the charming half-hours after tea at Hinton.

36

Ivo in his sailor-suit, so serious and manly at seven, and the heavenly baby...

And no child, thought Edmund at luncheon, sitting next to Alice. Her forearms were a sort of milk-brown. Thin, pretty hands. He felt a kind of unhealthy curiosity in himself to know how things were between her and Gerard. What they said to one another alone, how... She made him feel horribly tender, looking so like Kitty. Hers would be the body he had not known but had imagined. Slender legs and arms, small breasts with brown nipples...

He looked over towards Gerard, wondering what he could be like as a husband to this girl, trying to make out from his expression what he felt about Nina, wishing he knew more about them all before being closeted with G. after lunch, as the plan was, wanting in a treacherous way to know how the land lay before being drawn into one camp or another. He was pleased to see Gerard, but if the household was the battlefield Nina had suggested, then he would like to make his own dispositions, see for himself the truth of things. His conversation with Gerard before lunch had been brief, but not too brief for him to notice that Gerard had taken his support for granted, ear-marking him for a talk before he could fall into the clutches of his parents or one of the others, a need made apparent by the momentary but intense look of irritation on his face as he had come into the hall and seen that Nina had already staked a claim to Edmund.

'Did I miss much?' Nina put her glass down.

'A good view.' Gerard did not look at her. 'But then you don't really like that kind of thing, do you?'

'Oh, I don't know...' She looked at him sideways. It was naughty to tease, but she loved knowing she still had power over him, power to attract, liked seeing him have to struggle against her, even now.

William was a dear, of course, an absolute dear, but

one had to flex one's muscles from time to time, just to make sure the machinery was still in working order. She looked at Edmund and thought he was probably the most attractive man she had ever met: that extraordinary hair, a sort of marmalade colour, the way it parted not quite up the middle, the very blue eyes, most of all the mouth: the mouth was immensely sensual. He likes Alice, she thought, watching them talk, and found this did not please her at all. Alice Mouse.

He likes me. Alice said this to herself with confidence. His interest is unmistakable. I feel he knows me better than is possible in such a short time. I like the way he looks at me as if we were already intimate . . . or is he like this with all women? Nina had seemed rather pleased with herself when they came in. Look at me, she appeared to say, first to meet him, the prize: mysterious Edmund.

He had been very handsome like that in the hall, waiting for them, rising and going to Gerard; the arm round his shoulders was nice. She had liked that particularly, liked to see Gerard pleased too, for a change. Gerard and his darknesses, the anger with his father, the innuendo with Nina, the constant fencing that went on between them that was to do with attraction denied. It had been a mistake, really, to have them, but he had seemed so keen on the idea in London, and with things as they were at the moment it could only be family and close friends. But Nina. Was it that, she wondered, that spoilt things so between herself and Gerard in bed, her not liking it, his turning from her as if she had failed. . .

'. . . bed,' Edmund was saying, 'all summer.'

'Wasn't it dreadfully dull?'

'Nearly unbearable. One broods, rather,' he said, looking at her, wanting, impossibly, to see in her face . . . recognition, a secret sign. Looks should not mean likenesses, the similarity was, must be, the wildest of coincidences, and yet it seemed to him she was in some way what Kitty must have become: modest, intelligent, straightforward. Perhaps it was this that completed his captivation, the way she was without stratagems and pretence; good manners and a certain shyness acted as brakes upon her character, not at all the complicated diet of womanhood he had become used to and grown ... so tired of. He thought of the emotional checks and balances Hatty applied during their short meetings, so that he would come away not only worn out physically but exhausted by the effort of playing her games, of making the right interpretation of a look or gesture. He was not able to be himself with her, but then that had been all the fun of it.

'What did you read?' Alice asked, wondering why he was staring so.

Looks, looks. Was that how Gerard should look at her, but did not? Was this kind of flattery forfeit because she had been rescued? After her father ... she had gone to her mother's eldest sister, Aunt Bundock, a London neighbour of the Baillies', and they met there over teacups in Aunt's dark sitting-room, smelling of dust and whatever it was Ethel cleaned the silver with, when she cleaned the silver, and, very slightly, of old woman, the spaces under the skirt, under the petticoats, under the ... that Aunt wore.

Her aunt had encouraged the affair: 'He is a catch,' she said. 'This Catholic nonsense will probably pass. It is a good title, the family is ancient. They have money' – somewhere, she seemed to think, there were coal-mines – 'the house is hideous, not like Leith, darling, that jewel ... but they've got good pictures and plenty of plate. You will be secure. Love may or may not come, but have a baby or two, get all that out of the way, and then see what life has to offer...'

From the way it was put, it was difficult to know whether she meant good works or adultery. Or both?

They are getting on well together. Gerard watched his

wife and Edmund over the table, liking this, silently thanking her for making them a threesome. Edmund looked peaky but fixed, a little strained. Then it was always a strain coming into a party like this, already begun, and having to catch up with everyone. He caught his father's eye and looked away.

After lunch, he said to himself, after lunch Edmund will come with me and I shall tell him everything. I will make him understand.

'Tell me,' asked Lady Baillie, 'about Leith?' William was on her left. A nice young man.

'Nina is the person to ask about that,' he said, thinking from her tone it was as if nothing had ever happened there, that he had succeeded his father as other sons succeeded their fathers, in the usual way. He tried his best not to think of the end his father had prepared for himself in the gun room, the agonizing and untidy end, drink having made his hand unsteady; mostly he thought of his house in terms of regeneration: crawling with workmen, workmen on the roof, workmen in the hallways and passages restoring floors and plaster work, workmen who talked rot and beetle to him and made dire and incomprehensible threats about the fabric of his house, workmen in cradles in the garden hall putting back the famous Italian painted ceiling that had been shedding bits of angel and cloud like confetti for years.

'I think it's perfectly marvellous,' said Lady Baillie, making a secret sign at the butler to clear away for the pudding. 'Perfectly marvellous. It will be an occupation for Nina whilst you are away,' she added, suddenly wanting to put her hand on his and say what she really meant which was that she had fears, fears of a most profound kind about this war, that she only had one son and did not expect him to be spared. But she did not.

One cannot burden them, she thought. William's face had assumed a curious expression composed of sympathy and alarm. He is afraid of an old woman, she said to herself, leaning slightly to make way for the pudding, a summer one, rich with dark fruit that would leave purple stains on the table-napkins.

'You look forward to it, I suppose,' she continued, having decided to spare him her mother-pangs, and be instead what she imagined was expected of her.

'They must be stopped,' William said, firmly. 'We cannot let them get away with it.' He did not add that he had applied for a staff job. Nina had insisted on it. She was quite right, of course. One had a duty, after all ... next in line were some appalling Australian cousins who lived in a place called Alice Springs and went about on camels.

There had been enough trouble in their family for one generation. Still, one would have to wait and see what happened. The war was only six days old and might be over shortly. Personally, he hoped to be back for the best of the newly reared November pheasants at Leith. Nina was already talking about booking people now.

'They could always come back for it,' she had said, when he had mentioned his qualms about it being the teeniest bit tasteless. 'Leave it to me, darling. It'll be all right; after all, none of their guns could go if it wasn't for us and our ball-bearings...'

Which was quite true.

CHAPTER
THREE

The walk, the set piece. Edmund made a joke but Gerard did not laugh, said 'Yes?' at the end, politely, as if waiting for him to continue. After that, walking side by side, hands in pockets, they picked their way in and out of such neutral topics as the weather, not so neutral topics such as Edmund's head, fiddling about in the shallows of conversation, boring themselves to distraction.

To Edmund they seemed like a pair of intelligent but not particularly congenial strangers who knew everything about one another except what to do with all the information. It was apparent from Gerard's inability or reluctance to make small talk that he had nerved himself too long for this conversation and could not now think how to begin; Edmund considered tripping him up or pushing him into the rhodies, giving him a fright of some kind, longing for a shot gun to appear in his hand or a pair of castanets, stilts, anything. Tactless questions stacked up in his mind as a kind of counterpoint to the rambling inanities about polo ponies and the lies about tenants digging up cooked vegetables: What is it like to be an RC? Is the Real Presence Real to you? And the BVM – how do you manage that? It must be like employing a butler after years of answering the door yourself?

'I suppose you think I'm a complete idiot, like all the others?' Gerard stopped so suddenly that Edmund fell against him and had to put out a hand to steady himself.

'I've always liked the word "Paraclete",' he said,

'although I used to think it was something to do with sailing-boats.'

Gerard looked at him as if he had gone suddenly and inexplicably insane. He said nothing.

'I mean...' Edmund began to laugh, 'no ... that ... presumably, *presumably* you have a conviction. I'm sorry.' The words tripped over themselves. The afternoon air was like blotting paper. 'Look,' he said, starting again, 'tell me about it if you want to. I think you do want to, don't you?'

'Always people think it's so bloody funny,' Gerard said. 'My entire acquaintance, family and friends, are either hysterical with rage or laughter about my conversion. I had Nina yesterday on the subtleties of the confessional; like wardrobes, darling,' he said, aping her tone, 'doesn't it get rather hot with two of you in an *armoire*?'

'You mustn't mind what she says,' Edmund pressed his hands together behind his back. 'And, in any case, what on earth is she doing here if she's such a torment to you?'

'You know then, about her?'

'A bit.'

'Brother Ass,' said Gerard in a numb sort of way.

'Brother What?'

'Oh, you know, St Francis.'

'I knew he was an animal lover,' said Edmund carefully.

'Never mind.' Gerard walked on a step or two, then looked back. 'Shall we walk up to the monument?'

'My God.' Edmund stopped and pushed his hair back off his forehead. Sweat jumped out of his skin. They had come up through the bracken, across the winter bog, and on and on up, treading on sheep *crottes* which sprang out from under the soles of their shoes like marbles, through midge swarms, slapping and cursing, to the short grass at the plateau at the monument, this tremendous phallic

43

symbol which dominated the countryside for miles around.

The view, like an important painting, required his attention. He stared and sweated and turned away, dizzy with exertion and alarmed at the enormous interior sounds his body made when pushed.

'Not fit,' he said, sliding to the ground beside Gerard.

'What did you think of Nina?'

'Gorgeous. A bitch.'

'I'm still in love with her,' Gerard said, tiredly. He had given up pretence but it was not a relief as he had expected, just another admission of defeat, another smirch on the far from whited sepulchre.

'What about Alice?'

'I just can't think what to do about it all.'

'It must be very mortal that, isn't it?' Laughter banished, Edmund was doing his best.

'Very human?'

'No. Mortal. Categories of sin. Aren't you meant to know all this?'

'Oh, I see what you mean.' Gerard sighed. 'Yes, it's beyond everything. Adultery, just looking, is sort of top of the list with murder and not paying your employees properly.'

'Worse than buggery or fraud?' said Edmund, sympathetically.

'Much worse.'

'Being an RC hasn't solved any of this for you?'

'No. It's just complicated things because I believe it. Belief', and he realized this as he said it, 'doesn't protect you from anything, it only makes you more aware of your failings, the impossible standard against which you measure yourself, continuously.' He thought of his baptism and the priest saying the words: *'Exi ab eo spiritus immunde,'* a renunciation which had got him through several dinner parties and a shoot where Nina had been present, just. Having her here had been a colossal mistake, perhaps almost a fatal one. He had deluded himself that to be under the same roof would be a final test, a way of demonstrating to himself that he was over her, primed as he had been with an arsenal of higher thoughts, armed with sanctity, disdaining the creeping, crawling, flesh-loving world. But holiness was only a useful weapon if people took you seriously. Nina had laughed behind her hand at him, ganged up with his father, discussed him with his mother and Helena behind the half-closed doors of the morning-room, made life a misery.

'Why wouldn't she marry you?'

'She doesn't like the house and said we would quarrel all the time.'

'Would you?'

'Probably.'

'Where did you meet her?'

'Some dinner party. An aunt or a godmother of hers. You know, the beginning of a coming-out, the young girl produced, suitable young men to match. I think they were just running through the alphabet and B happens to come before C. She led me on though, in the beginning.'

'Did she indeed?'

'Oh yes – the works. . .' Gerard paused, remembering the shock of it: skin and hair and blood. Nina saying, 'So riding doesn't help,' and laughing; pliant but not tender, gone, up and off before he could extract promises from her . . . the door opening and closing, light from the passage but no noise, as if she had always been doing this in strange houses with a map of bedrooms and bathrooms in her head, knowing the times of Violet and Rory's waking and sleeping, what time Rory abandoned the bottle in the library, knowing where the dogs were and the maids, but leaving him with bloodied sheets and no excuses, having to corner Violet the next day with the most embarrassing of untruths about piles.

'Carnegie seems an odd choice, though.'

'Not really. He was at a perfect disadvantage after

45

Archie's death. Young earl, wonderful house. She'll be a famous hostess, a female king-maker.'

'I see,' Edmund said. The truth of the matter was dawning upon him at last: Gerard had married Alice in order to spite Nina, though probably not calculating it as exactly as that. It struck him that if William had been, as Gerard put it, at such 'a perfect disadvantage' after Archie's suicide, then so had Alice. Just as well he hadn't married Nina; it would have been an explosive combination.

'I like Alice,' he said. 'A far better choice in my view.'

'I like her too, but I don't love her.'

'Does it matter? I'm sure these things could happen later; you've got to give it a chance, though.'

'It shouldn't, but it does,' said Gerard stubbornly. He was not being given the advice he had wanted. He realized he had wanted Edmund to encourage him in his unhappiness, to say: 'Go on, old boy, don't give up, keep chasing her, she'll capitulate in the end...'

'Will you go on with this Catholic thing?'

'I can't go on without it.' Gerard stuck a cigarette in his mouth and lit it.

'What does your priest say? Do you have a pet one?'

'Father Kinahan, yes.'

'Why don't you tell him? Surely he can advise you?'

'You forget,' Gerard said, 'they're all celibates. They don't know Eros.'

The Gloucestershire Eroses, Edmund thought, the Worcestershire ones. 'No,' he said patiently, 'but they must be trained for this kind of thing. Or why don't you just give it all up and stop worrying?'

'Won't make any difference to the awfulness,' said Gerard, beginning to sulk.

'Give Nina up and stop worrying.'

'I can't.'

'Yes you can. You should think more about Alice. I feel sorriest for her.'

'Well don't.' Gerard was thoroughly annoyed now.

'She's all right. At least she has some kind of position in society these days.'

'If you don't mind my saying so, that is remarkably uncharitable.'

'As a matter of fact, I mind it very much.'

'But she seems so sweet. If you don't look out she'll fall in love with somebody else, or somebody else will fall in love with her. I could,' he added unwisely.

'You've always been quite good at that sort of thing, I seem to remember.'

'And I', said Edmund rising, 'seem to remember a time when you were quite good at it yourself. Before all this. What's happened to you, G.?'

'I've told you.'

'It seems lunatic to me to want to make yourself so unhappy.'

'It's not of my choosing,' said Gerard grandly, getting to his feet.

'So bloody pompous,' Edmund muttered.

'What?'

'Nothing.' Edmund frowned and spat a piece of grass out of his mouth. Hot and cross, he wanted tea and pretty women asking about his accident and when he was going to be brave and join the war. Gerard did not want help, not really, and, in any case, there was nothing he could do but leave him to stew in his own juice. You couldn't *make* a fellow listen.

'We seem to have got nowhere,' Gerard said at one point, but Edmund did not reply.

CHAPTER
FOUR

Tea amongst the pretty women restored Edmund. Nina sat next to him and cut her cake up into squares which she then fed to a dog under the table (they were outside); every now and again she licked the ends of her fingers. He began to see what Gerard meant. Alice, on his other side, was anxious and kept looking towards the house. After a bit she said, 'Is Gerard coming?'

'Thank you.' Edmund took his cup from her. 'I don't know.'

She looked at him accusingly. 'So it went badly, then?'

'I'm afraid so.'

'I so wish . . .' She looked down at her plate, running her finger round the rim.

'I would have helped you,' he said quietly, 'but he wasn't having any.'

'I just thought you might jolly him along a little.'

'He isn't really in the mood for it though, is he?'

'He needs an ally.'

'He's got you.'

'Oh yes,' she said, looking up, 'but I'm not enough.'

'Lord Bute,' Nina leant across him deliberately. 'Marvellous dark red; we're talking pelargoniums,' she said to Edmund. 'Are you a gardener?'

'Not really.'

'Mixed with heliotrope? My dear Nina, that's very adventurous.' Lady Baillie put her teacup down on the table-cloth without noticing.

'I have a little man who advises me. I can't take the credit,' said Nina, taking the credit.

'I must tell Macindoe.' Lady Baillie adjusted her spectacles.

The conversation had moved onto salvias. The dog had gone to bother William who was pushing its nose away. Next they would do herb gardens: houseleeks and liverwort, thyme and cotton lavender.

'Hate the smell,' said Lady Few.

'But so pretty . . . '

'I could try again this evening, if you would like me to.' Edmund looked at Alice and thought he would like to kiss her. Sad, vulnerable little woman. He must harden his heart. No meddling here. Kitty out of the under-gloom.

'You are very kind,' she said, and blushed.

Gerard stood in front of the mirror on his chest of draw-ers, staring. 'You disgust me,' he said to his reflection. He brushed his hair and threw the brush back amongst the small change, knocking over his stud box. A sort of black restlessness was taking him over, a drinking mood. He went and sat on the edge of his bed and put his head in his hands, sitting there for a wretched minute or two, but nothing would calm him. The more he tried to deny the force of his feelings for Nina, the worse they became: he had no innocent thoughts left.

His conversion had been a genuine one. Misery had carried him into Catholic churches, blind seeker without defences. Faith had rolled the stone from his heart and he had seen and believed. The time during which he met Alice had been a time of clear vision and planning, of lingering exultation. The clamour from his family, the amused gossip of old friends had seemed not to matter. He had been above it all, then. Now, the net of family and flesh was closing on him. He minded everything, noticed everything, felt an outcast. Prayer was increas-ingly difficult: just words into blackness, no answers, no comfort. He felt abandoned.

Only war offered the prospect of change, but even that he seemed to have got wrong, leaving the regular army at the wrong moment. Now he was attached to the Essex Horse whose chances of active service over the next few months were slim, or, worse, nil. He had applied to be taken on as interpreter to the expeditionary force and was waiting to hear. But he knew the army, *festina lente*. It might be months before he reached the war. There was nothing to hang change onto, only the same, old routine: south after the shoot, deposit Alice in London at St James's Terrace, train to Colchester where his battery HQ was. The bloody drill hall again. Months of slow damnation by paperwork and agonizing inactivity.

He got up again, looking at his watch. Time for some secret comfort before joining the others.

Is he tight? wondered Edmund, watching Gerard come into the saloon and take a glass of champagne off a tray held by a footman as expressionless as a tin soldier. Is he? Something tells me so. He had a look about him Edmund recognized from the old days: a carefully contrived composure, as if his clothes were the only thing holding him together.

'I have to go in front of a board,' he said to Lord Baillie, turning his back slightly so that he would not have to see what Gerard did next. 'Then off . . .'

'I envy you the opportunity of making our German cousins knuckle under.' Lord Baillie wiped his moustache with an enormous handkerchief. 'Potsdam's a nest of vipers, although to hear that b.f. Morrell talk, you'd –'

'Aggressive amiability transformed, what?' Lord Few turned his enlarged eye upon Edmund. He was carefully dressed as a highland chieftain, even to the lethal instrument in his sock. Edmund imagined fat Helena at knife-point lacing his pretty, patent dancing pumps. Curious how people who should know better could never grasp the difference between the Lowlands and the Highlands. Queen Victoria's fault really, the road to the isles and all that. Highlanders were a lazy lot of so-and-sos except when they were rushing out of the heather killing things.

They began to talk about Bismarck and Dizzy, the Junker and the Jew, the good old days when Prussia knew her place. There were stirrings amongst the gilt chairs. The old peeresses were enthroned, legs apart, petit point out of sight, being entertained by the young. William, hand on wife's bare arm, was describing something, leaning forward on the edge of the sofa.

'Careful!' shrieked Nina. The conversation stopped. There was a creaking as Gerard sat down heavily beside his wife. He crossed his legs, elaborately casual.

'Did I spill some on you? So sorry.'

'Thank you.' Nina took a handkerchief from her husband and dabbed. 'Now I shall smell of drink,' she said.

'Shall we wait dinner while you change?' Lady Baillie leaned forward and peered at Nina's lap.

'No, thank you. I shall suffer in silence. Finish your story,' she said to her husband, ignoring Gerard.

'Why didn't you come to tea?' Alice asked when it was safe. 'It seemed so odd.'

'Other fish to fry,' said Gerard vaguely.

'But, don't you think ... when there are guests?'

'I am so sorry that you minded.'

'I only mind for you,' she said, looking at him. There was whisky on his breath.

'I wish people would stop minding things for me,' he said unpleasantly, draining his glass. 'I mind them quite enough for myself.'

'You are not kind to me.' Alice spoke so softly he could not be sure whether she had intended him to hear; in any case, it was the kind of remark to which, in public, there can be no reply.

He looked towards the door where the butler was engaged in some elaborate semaphore with Lady Baillie. Edmund would take Nina in. He would be lumbered with Aunt Helena, as usual.

'You don't look well,' she said to him as they crossed the hall.

'Don't I?'

'You need a tonic, like Ivo has. Malt extract.'

'I thought they gave that to racehorses.'

'It has a universal strengthening application, I believe.' She gripped his arm. 'You were such a nice small boy,' she added tactlessly.

Gerard drank seriously from watercress soup to *bombe* whatever it was, but drink seemed to be having the wrong effect. He wanted to be witty but like a foreigner at a difficult dinner, his best remarks came too late and were ignored.

'You're staring,' Nina said. 'Have I a spot on the end of my nose?'

'What if I said yes?'

'I suppose I would have to have the vapours and retire to the lavatory.' She laughed, but vanity and champagne made her curious. 'What was it though?'

'I was looking at your earrings.'

'Oh, those . . .' She put a hand to her ear. 'Do you like them?'

'I think they're rather vulgar.' They were, too. Much too big not to be envied.

'Did I ask for that?' *O mignonne, mignonne*. She managed to look hurt and sorrowful. 'You're very cruel tonight.'

'Am I?'

'Alice was nearly in tears before dinner.'

'Now that is just nonsense.'

'You don't know your own strength,' said Nina, expert.

On the other side of the table, Edmund put his hand over his glass. 'No. I'm limited,' he said. 'Doctor's orders.'

'Gerard is drinking too much,' Alice said. 'What am I to do?'

The question surprised him into honesty. 'Nina is not good for him. She stirs him up.'

'Yes.'

'It's all rather a trial, isn't it?' he asked, pursuing this new and daring line.

'We were all right before we came here.'

'But living separately a good deal. Or are you at Colchester too?'

'Sometimes. More often he comes to London.'

'But what do you do?'

'The days go by,' she said, wanting to cry and put her head on his shoulder.

'There is change now though: the war.'

'Yes,' she nodded and swallowed. 'I don't welcome it. Do you?'

'In a way, yes. I'm tired of playing pretend.'

'It would seem like that, I suppose ... to a man.'

'The difference between doing and enduring, you mean?'

'Waiting and watching your friends and relations being killed.'

'You mustn't think of it like that.'

'I don't ... completely,' she said. 'I know the rules, know there's a job to be done, but it's not in me to relish it.'

'And you think I do?'

'I think all men do,' she said, rising. 'I must go.'

Lady Baillie was driving the female guests out of the room like an amiable satin-swathed sheep-dog. 'Don't be too long,' she said to her husband, who ignored her.

'Draw near, take a glass.' He cradled the port, displaying a hole in the elbow of his coat.

'Are you coming?' Edmund bent over Gerard who had not moved.

'I begin to hate this more and more,' he said, getting up but waiting for Edmund to take the seat nearer to his father.

William sat down and began to ask Lord Few respectful questions about parliamentary procedure.

'He hasn't spoken for thirty years,' Gerard muttered. 'Something about accredited sportsmen being used to cull pigeons in London squares.'

'You're not serious!'

'I'm not drunk, if that's what you mean.'

'It wasn't,' said Edmund crossly, filling his glass. He sat back in his chair feeling himself being eyed through the gloom by Kneller's goitrous women in their gilt frames; large-eyed, careless spectators at the rout.

'Tell me about your best man,' he said to Gerard suddenly.

'Patrick O'Hallan. I don't think you know him.'

'He's a recent acquaintance?'

'Quite recent.'

'With you now?'

'Yes, but looking for a transfer, like I am.'

'When do you think you'll hear?'

'Soon.' Gerard turned to him. 'I'm very tired,' he said. 'I want to get away.'

'From what?'

'Everything.'

'You can't ...' Edmund stopped. Silence had fallen at the end of the table.

'Keep it moving,' Lord Baillie said threateningly.

Edmund obliged and then tried to attend to a story Lord Baillie had begun to tell about dacoit hunting at Bandelkhand in which every character appeared to be called Singh, *sowars* and hunted alike. By the time Randhir, Wazir or Khushab had been brought to justice at Indore, he was nearly asleep.

'Goodnight.' Lord Baillie got to his feet and leaned forward, both paws flat on the table. 'Time you chaps were in bed,' he said. 'As you can see, Edmund, Gerard is no longer used to these wickedly late hours. Not in keeping with his new *monastic* habits.'

Gerard stared straight ahead like a soldier at a court-martial.

'G'night, Pa,' he said.

Thinking about it later, Edmund knew he should have gone to bed when Gerard suggested dancing. He had every excuse to beat it and yet something had kept him there, something he could not quite explain to himself, curiosity perhaps, the puppet master's desire to watch a controlled experiment between two dangerous personalities: for Nina had egged Gerard on, claiming the right to make the first choice of music; only William, who regarded this part of his career as over, was able to resist her animation.

Looking at Alice, Edmund saw her uneasiness and felt himself placed in the curious role of her protector; again he felt this dangerous tenderness for her, a kind of melting, not passionate but compassionate, a more or less new emotion to him; a rush of feeling which obliged him to behave towards her with affectionate courtesy, supplying by gesture what he could not say in words. They had, after all, only known each other for the inside of a day.

'Now,' said Gerard, turning to Nina. 'Come on.'

'You ought to dance with your wife first.' Nina sniffed. 'Are you tight?' she asked. 'Frightful smell of drink.'

'No,' said Gerard untruthfully. His head felt as if it was floating off his shoulders but his feet, independent of him, tucked and trotted, performed the extraordinary manoeuvres without a stumble or a slip. Like riding a bicycle, he thought woozily, one did not forget. He moved his hand so that it rested on the bare skin of Nina's back.

'Shall we?' Edmund offered Alice a hand.

'I'm not much good.' She looked up at him abashed, flattered, oddly trembly. There was something frenetic in the atmosphere she did not like.

'Neither am I,' he lied kindly, steering her adroitly so that her back was turned to the others. He watched Gerard's hand moving up and down, saw Nina leaning backwards slightly saying something arch, provocative.

'What are they doing?'

'Just dancing,' he replied, then, catching her look, added, 'Behaving badly, I'm afraid. Try not to mind.'

'I need lessons ... in trying not to mind.'

'We all do,' he said, noticing with ghastly tenderness a

55

little mole on the side of her neck. 'Do you want me to stop it?'

'What can you do?' she asked wearily.

'Send G. to bed and smack Nina's bottom. They're both asking for it.'

'Don't do that,' said Nina sharply.

'But you like it.'

'Your wife is watching,' she said coldly, trying to hold herself away from him.

'You little tart,' Gerard said, 'you love it.'

When she slapped his face he stumbled and nearly fell. At that moment the music stopped. The only sound was the scratch, bump, hiss as the needle jigged on the end of the disc.

'She bloody well hit me ... ' Gerard stood, utterly foolish, in the middle of the floor. A neat red hand-print over half of his face made him look like a man disfigured from birth. One had to give it to Nina for maximum effect achieved with minimum necessary force.

'Go and sit down.' Edmund pushed Gerard towards a sofa. He was tremendously angry. 'And you,' he said to Nina, 'go to bed for God's sake before you cause any more trouble.'

'He started it,' said Nina.

'That's a matter of opinion. You'd better go anyway.'

'Nothing would induce me to stay.' Nina could say dowagery things and get away with them, somehow, unfairly, failing to resemble Lady Bracknell. Her mouth changed shape like an anemone closing. 'You should keep an eye on him,' she said to Alice who was standing behind Edmund. 'Mark my words. He's not fit to be let out by himself.'

'Oh ... go,' Edmund felt at the end of his tether. He waited until she had gone round the bend in the staircase.

'I can't wake him.' Seated by Gerard, Alice looked round for help. 'He's too far gone.'

Edmund came and knelt by Gerard's head, gripping

his shoulders and shaking him. The victim groaned and opened its eyes. 'You'll have to help.' Edmund picked up an arm and let it fall again, limp. 'He's quite gone to pot, I'm afraid.'

They took off Gerard's shoes and dragged him up the long staircase. Edmund took the shoulders and Alice followed with the feet. Gerard was wearing silk socks which were difficult to get a grip of and his body sagged between their uneven strength like a piece of wet washing. Every now and again Alice looked at his comatose face, torn between fear and distaste.

'I should hate to be an undertaker,' Edmund said at the top. 'Is he still in his old room?'

'Yes.'

'He deserves two years of scrape for this,' said Edmund as, between them, they dumped Gerard on his high bed.

'Will you undress him or shall I?'

'Which would you prefer?' he asked, finding the sight of her across the bed from him with her dark hair falling out of its pins very disturbing. He looked down at Gerard who had begun to snore and then away round this familiar room in which so little had changed. Only the bedside table indicated a fundamental difference: there was a Bible, still rather new-looking, an ebony crucifix with its tormented burden, a rosary.

'I will,' she said. 'Thank you for everything.'

'It was nothing . . .' Edmund hesitated. 'Are you sure you can manage?'

'Perfectly,' she answered, wishing he would go and yet, at the same time, wanting him not to go but to stay and comfort her, only she could not bear to confront Gerard's hopeless nakedness in front of Edmund nor did she feel it was somehow proper for Edmund to do it alone. 'Truly,' she said, raising her eyes, 'I can manage.'

Alice made herself do the job properly, as if by excessive attention to detail she could somehow overcome the repugnance she felt towards Gerard, that knot in the pit of her stomach which tightened when she touched the waxy skin on his face, felt the slight clamminess of arms and legs, the pathetic loins; it was a body abandoned in spite of the snores and occasional groans, a sham Christ.

Was it for this? she wondered, bending over him and putting a glass of water on his bedside table, and supposed that it was. In sickness and in health, only that one thought of sickness as a hunting accident or being struck down by disease, oneself in pale colours – she paused, imagining it, the sweet-faced wife in the chair by the bed, the acknowledged self-sacrifice – not this thing, this torment, this invited form of self-torture that would require her own complicity, the ability to gloss things over, shrug them off, be normal. Just another disgusting little tragedy. My father, she thought, closing the door, and now my husband too. There are people who lead ordinary lives and have happy marriages whose private conversations could bear public scrutiny, there are...

'I waited.' From the shadows Edmund put out a hand, making her jump.

'Oh ... well, but I ...' For Alice this encounter was almost like being caught unclothed. Even in the half-dark she could feel the need somehow to rearrange her face: the frown line, the hair falling about.

'Are you all right?'

'Yes ...' But sympathy at this moment was fatal. Tears ran out of her eyes and down her neck.

'Don't cry,' and without really thinking what he was doing or being any longer able to stop himself, Edmund pulled Alice into his arms and kissed her. Women in tears always made him behave badly; he either became unduly harsh or, as in this case, excessively incautious, although the desire to kiss Alice, he now acknowledged, had been mounting in him all day.

'You shouldn't have done that,' she said.

'No.'

They did it again.

A noise from Gerard's room made them both jump.

58

He shouted something in his sleep and an object, impossible to guess what, fell onto the floor. 'I'll go,' said Edmund.

She waited with her back to the half-open door, listening to the sounds of Edmund retrieving whatever it was. 'Yes, yes,' she heard him say. 'Here it is.' Then he came out, closing the door behind him.

'He wanted his rosary,' Edmund said, moving her down the passage away from her husband's room, 'so I put it in his hands. He went back to sleep at once.'

'What fell down, what made that odd noise?'

'Do you really want to know? I'm afraid Christ parted company with his cross,' he said, suddenly wanting to laugh. 'The temple veil rent and all that. Darkness at noon and no birds sing.' He looked at her carefully under the passage light, seeing how tired she was, how strained. 'You should go to bed,' he said. 'I haven't made things any easier for you.' He did not add that he would like to take her into his own bed, but the logistics of the thing suddenly defeated him: the lateness of the hour, the thought of Lord Baillie, running the gamut of the energetic, early-rising housemaids, quite apart from the fact that she was Gerard's wife.

'Don't leave me,' Alice said, putting her hand on his arm, wishing all at once for an arsenal, like Nina had, of seductive talents, for the right formula to convey to Edmund that she no longer cared for anything but the re-creation of the feelings she had had when he kissed her. She would do anything for that.

'It's very late,' he said doubtfully, confused by her reaction. Previous experience with women interpreted the signals plainly enough, but his knowledge of her nature in the one day he had spent with her did not allow him to jump readily to ordinary conclusions over her apparent willingness. She was probably just tired and over-wrought. There were other factors too which made everything seem clouded and unclear: her likeness to Kitty inclined him to assume that he could only, as he had ever done with Kitty on account of their youth and circumstances, worship from afar and hope. Besides, quite apart from anything else, he had forgotten how shocking newly awakened desire was, how it swept everything before it. He could no longer imagine those first fruits, that frightful hunger. The women with whom he had associated in the last few years were experienced games players, able to give the impression without any difficulty that, like men, desire could be summoned and dismissed according to some larger plan. He had forgotten innocence and how easy it was to overwhelm. One kiss. A game, a dream. Playing with fire.

'Don't leave me,' she said again at her bedroom door.

'It's not wise,' he replied, looking down at her, terribly tempted. Only once more and he would capitulate. He was not made of cast iron.

'Why did you wait for me then?' she asked desperately.

Foolishness ... now completed, he thought, going inside her bedroom door and closing it with one foot.

'Don't go,' she said with pretended lightness, putting her hand on his shoulder.

'I can't be found here.' The hand was a plea, he knew that, but he did not look round; it was the hurdle he always baulked at, always forgot about until too late. What women wanted afterwards. Hatty, he thought, where are you?

I can't bear it, Alice wanted to say. Edmund, I can't bear it. Now the madness was over she was near tears again. There was nothing left her, no moral refuge, something she had not realized she had taken such comfort in: that feeling of being the injured party, of being the object of concern. Overcome with shame, it seemed everything rested on Edmund's reaction to her. The act bound her to him, cut her off from former sources of approbation.

'I can't bear it,' she said sniffing.

'What? What can't you bear?' Edmund took her in his arms, trying his best to comfort her, although he felt tired and rather ill, certainly not joyful. Illness, he found, had knocked the stuffing out of him; his prowess was not quite what it had been, although Alice of course could not know that. He had also been rather shocked to discover that, once in bed, even with a new and naked body beside him, all he had really wanted to do was to go to sleep. But it was to be by no means as simple as that. Alice would fall in love with him; he knew his way so well around these secret states of womanhood that he could tell. It was as predictable as the simplest calculation in arithmetic.

'I don't know what I've done,' she said, looking up at him, waiting, hoping.

'It's all right.' Edmund stroked her hair, staring over her shoulder at her little travelling-clock, torn between Alice's need and his desire somehow to extricate himself. Knowing what she wanted did not make him any more able to give it to her. What have *I* done? he wondered, feeling her heart beating against his.

When he returned to his bleak and rather uncomfortable room in the bachelor's wing, he lay in bed smoking, unable to sleep, forced to watch the dawn coming up.

What should I do? he wondered, knowing perfectly well that he would do what he had always done in these matters, which was to drift with the current of events. Wait and see. She was a fetching creature who deserved a bit of fun. Gerard was such a bastard to her; he was asking for everything that was coming to him.

I deserve a bit of fun, too, he thought, nearly asleep. Yes, and why not? After all, I've had a perfectly vile summer. And, for God's sake, there's a war on. I might be killed. 'Gather ye rosebuds' and the rest. Those Cavalier poets knew a thing or two, even if they did go about in wigs and high heels.

Edmund closed his eyes.

CHAPTER
FIVE

Gerard came to early the next morning out of some dark place, a hot cavern in which various routine but nevertheless extremely painful forms of torture were being administered to him. He had a raging thirst and the light hurt his eyes so that he closed them again as soon as the man had put down his cup of tea and drawn his curtains. Consciousness was not welcome: he had a blurred memory of the events of the previous evening accompanied by a distinct and uncomfortable feeling of shame. He could not remember how he came to be lying on his bed, had no idea at all who had undressed him and laid his things so neatly on the chair by the writing-table; there was something uncomfortable pressing into the upper part of his back which turned out to be his rosary and when he turned to put it back on the bedside table he found to his great distress that the crucifix given him by his confessor, Father Kinahan, had come apart. Christ reclined in the tortured attitude of a yogi amongst the detritus so necessary for the formal diner, cufflinks and studs and small change. How had this happened? he wondered. Had he fought the person who had un-dressed him, most likely Edmund, or had he got up in the middle of the night and thrown the crucifix to the floor? Had it all happened in a supernatural way? Was this a sign perhaps that he must take a pull on himself? If he had felt less ill, he might have been inclined to launch a personal court of enquiry, but even to think about thinking made his heart hurt. Some other time, he said to himself, later on today perhaps, or after the shoot. Some other time.

He sipped the scalding tea and remembered that Alex was coming on the train this morning and that he must go and meet him. Alex was Gerard's first cousin (the only child of Lord Baillie's younger brother, Halliday Baillie, who was in the Indian Political Service, that *corps d'élite* of Empire) and was now a sixteen-year-old Etonian who lived permanently in Britain, dividing his time between his mother's relations at Thurlby in Lincolnshire and his father's family at Kildour. Their closeness was both difficult and easy to explain: perhaps it was something to do with being only sons, but Gerard had watched over Alex since the time he had first come to Kildour, an infant in long clothes. It was Gerard who slipped Alex extra quids and wrote to him at prep school and Eton, Gerard who had taken him out shooting for the first time, Gerard who (when possible) met trains. Now the gap in age was beginning to close. It was as if they were brothers.

Gerard timed his arrival downstairs at breakfast to the second, knowing the clockwork precision of his father's routine would mean that he got up from the breakfast table at exactly a quarter to eight and would then retire to the thunderbox next to his business room with an ironed copy of yesterday's newspaper, where he would remain for thirty minutes in private communion with nature and the letters page of *The Times*.

'The sole survivor of the *vie galante*,' said Edmund when Gerard came in. He made an irritating face of mock astonishment and banged his cup back into its saucer.

'Well, you're here, aren't you?' said Gerard grumpily, turning his back on Edmund and making a great show of peering under various lids, although he felt far too sick to eat anything.

'Try the kidneys,' said Edmund. 'Brain food, Aunt says, and you know how alcohol desiccates the poor little grey cells. Makes them turn up their toes.'

'Oh, do stop it,' said Gerard, sitting down with a cup of black coffee. 'I don't know why you've got it in for me this morning. No, no.' He waved away the offer of a cigarette.

Edmund lit one for himself in silence, then crossed his legs, leaning one elbow on the table. 'Listen to me, Gerard,' he said, 'and forgive, if you can, a rather hectoring tone, but you were the cause of a nasty little scene last night.'

Gerard said nothing.

'Do you remember any of it?'

'Not much.'

'Where does sweet memory fade?'

'Look, I'm not a child, you know.'

'Then don't behave like one.' Smoke drifted from Edmund's nostrils as if he were breathing fire. 'Someone's got to tell you,' he said, staring at Gerard across the table. 'I watched you dancing with our beautiful resident countess, running your hands all over her in front of your wife. No wonder she smacked you.'

'Did she?' asked Gerard, betraying himself.

'I thought so,' said Edmund, putting out his cigarette. 'You don't remember a thing, do you?'

'I can't understand what you're making such a fuss about.' Gerard took a gulp of coffee. 'I should hardly have thought', he continued, 'that it was for you to adopt this rather holier-than-thou tone. I've seen you behave quite as badly.'

'That's rather beside the point,' replied Edmund, lighting another cigarette. To his irritation he found his hands were shaking. He never had been good at rages. 'Point one, I'm not married, and point two, for God's sake do it away from home. Alice was dreadfully upset. We had to cart you up to bed between us. It's not a pretty sight for a young girl to see her husband in a drunken stupor.'

Again, Gerard did not speak. He could find no words to express how he felt at what he saw as Edmund's unwarranted intervention in his private affairs. If he had been ticked off merely for having a bit too much he might just have been able to take it, but it was the extra he could not stomach, Edmund's self-righteous moralizing, his stance as Alice's spokesman that stuck in his throat; and of course he was right. He *had* behaved appallingly.

'Am I interrupting something?' William hovered in the doorway, polite but curious.

'Yes,' said Edmund, looking at him with irritation and contempt.

'No,' said Gerard, pushing his cup away and rising. 'I've got to meet a train,' he said, and left.

'What, if you don't mind my asking, was that all about?' William raised his eyebrows at Gerard's angry and departing figure.

'Never mind,' said Edmund, getting up, feeling himself incapable of polite nothings with William. 'The kidneys have had it,' he said as he passed by. 'I should address yourself to bangers.'

William nodded, as if in agreement with some important philosophical point. 'Lovely day,' he said.

'Is it?' Edmund paused in the doorway. 'I can't say I'd noticed.'

Gerard drove extremely fast until he was some distance from Kildour, then he stopped his motor on the hill road and was sick into the heather. After that he felt well enough for a cigarette.

He walked away from the car into the view, all hills, heather and sky, those hills that were so bare, coloured in patches dun and faintly purple, with the huge sky beginning at their shoulder and going up and up, so blue, so clear, and he had a feeling of being on the edge of some discovery. He stood, staring, the slight breeze lifting his hair, the cigarette burning down unnoticed, until a pheasant disturbed him, drawing his eye away down the valley in its wake, and he walked on again, thanking God to be by himself and not to have people at his elbow producing clichéd superlatives, one of the hazards of

house-parties, all those bored people needing enter-
tainment.

But I am like them, he thought suddenly, although I
may pretend not to be, I am one of them. I am bored. I am
here for the grouse, here, home, waiting to kill some
birds on an appointed day in the company of appointed
people, waiting for the time to pass. Waiting, endless
waiting: waiting for the grouse, waiting for the war,
waiting for ... something; something to happen that
would seem decisive, that would make some meaning
out of it all, some pattern.

And he thought then that he had expected marriage to
do that, to produce a pattern to which he could conform
eagerly and without effort. But he had done nothing; he
had expected Alice out of her inexperience to construct a
framework in which he could be seen to best advantage.
He had married her, not out of an exclusive preference
for her above all others, but because someone he had
previously cared for, still in fact did care for against his
better nature, was making a good match. It had been a
season of weddings; to marry had been a fashionable
pursuit, a repetition of blank-eyed brides, hideous
crowds and of endless speculation by the gutter press of
the subject of dynastic enhancement: Murray-Walker
equals Baillie. A photograph of Alice in a dismal dress,
arm in arm with him. Even the poor quality of the picture
had not disguised the look of slight astonishment on
both their faces.

Alice. He was suddenly overwhelmed by a most terrible compassion for her, a kind of love that was not love
as he had previously known it, but was more, in a way, as
if his vision were clearing after a long period of semi-
darkness, of blurred outlines and shapes. It was a most
unwelcome but keen sensation, almost a force, that
seemed at once aware of him and benevolent, but was
also neutral; something powerful in its own right. He felt
as if he were being coerced.

The absolute heartlessness of his behaviour towards

her. My wife. A cipher, useful appendage, sign of maturity, but not real, a person with feelings, all that: hopes, fears, blood rushing and ebbing along veins and arteries. For the first time he knew what it meant not just to think of another person but to be that person. He entered into her being and was horrified. How long, he wondered, could he have gone on thinking he cared for others, thinking himself a Christian, involved in pious, Pharisaical pursuits without making this vital connection between mind and heart, intellect and emotion, belief and practice. It had been akin to peering for the shortest of seconds out of the citadel of his own engrossing being, that secret knowledge of being the hub of the universe.

He went back to the car and sat a moment, loathing this grace, this change, that would make him what he dreaded most: the loving fool, the easy prey, and yet, when he thought of Nina it was not as he had imagined it, after all. How interesting to see at last that little passion in its right place. How he had taken or mistaken love for what Nina herself meant by the word, Nina, that daughter of earth and the shadow, dark goddess: an excessive emphasis upon what was merely a strand in one of the natural affections; how he had been led by that as if there were a curse on him, as if there were nothing else.

The boy was there when he arrived. The train had been early, disgorging its one passenger into the station yard. A gun case, a Gladstone bag.

'Is that all you've got?' asked Gerard, throwing the bag into the back of the car, going more easily with the gun.

'I left some things at Easter.' Alex put a hand to the back of his neck and rubbed it. He was sweating inside his tweed coat. 'Do you mind if I take this off?'

'Why should I? It's like the bloody tropics here at the moment. Was it the same at Thurlby?'

'What?'

'At Thurlby,' Gerard repeated. 'Was it hot at Thurlby?'

'I ... think so,' Alex said distractedly. Something in the movement of Gerard's arm as he took the coat from him made Alex think of the dream again, the simplest outlines really: himself in a chair and someone telling him ... a chair in a room with books in it, and someone telling him something he did not want to hear. Something about a death intimately connected with him. A death. The narcotic sweetness of death. Where had he read that?

'Get in, will you,' said Gerard, starting up, wondering what was the matter with Alex. This vagueness was not at all like him. He tried and failed to think of a way of asking what it was.

'How's Alice?' Alex shouted.

'Very well, thank you.' Gerard swerved to avoid a hen. The motor plunged onto the hill road again, noisy, uncomfortable; carriages had been better, only they made one seasick.

'When are you off?'

'Day after tomorrow.'

'Lucky brute.' Alex smiled at him.

Lucky? Am I? He had not thought of it as luck, more as a kind of *pietas*, the putting of obligation above inclination, only it was more complex even than that: there was a deep impulsion in him to embrace this war and accept it as something inevitable without examining the reasons for it in a more than cursory way: pushed, he would talk of Belgium, of economic sanity, of international insanity, the pride of nationhood grown monstrous and distorted since 1870, the excessive and intransigent militarism, knowing all the time, secretly, that it was as simple and as terribly necessary for him to go to war now as it had been for the Greeks to board their ships and rush to batter Troy. Belgium, like Helen, was an excuse in a way, a little, moral gloss on other, older urges.

Alice sat up in bed reading a letter from her cousin Pamela. Dizzy Pam, Gerard called her. They had met

68

once or twice and loathed each other. 'Why does she have to dress like some kind of Bohemian washer-woman?' he had asked. 'It was a sort of sack with cubes on it. I hate women smoking, too.'

Rather unfair, that. He was quite good at smoking himself. She held the letter up to her nose and sniffed. Smoke and turps, written on the kitchen table, no doubt. Pamela painted and had what her aunt called 'easy man-ners', which meant she went to bed with an assortment of men. From the letter it seemed there was a permanent one at the moment.

My dear (she read),
It is chaos here. War fever. What has happened to us that we should have become like this so quickly? Everyone is urgent, bestial. Dachshunds like my poor Rolf are all at once *persona non grata*. Some-one tried to kick him in the street yesterday because he has the misfortune to be a German breed. Civi-lization, always a thin skin as I would be the first to admit, has gone by the board. What moral justification can we use against an aggressor when we ourselves behave in exactly the same way?

Petersen (this was the lover), a *Dane*, settled here for years, has been questioned by men he thought his friends and forced to protest loyalty of a variety that should always remain unspoken, being of the most profound, unshakeable kind. Of course he has German friends, we all do. After all, the Royal family are German or the next best thing. There are rumours of strategic name changes amongst the demi-royals, whispers about Battenburg and so on. They'll put the cake on the Index next and then where shall we be? But truly, darling, these are shocking times. Did you see the poem in *The Times* on the 8th by the Laureate? If I had my way the man would be debagged. There was a line (I won't quote it all at you in case you did see it) that went something like this: 'To Beauty through blood' and another: 'But they that love life best die gladly for thee.'

We are truly at the end of things if good men are now made to lay their heads on the block for a poetic conceit that is neither true nor, in reality, beautiful. Beguiling, I admit, lulling, *Pro Patria Mori* and all that. What those amongst us who are spoiling for a fight want to hear, but when the blood begins to flow and the deaths to mount up, what then? None of them, Germans, English, know what it is they have begun. I shall go for a nurse, I think. I shall have to do something. Painting pictures won't save lives; I feel rather bitter that the kind of truths I have spent my life trying to interpret through my work should be so easily turned from, so quickly. Greed, that's all it is. Plain greed.

Forgive me, darling, for this rather incoherent ramble of a letter. We are not sleeping well here. There is a lot of noise in the street at night, a *danse macabre* at closing time, and various blood-curdling whoops and yells on into the small hours as if some sort of carnival had been announced. Really, it is too much. As a result, we have rather taken to the bottle ourselves and wake every morning with heads like footballs, so no work is done either. I wonder what it must seem like to you in your cocooned northern fastness? I know that enclosed life in big houses when everything outside the estate boundaries seems to be taking place on another planet. But when it begins to bite and the young men are no longer there to return to the woods and the rivers then perhaps the governing classes will sit up and take note.

I am becoming vitriolic, forgive me again. Come and see me the moment you get back.

Best love,
Pamela

Alice pushed the letter away without really taking it in. Pam's tone did seem a little overdone. 'Cocooned northern fastness' indeed! Alice leaned forward, drawing up her knees, putting her arms round them. Last night could not possibly have happened. She thought of herself closing Gerard's bedroom door and the way everything had gone upside-down afterwards, the way she had thrown herself at him. She had no idea what to do with this new knowledge of Edmund, body knowledge. What was he really like? The thought of him made her go hot and cold, a horrible mixture of fear and desire.

Would I do it again? she wondered, and lay back on her pillows considering the matter. He was kind . . . and wonderful in bed. Wonderful, wonderful. One night had made her a judge. She thought of Gerard almost with contempt, feeling she had moved on a step or two, grown up overnight. Her old self, yesterday's Alice, seemed an innocent little being in comparison with this new version, her tears when it was over almost disgusting. I should be calm and cool and confident, she thought. Why shouldn't I have what I want, a little pleasure? He has done nothing for me. Nothing. She thought of Gerard with anger: his coldness to her, his vileness last night. Play him at his own game, she said to herself. Now it is my turn to take.

She had not expected him to come. What cheek, she thought, when he put his head round the door in that irritating supplicating kind of way and said hallo. He wants instant forgiveness, I suppose, she said to herself; like a child thinking 'sorry' will do the trick.

'What is it?'

'I came to see how you were.' Gerard advanced into the room.

'I'm really very well, thank you.' Alice sat up, bracing herself.

'I came to apologize for my behaviour last night,' he said, not quite knowing what to make of her tone.

'Is she still so important to you?' The question pleased her. It seemed direct, sophisticated.

'No. She's . . .' He sighed and looked away from her as he spoke. Already it was turning out harder than he had expected.

'Then why?'

'I made a mistake,' he said, speaking without expression.

'A mistake,' she repeated irritatingly. 'I don't know what you want of me.' Alice stopped, rather shocked by how angry she felt, how, after all, it was not so easy to control the words.

'I made a mistake,' he said again. 'I came to apologize, to ask if we could . . .'

'Could what?'

'I don't know. Begin again, or something.' He turned from the window to face her, pulling his signet ring on and off his little finger.

'I suppose so.' She shrugged, wanting him to go now, but aware of some clever, hitherto undiscovered part of her, which informed her that to be collected, uninterested, was the best way of tormenting him.

'You won't accept my apology then?'

'I didn't say that.'

'I don't know what's got into you this morning,' he said, looking grim in an effort to resist losing his temper. It disgusted him to find his own good intentions so easily vanquished. 'I was brought up to believe one should always accept an apology.'

'So was I,' she answered.

'What do you want me to do?' he said too loudly. 'Crawl in here on hands and knees? Sackcloth and ashes, is that what you want?'

'Don't threaten me, Gerard,' she answered in a new bored little voice. 'If you can't behave properly, then go. I've had enough of your tantrums, your selfishness, your obsession with yourself.'

'Why did you marry me then?'

'I didn't know. I had to marry someone,' she said and burst into tears.

'And I was that someone?'

'You know you were. You *know* that. Don't persecute me,' she said, blowing her nose.

'What's to become of us then?' he asked, letting his hands drop to his sides.

'I don't know.' She looked at him. 'I can do nothing. Without you, I am nothing. I have no means. You *know* that,' she repeated, piteously.

'I'd no idea you could behave in this melodramatic way,' he said, provoked. 'I married you because I was fond of you, because of your charm, because I thought we could get on well together.'

'You married me,' she said, from behind her handkerchief, 'because Nina wouldn't have you and I just happened to be in the right place at the right time. Why don't you admit it?'

'That's not true,' he shouted, knowing of course that it had been true, but was not so, any longer. Not since, ridiculously, this morning. How could he explain to her and expect her to believe in his ... *metanoia*, this tremendous change of heart that had come over him on his way to the station? And the rage which he could not control solved nothing. He shook his head in despair, hating her for moving him so unbearably, for putting him in a position where he could not comfort her. We kill the thing we love, he thought, disgusting little cliché, but true, like all disgusting little clichés.

'Will you go?' she asked. More tears. He wanted to shake her, stop them.

'You won't let me do anything for you?'

'Leave me alone. I'll be all right,' she said, putting her hands flat on the bedclothes. 'I won't embarrass you or anything. You don't have to worry about that.'

He looked at her and thought of saying something, but refrained. I might have asked for that, he thought, closing the door, but it doesn't make it any easier to take.

'He is really almost too good-looking, don't you think?'

Lady Few removed her tinted sun-spectacles from the bridge of her nose, her 'colonial administrators', David called them.

'Who? Alex?'

'No, no, my dear, Maud's boy.' She wiggled her fingers in the air as if trying to summon up Kerr, E., Edmund's income and rank, prospects, childhood diseases, from the rows of similar young men whose credentials had been lodged in her mind for better or worse during dear Joan's two seasons. 'Edmund. He's like a young god.'

'He's only her nephew by marriage,' said Lady Baillie, sitting up, smoothing her hips. She had been half-asleep. The tennis court, around which they were arranged watching the young men's four, was in a dip; the hottest place. In her half-dream, the bat and slap of tennis-balls had been one of the house boys in the India of her distant youth knocking oranges off a tree with a long stick, the shouts of the contestants his strange song.

'Who will inherit, then?' Lady Few leaned a little nearer, plump shoulder to plump shoulder, lowering her voice importantly.

'Why, Edmund, of course.'

'And no bride in sight.' Lady Few raised her lorgnette threateningly and peered along the row of canvas chairs containing Alice and Nina, as if accusing them of concealing a vision in white satin and orange blossom.

'Alice is pale,' she said. 'Oughtn't she to go to a man about her insides?'

'I try never to interfere,' replied Lady Baillie sighing. 'And you know how Gerard has been.'

'Yours!' shouted Edmund.

Gerard swerved, tipping the ball with his racquet so that it fell defeated against the net.

'He's lost,' said Nina to Alice. 'Perhaps he's rather tired today.'

'Perhaps,' Alice replied non-committally. Last night had not been mentioned. It seemed better.

'I'm sorry you saw that,' Gerard sat down in the chair next to her, turning his head so that he could look into her face. 'Sorry generally,' he said in a lower voice, putting a hand on her shoulder. 'Next time we'll do better.' Edmund lay almost horizontal in a chair the other side of Nina, long legs crossed, exposing a gap of skin between sock and trouser leg. 'Do you play?' he asked, idly, pushing his hair back with one hand.

'I'm rather good, actually.' She smiled at him, said something Alice could not hear.

'Tomorrow then,' he turned his head towards her: brown neck, button-down collar, some throat.

'Tomorrow's the shoot,' said William from the ground.

'Before breakfast perhaps,' she answered, putting her hand on Edmund's arm.

'Why not?'

'Nina never got up before breakfast in her life,' said William, who was leaning on one elbow. 'That's for extreme youth, people like Alex.'

'What's for me?' He came up, swinging the tennis-balls to and fro in a string bag.

'Edmund and I shall – '

'Are you cold?' asked Gerard, moving his hand further down Alice's arm like a doctor.

'What?'

'You're shivering.'

'No.'

'Ma's gone in,' he said. 'Let's go and join her.'

She rose and allowed him to take her arm.

'That's better,' Nina whispered. 'You must have done the trick.'

'Mmm.' Edmund watched, trying to decide what he felt for her. She wasn't really so very like Kitty after all. The trouble was, the real, real trouble was that he couldn't remember what Kitty *had* looked like. She was in the wings of every photograph, a half-step from the cross-legged children but not old enough to have made a marriage and moved towards the centre.

Periods of abstinence, he seemed to remember, had produced romantic yearnings of this kind in him before: dreams of an ideal, the one, the perfect woman; yet, for all that, she was very touching, she affected him ... going obediently with Gerry up the steps like a sleep-walker. And G.? What of him? Where was the guilt he should be feeling? Off-stage somewhere, waiting for a prompt. G., it seemed, could take a telling and act on it, in faith. Perhaps it was this that removed them so far from one another now. I would not have been able to do that, thought Edmund, but then I would never have got myself into such a situation in the first place ...

'What are you thinking of?' asked Nina. Their little chat before luncheon, however ambiguous, allowed her this pleasing intimacy.

'I couldn't possibly tell you,' he replied, getting up and nearly treading on William who was half-asleep, holding out his hand to Nina.

'I think you are really quite heartless,' said Nina teasingly. 'People with perfect manners nearly always are.'

What rot she talks, thought Alex, waiting politely for William to get up. All she needs is a spoon and then she could eat him. If she was my wife, I'd shoot her.

'All set for tomorrow, are you?' asked William. 'What kind of gun?'

Alex told him.

'Good boy's gun that,' he said. 'Excellent.'

'And you?' Alex felt obliged to ask.

'A pair of Westley Richards, new ones,' William answered immodestly. 'Nina gave them to me as a wedding present. What's so funny about that?' he asked, joining, in spite of himself, Alex's laughter.

'Stupid, schoolboy joke,' said Alex. 'Couldn't possibly explain.'

CHAPTER
SIX

Breakfast. Lord Baillie: didactic, lairdly, monumental in hairy tweeds directs operations; an enormous stopwatch sits by his plate: the one day in the year when defecating will take ten minutes, short, sharp and to the point.

The guns: old David, spindle legs lost in bulging pantaloons. Flask, eyeglass, handkerchief. He pats his body surreptitiously, checking.

Edmund: well-made body in well-made clothes talks with animation to Gerard on the neutral but fascinating topic of grouse. There are no *doubles entendres* in this conversation, no innuendoes, no complaints. Bird slaughter restores them to one another completely.

Alex sits in the shadow of his uncle, saying nothing but eating as fast and as seriously as possible. It will be a long morning. He watches Gerard and Edmund, obscurely worried by Gerard for some reason as if, as if . . . always it is in the movement of an arm, as if he is warding off a blow; but that is ridiculous, he is simply making an arc to describe a falling object . . . *amarae morti ne* . . . Who is telling him this? Is it God? But it cannot be God. God is the Headmaster of Eton, with his beak nose, his handsome, ascetic face. And the cup falling from his hand like some bloody, cheap melodrama; it is black now, black stripes, but with voices and Lord Baillie calling 'Hi' in rage and alarm.

Black with faces coming and going.

And they turned the victim's body westward, his head being placed at the altar's foot.

77

But he spake of the temple of his body.

'Is he ... is he epileptic?'

Autistic, Havelock Ellis's victim, catatonic. Words not in general use yet. His Dame's voice: 'Give me, give ... me, me ...'

Ammonium carbonate.

Alex sniffed and reared. Eyes anywhere. Tongue like wet felt. Dining-room. Birley of Gerard. Battonis. Valuable, valuable Battonis. Knellers. Lelys. Miss Baillie by Lely. Miss Baillie the traitor's daughter. Hoppners ... no, that was Thurlby, and all those bloody battle pictures. Gonville at Rorke's Drift. Pip, his dog was called, behind the biscuit boxes and mealie bags. Pip. Good dog. Sit now and don't mind the flames...

'There now.' Gerard's voice. A voice out of the world of order and sanity. Calm voice. The smell of sick somewhere.

'I'm sorry ... ' Alex raised up his head and looked. They had taken him to the library and left him with Jorrocks. And Gerard.

'Don't talk. The doctor's coming.' Gerard on his knees by the sofa, face level with his. His own face but with a moustache tacked onto it. Alex stroked his upper lip.

'I've tried but it won't grow – '

'Don't talk,' said Gerard. Alex's legs were shaking as if a current was running through them.

Gerard got up and went out into the hall. It needs words, he thought, this: shape and form. He was possessed by some enormous but unattached sense of foreboding. Words then. What? Insanity. *Petit mal.* A young man's aberration. None of them fitted. The darkness persisted, edgeless, weighing him down.

Nothing came to him standing there in the hall waiting for the doctor to arrive, nothing but an idea that appeared to have no relevance to Alex: that time was somehow out of joint, as if his own actions had taken on a significance he could not possibly understand. He felt, now, that everything rested with him, in an odd way that his apprenticeship had come to an end.

And he thought of Alex lying there in the library with his eyes shut, seeing who knew what horrors, calamities, with his legs twitching as if they were full of electricity, and it seemed to him then that his life had stopped and begun again during that unlooked-for moment of truth yesterday: the pits and traps of proper love. Hostage. He would not now be free again.

With Farquhar came his mother and between them they reduced Alex's agony to over-stimulation, growing pains; antediluvian theories couched in quasi-medical language. The boy was taken away to bed and given broth. Gerard was suspicious and then grateful. Better thus. The plain, matter-of-fact nursery theory of life. Maladies without a name do not exist.

They killed things all morning.

Gerard went up the hill at lunch-time armed to the teeth. He found them all at their pik-nik on rugs eating fowl drumsticks and pieces of pie; rows of feet, it seemed to him, tweed laps, hands holding bones half-way to their mouths, wind blowing away someone's hat. It was like entering a photograph.

'Here,' Edmund called, pointing. He was sitting next to Alice who also waved and got up.

'All well?'

'Now, yes.' She was easy with him, looked pretty and relaxed; colour in her face. He could love her. It was happening at last, taking on nearly a physical shape, easing and straightening.

'Gerard. Food.' It was Nina with a plate. 'Is Alex all right?' For once she was natural with him, her tone bland, unprovocative.

'He is now, thank you. Ma and the doc put him to bed.' He took his meal from her, missing the look that passed between Alice and Edmund. Complicity. It had been fixed for London, put on a proper footing; the morning's sport had excited Edmund, made him aware, as shooting always did, of the enormous physicality of things: earth and sky, some excellent marksmanship, the erratic, moving target. Morals did not exist in this landscape. There was only oneself and an immense and satisfactory feeling of well-being. If, after that, an attractive woman made herself available, then it seemed to him almost deserved perks, a reward for an outstanding performance. In any case, once done a deed of that kind was hard to ignore. It brought with it obligations and special courtesies, small tendernesses. Of course, he had to be careful, extra careful here, waiting for the rhythm of things to deposit Alice by his side without contrivance and without other ears.

Meals were hopeless. When you were trying to say something to someone, something particular that was, conversation invariably tapered out and ceased altogether at the crucial moment. He had been aware that she thought he was being deliberately cruel, so that to be able to sit next to her here, part of and yet apart from a large and noisy group, outside, without exciting any suspicion, particularly with Gerard absent and the topic of Alex's mania or whatever it was overlaying what had gone before, occupying people like Nina, who seemed somehow to be always on the verge of knowing everything about everybody, had made the conversation they had had doubly pleasurable; repairing and achieving at the same time. He would not like her to think he was a cad.

'Sit down, my dear fellow,' he said to Gerard. And they began again the conversation they had been having at breakfast, each careful to include Alice, so that it seemed to Sir John Kerr as he rose with some difficulty onto his stout, stockinged legs after luncheon, that Edmund was not only well but was on the old footing with Gerard again. A threesome. Nice, eh?

And there was a moment during the afternoon when Gerard raised his gun and found that he did not want to kill the bird that was his, allowing it to go by; but the damaged pride of his loader prevented this from happening again. In any case, the next time, hands, eye, aim, went ahead of thought, and it was over before it had begun, so to speak.

'*The night is dark,*' shouted Lord Baillie happily from his bath, soaping his fat, furry shoulders, annual pride-taking salvaged by a good bag, '*and I am far from home.*' Gerard wanted to see him. Why, he wondered? '*Lead thou me on.*' Boy off soon. Not good to let this bad blood continue between them; besides he wanted to know what Gerard thought about Alex. Good of him to wait behind like that. Women could have done it but he insisted. Doing the decent thing on the best day of the year. Hmm . . . He called for his towel and the man came in, laying his dressing-gown on a chair.

'Won't need that. No time. Straight into stiffs.'

And to think of old David coming down the night before in a kilt saying something about his granny being a McHoddle of Muck or Eigg, one of those God-forsaken outcrops of rock off the West Coast. Lord Baillie snorted with laughter. 'Go and tell Lord Few not to wear a skirt to dinner tonight, will you?'

'Very good, m'lord.'

Lord Baillie twiddled his moustache and then went off to his business room, still singing: '*Keep thou my feet; I do not ask to seeeeee . . . The distant scene – one step enough for meeeee . . .*'

He had forgotten it was by the traitor, Newman.

'You look nice.' Alex turned his head on the pillow. His pyjama jacket was buttoned right to the top. A book, *Mr Sponge*, lay collapsed on his chest.

'What is it?' Alice leant over him, all scent and flesh, ivory and black draped satin.

'Surtees.'

'Ah, yes.' She replaced the book carefully.

'Is it difficult to get them on?' he asked, looking at her gloves; buttons at the wrist and then a casing of kid all the way to the elbow. So pretty.

'You can't be in a hurry.' She looked at him indulgently.

'Do they think I'm a lunatic?'

'No.'

He watched her touching her pearls with absurdly delineated fingers; obviously it would be difficult to wear rings underneath.

'No.' But she didn't smile. 'They don't.'

'They?'

'Gerard. And Lady B.'

'What's the verdict then? I feel like a prisoner here; there's nothing the matter with me.'

'I can see that,' said Alice cagily. Gerard had expressly told her not to come, but she had wanted to.

'Are you on a recce of some kind?' Alex asked suspiciously. 'Spying for Dr Farquhar?'

Now she did laugh. 'Of course not. The general opinion is that you'll be all right in the morning, but Gerard...'

'What?'

'I don't know ... I'm not withholding information,' she said, putting a hand on the bedclothes. 'Gerard seemed strangely upset; he shot very badly, almost as if...'

Alex waited.

'As if he was trying to miss things on purpose.'

'That's not like him at all.'

'No, I know.'

'And you think the two events are connected?' he asked, looking at her as if he were considering something.

'I can't help thinking so. To shoot badly is one thing, understandable if you like, but to miss almost deliberately – that's not like Gerard.' It was becoming clearer to her why she had come: she had to know whether Gerard had sensed, God knows how, the new relation between herself and Edmund, or whether it was this: this business with Alex that had put him off his stroke.

Alex put his knuckles to his mouth. Silence. A distant male voice singing somewhere in the house.

Gerard counted ten and went in.

'Ah, good,' said Lord Baillie, then paused. 'Who wanted to see whom?' he asked.

'I wanted to see you, Dad,' said Gerard, ignoring his father's ploy, and using the name in a deliberate attempt to resurrect an ancient and almost forgotten kind of joky tenderness between them. 'I'm going tomorrow, as you know, and I don't want to go without a proper goodbye.' His father's surprisingly benevolent expression suggested that their difficulties could all be water under the bridge; an unexpected bonus. He had been prepared for the usual intransigence.

'There are things I ought to say to you,' said Lord Baillie, opening and shutting a desk drawer, 'but I'm damned if I know what they are. Chaps used to send their sons off to the wars to get them out of their hair. I can't say those are *exactly* my sentiments.'

'That's very good of you, Dad.'

'Well, well, enough slush,' Lord Baillie replied hastily. 'Two things I want to know,' he said briskly, 'why can't you shoot straight any more and what's the matter with the boy? Is he sixpence in the shilling or what? Your mother said something about outgrowing his strength. I never heard such rubbish.'

'I don't know,' Gerard answered, ignoring the first question, 'and I'm not sure he knows himself. But I don't think it'll happen again.'

'You don't.'

'No.'

'And why don't you?'

'What happened to me is very confusing,' said Alex,

83

speaking slowly. This was only partly true, but, assuming the event as a kind of wounding, he did not wish to look under the plaster to gauge the extent of the injury only to find it worse. He had a feeling as well that words would make his shapeless foreboding a certainty; words would give the thing edge and identity, words would make ... whatever it was happen. He wished Alice would go away and stop needling him. 'I don't really know myself,' he continued, avoiding her eye, 'what or why, but it is to do with a dream I had. Some kind of premonition of disaster...'

'General or particular?'

'Particular,' he said coldly, making up his mind to say nothing more. The truth or whatever it was had passed through him; he was not the god, only the mouthpiece, the vehicle.

'I see.' She put a hand to her face. 'Did you tell him any of this?'

'I can't.' Oh, leave off, please. He rubbed a sore spot on one of his knuckles where he had a habit of biting the skin when perplexed or distressed. With an effort he resisted putting his hand to his mouth.

'Do you think it's true?'

'I don't know,' Alex shouted. 'I don't know and I don't want to know.'

'I'm sorry,' Alice said, rising. 'I'm sorry. I shouldn't have come. It wasn't fair on you.'

'I didn't mean to shout,' said Alex, wiping his eye, 'but it's been such a bloody day. He was so good to me downstairs, staying with me like that.'

'He loves you, perhaps the most.'

'Don't be stupid,' said Alex looking cross and uncomfortable. He hated it when people said things like that. Horrible sentimental talk. There were no words for what was between him and Gerard. And that was right.

'Don't you tell him any of this,' he said.

'There's nothing to tell.' Alice had her hand on the door-handle. 'Is there?'

*

It was a brilliant dinner. The dining-room all candlelight and reflections, the breeze from the open window stirring the flames so that the light was a moving thing catching sometimes the tip of one of the silver horsemen's spears on the épergne, or a jewelled hand. And the young men, the fine, fine flower of their generation, so noble, so forbearing, aware of the shadow that lay across their path. There was a feeling of romance in the air, of ending, of change held off whilst the last drop in the cup was drained...

Of course this is all nonsense, a kind of *Daily Mail* myth. The weather was changing and the windows had to be shut because it was too cold for the women, half-nude in Worth and Poiret. The épergne had been taken to bits for cleaning and left in pieces in the butler's pantry. Everyone was tired, particularly the men, much, much too worn out by killing birds to contemplate slaughtering the next target, even if it was a two-legged one with a spike on its head ... 'The Greater Crested Pomeranian with its ungainly gait and strange, guttural call is commonly found in the flat lands of northern France and Belgium; grey plumage, lethal if disturbed ...' Nina's calf-muscles ached and Edmund could feel one of his heads coming on. Gerard yawned and thought about bed not Destiny. As for the last drop: well, that was drained by the mildly dipsomaniac butler after the company retired to the saloon.

CHAPTER
SEVEN

Gerard was on his knees when the man came in with the telegram. It was from O'Hallan at Colchester. 'WE GO TO WAR STATION TONIGHT', it said, 'AT WOODBRIDGE. YOUR PRESENCE REQUIRED SOONEST AT CROWN HOTEL, WOODBRIDGE.'

When he went downstairs to breakfast there was a letter from O'Hallan as well, posted two days before.

Dear Baillie,

We live in an atmosphere of scares and alarms, houses blown down, trenches and barbed wire everywhere. Today we have been asked by the War Office if we are prepared to go abroad, and all officers and 90 per cent of the men have volunteered, but I doubt if we move for a month at least. The 'on dit' is that the Guards and 1st Army Corps go in about a week and not in driblets, but one must wait and see. Each rumour is replaced quickly by another which appears to display the same amount of verisimilitude even if what is said runs directly counter to the previous one!

The East Coast, Harwich, is thought of as rather a 'hot spot'. There is a report that three German ships were off Harwich this evening with the aim of destroying the naval oil tanks there.

Hope the grouse was good but can't imagine it was as exciting as life here.

Yrs,
O'Hallan

*

'Telegram,' said Gerard to Edmund at breakfast. 'War station at last.'

'Does it mean anything?' Edmund felt a prick of envy that Gerard should be the first of them directly involved.

'A month in uniform at least, he says in the letter.' Gerard handed it to him. 'Read it if you like.'

'When shall we three meet again?' said Nina. 'You were lucky to get in your shooting as if nothing was happening. Mummy says,' she brandished a letter too, 'that all the young men are rushing back to their depots and that she is knitting socks frantically.'

'Whatever for?' asked William, who could not imagine his mother-in-law knitting anything, let alone a sock.

'For the volunteers, my darling. K.'s boys. Daddy lunched with Sir George Arthur,' she looked at the letter in her hand, 'Kitchener's Private Secretary, and says that he is having the time of his life. What else? Oh yes: Daddy says they are getting ready six divisions each to be 27,000 strong and have sent or are sending four, the two left are in reserve, and that he will get into trouble if I repeat this, so please don't ... Oh dear...' Nina put her hand to her mouth and giggled.

The entire room had fallen silent.

'Well,' said Gerard rather heavily, 'you seem to be better informed than I am.'

'I am going to be a nurse,' said Nina. 'What are you going to do, Alice?'

'I hadn't thought. Knit sleeping helmets or something, I suppose.'

'Can you knit?' Edmund asked her, smiling.

'No, but I can learn.'

'I like the idea of laying my magic hands on fevered brows,' said Nina, 'like dear Flo.'

'It isn't all brandishing a lamp about, darling,' said William, indulgently. 'Scutari was a nightmare of dirt and disorder when she arrived.'

'She went to bed for forty years to recover.' Edmund laid down his knife and fork. He handed the letter back to Gerard. 'I'm glad for you,' he said. 'What? London tonight and then on, or will you go direct?'

'London,' said Gerard looking at Alice.

'They say London is decorated with posters taken from the cover of that cheap newspaper,' Lady Baillie offered.

'*London Opinion*, you mean, dear,' said Lady Few.

'Do you read it?'

'No, but Cook does and then I have it afterwards.'

'I know the thing,' said Lord Baillie. 'Tells women to go to bed in gloves and handcream every night.'

'You're very well informed,' Lord Few looked at him in amazement. 'How the devil do you know that?'

'As a representative peer,' said Lord Baillie, 'I made it my business to know about public opinion, a way of keeping in touch with the common people.'

'He likes the scandal,' whispered Nina to Edmund. 'Vicars doing unspeakable things to their parishioners.'

'Hush,' replied Edmund, but his lips twitched.

'I'm off,' said Gerard to Alex, sitting down on the end of his bed. 'It's happening at last.'

'God, you're so lucky. I wish there was something I could do.'

'You're in the O.T.C.,' said Gerard, 'that's something.'

'It's like being in the kindergarten; little boy stuff.'

'We all have to do it,' said Gerard. 'Anyway, this won't be a quick war for all they talk about Christmas.'

'No.' He looked at Gerard wanting to say he was pleased for him but that he must be careful, only he couldn't think how to.

'Write to me,' said Gerard. 'I'll want to hear how you're getting on. Are you ... better now?' he added.

'Yes.'

'Would you like to tell me,' asked Gerard, 'but don't if you don't want to, what it was all about?'

'I can't remember much,' Alex put his hands under the bedclothes. 'Something about Gonville –'

'Gonville!'

'And his dog.'

'Are you pulling my leg?' Gerard looked away.

'I'm not, truly.'

'All right.' Gerard got up. 'Write to me, remember, and I'll try and reply.'

'We should make a code so that I know where you are.'

'There isn't time,' said Gerard, smiling. Perhaps it was all a nonsense, after all. 'Don't let Ma mollycoddle you.'

'I won't.'

When he had gone Alex lay down with a pillow over his head, so that nobody would hear.

A house near a park. Number 1, St Luke's Terrace, Regent's Park. A fanlight and a black-painted front door which stands open revealing a black and white tiled floor of a kind sometimes seen in those intimately domestic Dutch paintings. Move your eye up and beyond, past the hat stand and the vase of flowers, through an open doorway into a room which seems to be full of light. People are going up and down the steps with luggage; Alice's Noah's Ark is humped into the house; there is an altercation with a cab-driver and then the door is shut. A woman raises a blind at an upstairs window and stands looking out at the street.

Gerard went across the hall into his library. They had journeyed all day to reach this place and yet, now he was here, the journey, or rather the mechanics of it, had vanished, leaving only an immense feeling of distance between here and there which was not to do with miles but instead was measured in tempo, pace. It was a different world here: the city, the fever of it coming up through the paving stones, the flags, the crowds, the new recruiting posters. K.'s face, the walloping moustache, the

89

stubby, pointing finger, the written assurance of worth. And he remembered how, this morning, coming in from the garden, he had seen Macindoe in the border weeding: the bent back, the slow, deliberate rhythm, the unhurriedness of it, the violent contrast between that and this: London flushed and hectic in the embrace of the people's war, welcomed, it seemed, on every street. Where was Ireland now? Fermanagh and County Tyrone, the disruptive female suffragists; all gone, old hat, replaced by news of impending battles, rumours about the BEF; the chosen few assembling into their waiting ships, action, purpose. Suddenly it all defeated him, seemed beyond his reach, ungraspable; his own contribution would be a mere nothing in these enormous movements of men and equipment in the iron, impersonal fist of war.

He sat down and began opening his post, taking up his paper knife which was the foot of some dead animal with an ivory blade attached. He had left home that morning with purpose, excited himself and feeling that excitement honoured by the others who had, because of it, placed him in a special category: cramming into the motor with Alice, waving at them all as they stood about on the steps. How Edmund had come to the window saying something about meeting soon. 'London,' he had said, 'or out there,' magic words, putting his hand in and pressing his shoulder, a way of saying all right, no hard feelings, everything just the same as it always was. But was it? This distracted him. Was it? He found himself thinking rather sceptically about that gesture, not quite believing in it; looking back, he sensed in Edmund a kind of shallowness, a glitter, an insincerity that was new. They hadn't seen each other for a long time, he had to take that into account, but distanced from the party now by a day's travel, a return to normality here in this quiet house, time to think, to be objective about his own actions, it seemed that behind the façade of an old friend who could tell a home-truth or two, there was something else, a hardness, almost a kind of cruelty fleshed out and practically invisible behind the good looks, the perfect manners. *Edmund had enjoyed having the whip hand.* For some reason, Gerard found the word 'unscrupulous' appeared to fit these half-formed impressions.

He had passed through hell during that house-party and come out the other side into the quiet: to review in this way was somehow salutary, a kind of stock-taking. When he thought of Nina now it was almost with amazement, amazement that she could have inspired such passions in him, such foolishness, and yet it was only a matter of days since he had been carried upstairs to bed drunk out of his mind. It was the nature of change that puzzled him, its deceptive faces. He had thought becoming an RC had changed him, as if an intellectual belief was enough, a new label: I am a Catholic and therefore a good man. Real change was felt all the way from the bowels to the brain and bore no relation to time, was from one minute to the next, conviction, a certainty of things. The trouble was to convince others, to convince Alice of this. There was a distance between them which had become apparent once they were alone together. The train journey had quickly revealed this to him. It had been as if she was with him and yet not with him, something he couldn't quite put his finger on. Since that unpleasant scene on the day of Alex's arrival at Kildour, Gerard had tried to show her by both word and gesture how much he would like her to mean to him, if she would allow him to, but somehow, by a process whose workings were not detectable in any outward form, she had countered him. His remarks were met by replies, his smiles by her smile and yet there was no meeting point, no connection. Not once had he had the impression of getting through to her; she was composed, affable, but absent; it was extraordinary how ridiculously little he knew about her, the secret workings of her inward being. They had to talk, he thought, had to. To leave tomorrow without making contact would be fatal. God alone knew when they would have another opportunity.

'My dear,' Edmund wrote, 'I am now returned to my little cell where I have spent most of this dreariest of summers ... ' The letter was to his old love Hatty. It seemed to be a time to write letters, poised as he was on the brink of an event he had prepared for all his working life; he wanted to share his euphoria with everyone, scatter compliments and *bons mots* all over Europe. He had come back to Kincraig to find instructions waiting for him and was leaving for Ayr in the morning to rejoin his regiment. Somehow or other he hoped there would be a few days' leave to spend in London, time to see Alice and to drink deep before going abroad.

> My recovery was celebrated by a splendid grouse shoot at Kildour, over the hill from here, my old friend Gerard Baillie's place, and, I am afraid, the introduction of a new [he paused] 'object'. Gerard's little wife Alice, who quite literally threw herself at me.

Writing, he was beginning to find, tidied things up, was a nearly perfect way of remaking past events so that one could believe that it actually had been like that. He left out Kitty and all the ... sentimental nonsense; it would look pretty silly on a page to say that one had romantic dreams about a girl on account of the fact that she vaguely resembled a long-dead cousin who had been his first and perhaps only love. Alice had thrown herself at him, nothing new in that, after all.

> They are not happily married, it seems, and I appear to have been cast in the rôle of rescuer, knight on horseback, what you will. Not quite my normal line, but in your absence, dear, an absence I might add that looks like continuing indefinitely now that this

war has been announced, what is a fellow to do? And married women are fair game, are they not?

Gerard has recently become a Papist and is displaying all the usual signs of wear and tear that the excessive demands of the Holy See produces in ordinary fellows when they start thinking too hard about God and Life and Death. He made the marriage to cancel out the attractions of a previous *amour*, now married to his wife's brother. All very complicated and ironical, like something out of one of those novels you were always reading.

I do miss you, Hatty dear, but wish me a glorious war.

Love, always,

E.

At dinner he thanked God to be going, to be getting away from it all, forgetting how he had squashed Gerard flat on that account. It was, he supposed, looking round the room, all this that he was fighting for, but it couldn't keep you until you were ready to keep it; it needed danger, close shaves, a certain amount of calculated recklessness, and then one would be ready for the old, comfortable embrace of the house, its quiet routine, the endless rotation of meals, their length and absurd formality, the way nothing was done all day and found exhausting. One day, sooner or later, sometime, he would be old and dull and grateful.

CHAPTER
EIGHT

'Are you sad?'

'Yes.'

'You don't sound very certain.'

'I don't know how I am supposed to convince you of it,' said Alice, who was talking on the telephone to Pamela.

'Come to a party. I should love to see you.'

'I wouldn't fit at your parties. I'm not unbuttoned enough.'

'Don't be absurd.'

'When is it?'

'Tonight.'

'I can't – ' Then she thought, why not? There was nothing else to do. 'All right. What time?'

'After eight and don't dress up.'

'Is it in aid of anything?'

'No, just to keep ourselves going. Some Hungarians Petersen knows are going to play Mozart.'

'How's Rolf?'

'In purdah, darling. He's a German, you know. If they smash Appenrod's what'll they do to a poor, elderly Bavarian sausage?'

'How do you know he's Bavarian?'

'I don't. I'm just making it up. Southern ones are better than the northern bunch. Gerard would tell you that.'

'He can't tell me anything at the moment.'

'Sorry, I forgot. Now you do sound sad.'

'Goodbye,' said Alice.

Gerard had gone away on a train some days ago; it had all been most unsatisfactory. The night before he went, he came through the dressing-room holding his book in his hand and asked her to come and see him when she was finished undressing. She had not liked the sound of this at all. There was a look on his face she had seen several times in the last few days: a new expression of interest and concern, but with something stern in it, a hint of the change in him she could see but not understand. People did not change, not really, not profoundly, and certainly not after twenty-five or so. It made her feel very unsure of her ground; the discussion, whatever it was he had to say, would be conducted on some new basis now, a situation in which she was sure he would arrange for her to have a fair say, a situation for which she felt entirely unready on account of her betrayal of him. Between them it was not the moment to talk, but other events, the outside world, were forcing this on them; in the morning he would be gone, they might see one another again, briefly, before he went away to the war, then anything might happen. He could be killed. And of course that would leave her with a life-long feeling of guilt and shame, but in spite of knowing all this she still felt perverse, unwilling, elated by her secret, determined to follow things through with Edmund, about whom she found herself having the most romantic, absurd thoughts. He had nearly defeated her hopes of him at Kildour by his extraordinary social deftness, the way in which he was able to look at her as if she was nothing to him, the way he flirted with Nina, talked shop with Gerard. He had explained all this to her at that lunch, made it plain how necessary it was to dissemble, so that she had ended slave to him, suppressing thoughts that he could have been deliberately cold to her, unfeeling, that he was playing games with her.

'I'm sorry if you're tired.' Gerard looked up as she

came in. He was sitting on an upright chair at a little table, writing something.

'It's not late,' she said. 'Are you ready?'

'Nearly. Most of it's in there.' He elbowed in the direction of the dressing-room, bringing up a chair for her, the twin of his. 'Sit,' he said, 'do. I like that.' He touched the edge of her wrapper. 'Have I seen it before?'

'It was in my trousseau,' she said, 'but I haven't worn it much.' This was not strictly true, but she didn't want him to have the advantage over her so quickly by apologizing for not noticing it. 'What was it?' she asked hastily, trying to read upside-down the letter he had been writing.

'Look at me, Alice,' he said and took her hand. Reluctantly she did so. 'I can't go,' he continued, 'without knowing that things are right between us. You have such an odd expression on your face. What is it?' He dropped her hand and put a finger under her chin. 'You look mutinous,' he said. 'Can you not forgive me, believe that I know I have treated you badly, that I should like us to begin again? Nothing can be so bad that it cannot be fixed, if both parties want it to be so. Do you want it, Alice?'

'Of course.'

'You say that,' he said, 'but I cannot get through to you. You are unreachable.'

'You know me so little,' she answered, sitting back in her chair, 'that you cannot see that I am all here. You're inventing me all over again because of something that has happened to you, some change that has come over you.'

'I have changed,' he said, 'that is true, but it is, if you like, an uncomfortable kind of change. I've become aware of things that escaped me before, when I was so busy thinking about myself all the time.'

'What do you mean?' She wondered if he was claiming some kind of supernatural power.

'I mean,' he said, 'that I know perfectly well you are keeping yourself hidden to me, whatever you say. I know that my father means well towards me, even if it has appeared sometimes that he almost hates me. I know that Edmund is an officer and a gentleman but that behind the perfect façade he is somewhat unscrupulous. All these things I know and now acknowledge that I know.'

'You're going too fast for me,' Alice said, panicked by the reference to Edmund. 'You only say that about Edmund because he saw you at your worst and gave you a dressing-down.'

'He enjoyed it,' Gerard emphasized the words, 'and, in any case, how do you know that? I didn't tell you.'

'Edmund told me,' she said, improvising madly. 'Surely you didn't expect we would avoid all mention of it. How could we?'

He looked at her very hard. 'I suppose not,' he said, 'but it is uncomfortable to know that you were discussing me.'

'What you did with Nina was uncomfortable for me too.' O infallible accusation!

'He feels sorry for you,' Gerard said, 'he told me so. It's only natural . . .' He looked down at his hands; these words were for himself. For a moment he had felt quite like the Prince de Clèves. 'We can't argue,' he said. 'Time is so short. Just forgive me, believe what I say.'

'I do.' Alice was made eager by relief. 'But it applies to you too.' A tremendously good liar, which she was not, would now have talked about love. She admired him for his courage, but felt she had gone too far in the other direction for a true *rapprochement*. He would never forgive her for Edmund after this, whatever happened. It was all reversed between them now. She could see that she was no longer good enough for him.

'There is one other thing,' Gerard said, getting up and walking about. 'But it's very delicate . . . I don't know if now is the right moment.' He looked across the room at her and she saw that he was fiddling with his signet ring, twisting it round and round on his little finger.

'I think I know what you're going to say. It's about a child, isn't it?'

'Put like that it's so ... blunt.'

'Your mother said something about it.'

'Oh God, I wish she wouldn't meddle.'

'She meant well,' said Alice who, above everything – modesty, failure in her duty and so on – was glad of a new subject, particularly an engrossing one such as this. As yet the idea did not touch her personally, was only something that other people worried about. It did not occur to her that she might have conceived a child from Edmund; the two functions, pleasure and duty, seemed so separate somehow. She supposed her body would know the difference, when the time came.

'What did she say?' He was anxious for her, embarrassed. Perhaps it was this that had so strangely separated her from him?

'That I should go and see someone.'

'It doesn't matter to me,' he said, coming to her and putting his arm round her. Nothing mattered but that they should be on a right footing again. He pushed the idea of a son away. 'It could be my fault.'

'It's nobody's fault.' She bent her face into his silk arm, feeling so sad for him suddenly. As if the world was always this: betrayals, half-truths. She remembered Alex. What could any of them do?

And so he had gone, leaving her not knowing whether to be glad or sorry. In his presence she was filled with the most unwieldy, conflicting emotions; gone, she felt sad for him and irritated and unworthy.

The afternoon of Pamela's party she finally went to see a man. A Harley Street man: Mr James, gynaecologist and obstetrician to the quality (he had delivered some minor royalty) whose plump white hands and insinuating manner she found slightly repellent. He wore an immaculate suit and sported an enormous and improbable carnation the colour of blood in his button hole. She supposed this bloom to be fed from one of those little holders cunningly concealed behind his lapel and wondered what happened when he bent over – whether the water ran out – or whether the flower simply existed supernaturally on the strength of Mr James's tremendous vitality. He walked lightly, bobbingly on his fat feet, leading her to her chair when she came in, seating her.

From the other side of his enormous desk he asked questions. How long, how often, do you have pain, does your husband...? He talked ova, and cycles and menstruation. Timing, apparently, was the thing. It was all a mystery to Alice. One either did or one didn't, she had thought.

'Let's just have a little look, shall we?' he finished up, gesturing her towards a curtained cubicle. 'Bottom things off.' It was like Nanny, only faintly prurient. She lay down on an object like an Empire sofa but with wheels, listening to Mr James rustling round the room, running taps, pulling on rubber gauntlets, whistling *Gilbert the Filbert* under his breath.

'Like this, please.' He bent her legs into a most embarrassing position and proceeded to guddle and prod. 'Does this hurt?' He dug his rubber fingers into her left side near the groin.

'No.' It had, in fact, but she wasn't going to tell him that.

'This?'

'Ouch.'

He didn't apologize. 'That's it then. Put on your things and we'll talk.'

'You have a displaced womb,' he said, making a little pencil sketch on his pad and pushing it across the desk. Alice stared at a picture closely resembling the outline of a ram's head. She could think of nothing whatever to say.

'Conception is not impossible, but it will be difficult. There are various things you can do to help yourself.

Don't be downhearted,' he said, seeing her expression.

'I'm not, I'm just baffled.'

'Shall I tell you what they are?'

'I suppose so.'

'Hips up afterwards,' he said briskly. 'Legs in the air helps too, but I admit it is a little undignified.' He smiled urbanely. 'Come and see me again in a few months if you have no luck. Husband away, is he?'

'A week ago for an indefinite period.'

'Hard lines on you. You should have come to see me sooner.'

'But I had no idea there was anything the matter.'

'It shouldn't take more than three or four months for healthy young things like you to conceive a child, my dear.'

'One is not told these things in the schoolroom,' said Alice, crossly.

'Indeed, no.' He looked at her for a minute then jumped to his feet. 'Don't hesitate,' he said at the door, 'at any time. Always at your disposal...'

Alice went home and had a bath, feeling she smelt of consulting room and rubber glove, perfumed yet antiseptic, most unpleasant. She found herself in tears. The numbness she had felt during her interview with Mr James had worn off. It seemed hard to find out how much she wanted a child after she had been told it would be difficult to have one. The traitor body. In a way it almost justified Edmund, any sexual activity being better than none, any child better than no child. The more the merrier. It was extraordinary how quickly, she thought, one could pass beyond the moral pale, how secretly, and find oneself thinking the unthinkable, doing the unthinkable, justifying it all by any old aphorism: that one might as well be hung for a sheep as a lamb. She suddenly found herself filled with a kind of wild and desperate gaiety, based on a sense of her own inevitable damnation. She would go to Pamela's party and find some sort of oblivion in hot rooms full of smoke and people; possibly she might even drink too much, there was nothing now, nobody to stop her.

Pamela had attic rooms in Bloomsbury, a tall house in a square of tall houses with sombre gardens in the middle. Alice climbed to the top, guided by the sound of voices, and with some difficulty made her way past a group of people clustered round the doorway who showed no inclination whatever to make room for her. There was a long passage with a sloping roof and rooms leading off it. Each seemed to contain an inordinate number of people. It was very hot and already the smoke was making her eyes water. She took off her coat and looked round for somewhere to put it. Nobody so far had paid the least attention to her.

'Allow me.' A young man wearing a tobacco-coloured velvet jacket and a white shirt unbuttoned rather too far appeared at her elbow. He had round spectacles and fine, dark hair which he pushed self-consciously off his forehead.

'Thank you,' said Alice, grateful for any attention. He stuffed her coat onto a chair already piled high and took her arm.

'Now you must have a drink,' he said. 'It's the most ghastly party. I can't think why any of us are here. The usual hogwash to drink too, but one is fond of Pamela, and of course her work is...'

They were now in a room that Alice with difficulty recognized as Pamela's sitting-room. The blotched mirror over the fireplace reflected the backs of heads and shoulders. 'Stay,' her young man had shouted. 'I'll fetch a drink.'

Obediently, she remained; indeed it was not really possible to do anything else. Her attention was caught by a man with fair hair, rather older-looking, half-turned from her, his shoulder pressed to an unframed oil which threatened at any minute to fall from its moorings.

'Now I find you. Have you been here long? You

101

missed the music.' It was Pamela, flushed and pretty, hair up, low dress, clutching a glass in one hand and a cigarette in a long holder in the other.

'No, but someone's been nice to me. I don't know his name, he's gone for a drink.' Alice felt miles behind in the league of gaiety. Pamela was all party spirit, shiny eyes, enjoyment.

'Come and meet Petersen,' said Pamela. 'He's longing for someone to have an argument with. You might be able to do something with him. It's rather like living with Nostradamus; he's terribly doomy, gloomy – thinks Lord Northcliffe's the Antichrist. Thank you,' she said, taking a glass from the young man with dark hair and giving it to Alice. 'Now go away, David,' she said to him, 'she's my cousin and she's not for sale. Her husband's gone to do his bit,' she added, leading Alice towards the man with fair hair, now looking for somewhere to put out his cigarette.

'This is Alice,' she said to him, 'remember? Now I shall leave you,' and she vanished.

'So, Alice, yes . . .' He was lighting another cigarette as he spoke: bony hands, dirty fingernails. 'Pamela's cousin, I remember now; she was speaking of you only this morning. Do you sit for her?'

'No, I don't.' Alice was embarrassed by his candid stare, the way he had come too close.

'You should. Perhaps you would sit for me?'

'Well, I don't know. I'm not very good at being still for long periods.' She could feel herself blushing.

'Lovely bones,' he said, 'and hair.' He touched her jaw and, without meaning to, she jerked her head and took a step backwards, loathing the familiarity.

'Look out,' said a voice. A girl shrieked.

'I'm so sorry,' Alice turned and made apologetic gestures, hoping for an excuse to get away from Petersen.

'Don't go,' he said. 'It's a terrible dress anyway. Tell me about yourself.' He moved her from the girl in white who was tutting and dabbing. 'I understand your husband has gone.'

102

'Yes.'

'You should have stopped him; such folly all this. We are returning to the Dark Ages in ruin, degeneration, intolerance. When I think of France I want to weep.'

'I didn't want him to go,' said Alice, 'but how could I stop him? How can one stop any of them? They have a duty to fight.'

'Pamela told me he had recently become a Roman Catholic. He must be aware of the Sixth Commandment.'

'Are you one too?'

'I was. Once. Now I am what they call lapsed.' He smiled for some reason.

'But an invasion of territory,' insisted Alice. 'Belgium. Are we to stand aside? Surely you are not suggesting that men like Gerard who are acting in the most honourable way open to them can be murderers?' The conversation seemed to be taking the most violent and exaggerated turn.

'Why is it different to kill a man in war? He dies just the same. It is all a matter of labels, you see, exoneration; men like Grey offering up our youth on the altar of barbarism.'

'Officers, you realize, don't as a general rule kill men,' said Alice coldly, remembering something Gerard had said.

'You mean they merely direct others to do so.'

'You deliberately misunderstand me.'

'What is Belgium to us?' he asked, flicking his ash onto the carpet, 'or the original, absurd quarrel over the Slav business. It could have, should have been resolved peaceably; all those diplomats jumping and waving their arms, achieving nothing. We should have stood aside. It is not our quarrel.'

'Not *your* quarrel, perhaps,' said Alice rudely.

'There you are wrong,' he said. 'I am a British subject ... but I see that I am making you angry. I'm sorry.'

She looked at him in silence over the rim of her glass. 'I think, perhaps –'

'One more minute.' Petersen gripped her arm. 'This is important, I'm sure your husband would understand –'

'I can't for a second imagine why you should think that,' said Alice. 'Please let go of my arm.' She tried to move away but he tightened his grip.

'Listen,' he said desperately, 'if your husband had read more he would understand that it is a patristic error to suggest that God's judgement is put in suspension when it suits man's purpose. I know the Roman Church is well primed with evasive dogma on the subject of Holy War, Just War, but these are only more labels for wars, killings, conducted in the interests of the State which reflects also the interests of the Church. That is why it is considered so treacherous to dissent, to be a pacifist, as I am.' He let go of her arm. 'Go now, if you wish.'

'But we're not talking about a crusade,' said Alice, feeling that she must somehow see this extraordinary conversation through. 'That was all so long ago.'

He muttered something under his breath. She caught the word 'snobbery'.

'What?'

She wanted to take him by his angular shoulders and shake him.

'There is very little difference, really,' he said, looking at her rather sadly. 'People are wearing different costumes, that's all; the sentiments, the underlying feelings are much the same. The young men have been sold a kind of romantic militarism, approved by the clergy, spiced with sanctity and patriotism. They have been given something to die for. Peace will be a dead word until there have been enough deaths . . .' He looked away and she saw that there were tears in his eyes.

'What will you do?' Alice asked, looking at him with distaste and admiration; one had to admire such passionate conviction.

'Stay,' he answered, draining his glass. 'Wait. Work. Then there will be conscription because it will be a long and bloody war. After that I shall go to jail. Come and sit for me,' he added suddenly. 'I should like us to be friends. You have a lovely face. Let me paint you as a present for your husband, for Gerald.'

'Gerard.'

'I'm sorry, Gerard. You must forgive a bloody foreigner,' he said. And smiled.

'What did Petersen do before?' Alice asked Pamela as she left.

'He was a monk, darling. Didn't I tell you? Frightfully ultra-montanist, so much so that he made himself ill. When he got better he found it had all sort of washed off, so he had to leave. He is a little dotty, isn't he? But his heart's in the right place. Paints like a dream, although this damn war's put him off his stroke a bit. Says it's the end of Christianity, the lot.'

'He still believes, doesn't he?'

'Oh, you know how that sort of thing lingers like a bad smell. Look, do go, I'm frightfully tight. Come and see me in a couple of days and we'll have a talk.'

Alice kissed and went.

CHAPTER
NINE

'Yes?'

Gerard looked up in exasperation, wondering who the hell it was this time. His watch said half-past ten which, according to his upbringing, was a guarantee of solitude except in the direst emergencies. And he was in need of solitude merely to keep abreast of the enormous amount of paperwork that had deluged him in the three weeks he had been at Woodbridge. He doubted he would finish even if he worked all night.

'Sorry to disturb you, Captain Baillie.' It was the vicar of St James's, Colchester, who was also acting chaplain to the battery, with them for a couple of nights to test the spiritual temperature of his flock and to enjoy, in a way that rather amused Gerard, being military. 'A word', he said, coming round the door, 'about the relief fund. Would you mind?'

'No, of course not.' Gerard rose from his writing-table by the window, loosening his collar, and came towards the padre, waving him into one of the armchairs by the fireplace.

'I'm glad to see you, actually,' Gerard said, kneeling and poking at the fire. 'My head's going round in circles. The paperwork is fearsome: I was just making up my observations on the equipment and store account and trying to get the gunnery rules ready in time to go to the printers in the morning. Let's have a drink,' he said, sitting back on his heels, still holding the poker. 'Whisky, if that's all right. Help yourself – it's on top of the chest of drawers. Do me one too, would you?' He looked at the fire where one feeble flame had poked its head out of the glowing mass then died away again. Hopeless.

'You seem very cosy here,' said the Rev. Naters over his shoulder, holding a glass up to the light. 'Nice little place, isn't it? They're very civil at the desk and so forth.'

'It's not bad, I must say.' Gerard scrambled up with difficulty, feeling stiff and awkward. He had missed two days' riding on account of a cold in the head and was already paying the price.

'Here you are,' said the padre, 'Your reward. And well earned, too. Things are going pretty smoothly, aren't they?'

'Oh yes.' Gerard sat down rather carefully opposite Naters and raised his glass to him. 'Chin, chin. Yes. The poster's had a good effect, everything's going well there; it's just the paper. The army breeds forms: everything in duplicate, triplicate, telegrams here, notifications there, all on a daily basis, couched in a style peculiar to the army which renders even the most simple statements almost unintelligible to the ordinary person; really I think it is to disguise the absolute unimportance of all the balderdash that goes to and fro in cartloads. I fully expect to be crushed to death by paper rather than a German.'

'How soon will you go?' asked the padre, smiling a little.

'Anyone's guess,' said Gerard, getting up again to look for his cigarette case. 'Between you and me,' he continued, going over to the table, picking up various pieces of paper and putting them down again before he had found what he wanted, 'I've applied for a transfer to go out as an interpreter. I expect to hear from the War Office any day now.'

'I didn't know you were a linguist,' the padre said, waving away a cigarette. 'What do you speak, apart from French?'

'German,' said Gerard. 'I lived there once as a young

man. Later I had friends in the White Dragoons. Dined with them in January at Darmstadt...' He paused, leaning back against the table. 'Now I hear they've been annihilated near Strasburg. It seems unbelievable, really, they were such good fellows.' He tapped his cigarette on the lid of his case, remembering the dinner which had been in celebration of the Kaiser's *geburtstag*. January. A different era. 'It's so sad,' he said, 'that when we think of a typical German now, we think at once of a Prussian: the new German with his *"weltanschauung"*, and forget all the rest.'

'I know what you mean,' said the padre. '1870 was the turning point. Something went wrong then in the fledging of their sense of unity, as if some grievance at being blamed for what they had not begun was incorporated into the formation of the Reich, affecting their new nationhood: the nearly civilized child falling back into an infantile kind of aggression and unreasonableness. The Kaiser seems to me a perfect example, really. Powerful, cunning, but a child, with a child's lack of proportion and discretion.'

'How well you put it.' Gerard sat down and crossed his legs. The talk and drink were doing the trick. He wanted more.

'I envy you,' said Naters, putting his glass down on the table beside him and unconsciously putting a hand to his collar. 'We're so circumscribed in what we can do. Your lot are sending priests into the fray, I gather, and of course the nuns will go on doing what they have always done: nursing the wounded, caring, being useful.' He turned his glass this way and that on the table. 'If it's not a rude question, when did you convert?'

'No time ago at all, as these things go,' said Gerard, 'but it wasn't crossing over from one thing to another, nothing Newmanesque in it. God was always doing geometry before that, as far as I was concerned. Religion meant very little to me; I was confirmed with the herd,' he made a gesture with his hand, 'one autumn, like

108

passing trials, something else to be done; disappointingly blank, the whole thing. I don't know what I'd expected: pillars of fire, doves, orchestras...'

The padre laughed. 'Go on.'

'I sailed along,' said Gerard, 'like most other young men. Sandhurst, Guards, London life; it all seemed a wonderful picnic, too easy to be true. Then something went wrong: a girl I cared for deeply and wanted to marry, who allowed me to hope before throwing me over. I began to find myself in churches, Catholic churches; the C of E didn't seem complete enough somehow, had too many old, almost frivolous associations in my mind, seemed – forgive me – just an extension of my social life. It had to be something new. Between one day and the next I made some kind of connection, believed, although the process by which this ... conversion was achieved is still extremely mysterious to me. It seemed time to tidy up, to change, so I left the army proper and attached myself to the Essex Horse – just before your time.' He stopped. 'Do you mind this? I don't usually talk of it. I can't think what's come over me.'

'Of course not.'

'I became exultant,' Gerard said, throwing his cigarette end into the fire, 'as if I had acquired some kind of immunity to life's difficulties. I converted, much against my family's will; my father was so enraged he threatened to disinherit me. He loathes Papists, the whole thing in his mind being tantamount to treason. Then,' he continued, 'I met a girl whom I thought I would marry. And that's when everything began to go wrong again.'

'It very often does after an experience of the kind you have described to me,' said the padre. 'Belief, as you obviously know, is only the very beginning.'

'Yes. We married but, by some hideous irony, my first love, Nina, married my wife's brother.'

'Could you say that again?'

109

'A brother and a sister,' said Gerard holding up his hands. 'I married the sister, Nina the brother. We met everywhere. I retreated into a kind of excessive piety as a form of protection because I found ...' even now it was difficult to talk of this '... or thought I found that I still loved Nina. I was horrible to Alice. Nina became a sort of Herculean task I set myself, a trial of strength. I wanted both to make her love me and yet, at the same time, to convince her of my immunity to her. Of course she saw straight through it. She is not really a very nice person. Then the war came, but I went on with the plan to go to Scotland, home, to shoot. Nina was there too. I behaved disgracefully one evening, was carted off tight as a tick by my wife and my best friend, then, the next day, suddenly, like one of the seven sleepers, I came to my senses, properly, horribly. It was not easy. I still feel rather battered by it all.'

'You don't show it,' said the padre. 'And now there is a new ordeal for you to face.'

'I long to be allowed to,' Gerard said, gathering up glasses and refilling them. 'Is it a Just War in your view?'

'As much as any war is,' the padre replied. 'Personally, I think Augustine made rather a hash of all that. It would have been more honest if he'd taken a bolder stand, either for or against, instead of laying down rules for the middle ground.'

'The Christian behind the gun,' Gerard paused with his hand on the bottle. 'You can't square it, can you?'

'Not really ...' The padre, Gerard noticed, was beginning to look a little uncomfortable. *'Deus le volt,'* he added, rubbing his moustache.

'I beg your pardon?'

'God wills it,' said Naters, taking his glass. 'Three most dangerous words in history ...'

Gerard looked at him but said nothing.

'What amazes me,' went on Naters, changing the subject, 'is the men, the courage they have; even untried you can tell. They flabbergast me by their very simplicity. A

110

rich harvest. There's not one of them that wouldn't be gone in the morning if ordered to.'

'I know,' said Gerard. 'When Lord O'Hallan was with them on the eighth he sent a telegram to the War Office about their willingness to serve. They cheered him when he'd done it, too. He has some odd ideas, O'Hallan, though, thinks none of us will see a shot fired and that we shall probably garrison some town like Cologne and guard the lines of communications if the main armies have gone on towards Berlin.'

'Sounds a little optimistic to me,' said the padre.

'A little! I should say so.'

'That reminds me,' said the padre, putting down his glass. 'The relief fund. I'd quite forgotten what I came here for. I had an idea, and I wondered if you might sanction it, that we put an announcement in the *Essex Herald* appealing to the county to raise a fund to relieve distress amongst the wives and children when the men have gone. Many of them are in positions where they're highly paid, but being called away on active service will mean they only receive the same pay as soldiers of the regular army. I wondered if we might have a committee formed of the wives of the battery officers: Lady Alice, Lady O'Hallan, Mrs Maynard and so on?'

'Excellent idea,' said Gerard. 'Alice would like it and I'm sure the other wives would be glad to be of some use. I shall write to her at once about it.'

'Subscriptions could be sent to me at the rectory.'

'Or to the bank,' said Gerard, getting up and going to his table to make a note of it.

'There was one other thing ...'

'Yes?' Gerard looked round.

'I've been going through the parish records,' Naters said, 'which are all in the crypt. The muddle is beyond words, but I found this.' He pulled an envelope out of his pocket. 'It's a copy,' he said, 'not a very good one. I'm not much at typewriting, but I thought you might like to have it.'

111

'What is it?' Gerard came and took the envelope out of his hands.

'An old prayer, not dated, but it seems rather appropriate. Read it when I'm gone,' he said, draining his glass and setting it back on the table. 'I have enjoyed it,' he said, shaking Gerard's hand. 'Oh, and good luck with all your arrangements. We shall be sorry to lose you if it all comes off.'

'I shall be sorry to leave,' Gerard said, holding the door open, 'but I must get there. Can't have a Master of Kildour shirking his duty in the greatest war the world has ever seen.'

The padre hesitated. 'God bless you,' he said, quietly.

A good man, he thought, going slowly down the passage after the door had shut behind him, but with something a little tragic about him. Nothing conscious, not a pose, perhaps connected with his excessive awareness of his own failings. An unusual man certainly. Spare him, he sent upwards, going into his own room. Spare all of them.

When the padre had gone, Gerard looked at his glass but decided against another, knowing the futility of whisky drinking as a stratagem to encourage coherent thought, and went back to his writing-table.

He sat down in front of his Blick and opened the padre's envelope.

'A Prayer,' he read. 'They who shall repeat this prayer every day shall never die a sudden death ... nor shall they be overpowered in battle.' His eye moved farther down the page: 'O adorable Lord and Saviour, Jesus Christ dying on a gallow tree for our sins, O Holy cross of Christ ward off from me all dangerous weapons, O Holy cross of Christ ward off from me all dangerous deaths, and give life always...'

In Hora mortis nostrae ... How interesting this should have found its way to him now, the smallest fragment of the prayer life of the common people out of another world. It was a devotion centred on the ancient idea of a 'good death', the notion of preparedness, of a kind rather frowned upon by the élite in the Church, but clung to nevertheless by the commonality for obvious reasons; and it was affecting. He read it again '... ward off from me all dangerous deaths, and give life always ...'

The power of faith, he thought, the magic potion or prayer, the scapular. A kind of amulet really, a charm. What a pity in a way it was to be twentieth-century man, to be too grown up for all this, to know that one stood alone, relying on a good life to make a good death, no use retiring to the cloister if one had an inkling or rustling up some quick, last-minute penitence. Like St Louis of Gonzaga one would simply have to go on playing ball or cleaning one's teeth ... It was no good, either, trying to ward things off, hoping not to suffer. Nothing, he now knew, could or indeed should avert one's own suffering; suffering was being worn thin and at the same time burnished; it was the way to knowledge. It could almost be equated with a hand being taken in the divine grasp and pressed very hard, so that in the end the pressure would be recognized as the pressure of love.

With a kind of shock he realized that the tortures he had undergone at Kildour had been suffering. It was something to do with his upbringing – the unwritten code – that emotional turmoil, crises of faith, unhappiness without 'proper' reason, was anathema, not spoken of, not counted. Until now he had always equated it, for this reason, with physical damage only, some illness or other, something Job-like and definite that could be seized upon and catalogued: an obvious grievance, a death, not this kind of private agony, the self-made abyss, misunderstood by family and friends.

And it continued. Alice. By her absence present. Pascal had been right about staying in one's room; he wasn't sure about 'sole cause of unhappiness' but it was certainly a contributing factor. Inactivity conjured her. She was much less in his mind when he was doing physical things, riding and so forth, but the long nights here, the early dark, the way his mind was only half engaged by the routine inanities of paperwork, made him constantly aware how much he thought of her, how much he regretted her. And it was regret, and dissatisfaction; these had been the twin colours of his departure. The immediate relief afforded by their last, long conversation had not lasted; making love had been instant but sham anodyne, too good a way of testing deficiencies; afterwards, when she had gone, he lay in his bed, sleepless, trying to read his Tacitus, pretending to draw clever analogies between AD 69, the long and single year of the Histories, and AD 1914 ... and failing, manifestly failing. He could not make her love him, neither could he stop the strong feeling of despair that it might never happen; there was a horrible feeling of urgency to it all now, the idea he had that if they were to have a child, it must be conceived in love.

This idea of a child plagued him as much as the shade of Alice. Sitting through the long nights over his paper mountain, smoking one cigarette after another, he would pause again and again involuntarily, staring into space, imagining young Freddie, Robert, John ... how much he would like to know now that if he was killed there would be a successor at Kildour that was his own particular flesh. He did not mean this as disloyalty to Alex, but cousin, brother, brother, cousin, however close the relation was, it was not like knowing that his own son was being grown on the top floor in the old nursery that had been his; a boy who would look in the bookcase and find books inscribed in his own childish hand: Gerard Alexander Baillie, Kildour, Lanarkshire, North Britain, Europe, the World, the Universe ... chivvied by Nanny, terrified by Grandpa.

He put his feet on his desk and lit a cigarette, thinking he was becoming disgustingly sentimental in his old age but that perhaps one was allowed these thoughts on, or nearly on, the eve of active service. To be without a child now, a son, was to be incomplete. If I am killed, he thought, and I must accept the possibility, it will be such a bad, such a messy moment to go. Everything undone, unresolved. At a distance like this, death seemed improbable and yet alarming; it made him think of something of the Abbé de Tourville's he had read once about death only being frightening when it is a long way off. How would that apply, he wondered, when death was both near and far, touching oneself and yet not being oneself; it was all such a frightful lottery, war: tantalizing, impossible to imagine, exciting, terrifying.

He unwound himself and walked to the window, restless and dissatisfied, full of longings he seemed to be unable to do anything about. He had letters to write to his mother and to Alice and there was an idea in his mind about keeping a journal, but he could not find the necessary energy. In the beginning, when his thoughts about Alice had been taking shape, he had once or twice attempted to put in a letter to her his new feelings, wondering if words on a page would somehow make the impact that spoken protestations had failed to do, convey to her his tenderness and longing for her. But words of love sat awkwardly in between requests for fur-lined sleeping bags, haversacks, Jaeger socks and all the rest, so that he had rather given up, and that applied to the journal, too. It could only be of interest, he felt, once he was abroad on active service, once the blasted War Office had stirred itself into dealing with his request to be taken on as an interpreter.

He turned to survey the room, the so-familiar room with its two single beds, the crowded writing-table, the armchairs facing one another in front of the fire, the chest of drawers with its tooth-mugs and whisky bottle, hairbrushes, stud box, thinking he had never expected to have such a long period of waiting, all this time for painful reflection. 'War Station' had seemed so imperative, so urgent, not this enormous patience-tease, taking the edge off everything, this waiting for red tape to be unravelled, waiting for the telegram to come, so that one could say to oneself: Now, now the moment is arrived, now I can *do* something. But general war, he supposed, going over to his bed to sit and remove his boots, was as much an industry as any other large-scale enterprise. Somebody hadn't done their job properly, so that the machinery which depended on a thirst for *gloire*, a desire for immediate action, ran down a little, stopped functioning, leaving the vital ingredient – the man who wanted to do his duty – impatient, dispirited. There is nothing worse, he thought, removing his shirt (flannel, drab) and his underwear (underclothing, suit of) then his socks (Jaeger, expensive), than being kept waiting by a pack of bureaucrats who would probably never see the war at first hand. And neither would he, if it went on like this.

When he came back from the bathroom he said his prayers: last, tremendous test of concentration ... quick canter through the Paternoster without once thinking of forage; if you do, start again. Two Salve Reginas without wondering how long the printers would take. After that, stare into fire and smoke; the ragged, real prayer this: getting God in a half-nelson: Alex, make him well and stay well, Alice, make her love me ... *in splendoribus sanctorum* ... you are my son, born before the morning star ... make it all work, O Lord who ... has broken kings in the day of his anger.

CHAPTER
TEN

Two days later, somewhere about 4 October, a telegram came for Alice from Gerard at Woodbridge. She supposed, taking it from the boy, that she had expected this: 'I HAVE BEEN APPOINTED INTERP ATTACHED TO 7TH DIV,' she read. 'GO LYNDHURST AT ONCE STOP WE GO FROM S'HAMPTON IN 2 DAYS STOP PLS BOOK ROOM IN HOTEL FOR 2 US, NIGHT 6TH STOP G BAILLIE.'

'No reply.' Shut door in boy's face.

She had thought it might be from Edmund. Disgusting, faithless creature. She was awaiting him. In seven weeks there had been two letters; having no idea of the rights of an adulterous wife, she could not decide whether she was lucky or hard done by. And the letters themselves had been ... unrevealing: amusing, entertaining, full of rather well-executed little sketches: 'Oneself as a Fusilier', Edmund pencilled in pretty Hunting Erskine trews, blue facings. 'Kilmarnock on a Wet Sunday': huddled town, arrow storm in sky, or were they meant to be stair-rods symbolizing rain? But nothing much about how one's opposite number in London might be feeling. She wanted reams of purple prose, passionate declarations, avowals. The mind might say one thing, warning of the dangers of hoping too much, but the heart said another. Heart said, if I can just see you once more, you shall be mine.

By contrast, Gerard's letters were much nicer and more revealing. There were lots of things he wanted, from socks to plum cake, so she was kept busy. He wrote

117

of boredom, of long nights on his own, allowing, by inference rather than direct statement, the assumption that she was in his thoughts more than he could say. Again, it was a question of mind and heart. Mind said a good man, who wants you now, believe in him. Good? Gerard good? Not an adjective she would have chosen at the beginning of August. Interesting. Heart said, no thanks, available space for loving and wanting occupied by Fusil Jock.

She went into the library, thinking to keep the wire. Gerard had said to keep everything. An historical moment, perhaps, but a pity the summons to arms should be written in pencil on something resembling the lavatory paper the servants at Kildour used. One wanted a scroll really, tassels and sealing wax, trumpets. She opened the folder of Gerard's letters. The morning's project was to go through them, making sure she had all the things he had asked for ... Dear God, what if Edmund comes while I'm away? He might only have one night. You can't tell any more. It would be sure to happen like that, my luck completely...

Map case. She put a tick against this. Must keep calm.

Vicuna square for neck. Yes.

Rubber boots.

Electric torch with refills.

String gloves. Impossible.

Plum cake and Captain's biscuits. Fortnum's.

Spare lighter. Boots.

Shirt and socks. Harvey and ...

'Yes?'

Another telegram ... from Edmund, of course. But it wasn't. 'FURTHER INSTR,' the paper said, 'INTERP ADVISED SUPPLY THEMSELVES WITH "DICT OF ENG & FR MILITARY TERS" ALBERT BARRERE, PUBL LIB HACHETTE, 18, KING WILLIAM ST, CHARING X, PR.2/-+ "TECH MILITARY TERS FOR MILITARY STUD" MARIUS DESHUMBERT DAVID NUTT, 11, GRAPE ST, NEW OXFORD ST 2/6D STOP PLS OBTAIN & BRG WITH YOU STOP G BAILLIE.'

Military Stud? Stud? Student, of course, how stupid of

118

me. A new language. It made her feel she needed an interpreting course herself to cope with this barrage of telegraphese.

Alice put on her hat and went out shopping. The shops were stuffed with people and she was kept waiting hours in one place whilst they searched for Gerard's new but mislaid field boots. The chemist was out of lighters. In Fortnum's she met Nina procuring rare delicacies for William who had got a nice job as a transport officer with the Scots Guards. 'Brave but safe,' Nina said triumphantly. 'I was going to ring you. Helena needs knitters and bandage rollers. Are you interested?'

'I must do something,' said Alice. 'But aren't you going to nurse?'

'Sartorial insufficiency.' Nina made a face. 'The uniform just wasn't me.'

It was a mistake to go to the A. & N. but she had been intrigued by the idea of ear protectors as a present for Gerard. And it was a present, she insisted to herself, not a sop to a guilty conscience, but it made her late home for lunch with Pamela whom she had not seen since the party. The hangover had turned into bronchitis in some mysterious way and Pamela had been *incommunicado* for weeks. The traffic was dreadful. At one point Alice was able to get out of her cab, purchase a copy of the *Daily Herald* and climb back in again without having to run after the vehicle.

Antwerp had fallen or was falling. Moltke was about to be dismissed. Antwerp, though. She remembered going there with Gerard on honeymoon. Hours and hours in the cathedral waiting while he went over every carving with a fine toothcomb. Cold and bored on a chair by the great door, waiting, listening with half an ear to the ugly, incomprehensible language. Now the cloisters where she had spent a slow half-hour in the sun, idly watching the other visitors with the gentle breeze in her face, would be full of soldiers disturbing the ancient peace, the quietness and shadows of the interior echoing to the thump of the big guns. What did it say? 'Cathedral used as observation post' ... and the carvings, the stone saints, hands outstretched beneath a mountain of sand-bags.

The absurd façades of Wigmore Street moved and swam as she watched. The tears were for ... what? She wished she knew. For herself or Europe's agony; a past whose richness she had not valued enough which now, in her memory and because of what had happened, was becoming somewhere she had been happy, at any rate untroubled by more than minor, fleeting discomforts. The traffic was moving again at last. Had she been happy there, then, in that place? She had not thought of it as such, or perhaps happiness was exactly that: when one was not aware of being unhappy, when there were no questions. Just the days passing, the meals, good, bad or indifferent consumed, the wine commented upon and drunk, the carvings assessed, the bodies joining in the dark and moving apart again, the light from the street coming between the gap in the curtains and herself, with Gerard asleep by her side, passing her hand to and fro across the line of light as a child might do, waiting for sleep.

They had not known each other then, but the echoes of the enormous promises made were still with them. Sometimes at meals, or walking, she had looked at him and thought: you are mine, we are bound by the most solemn declarations, yet I do not know you. He was a good-looking man, striking, quite tall. She would see people making assumptions about them in hotels and restaurants and longed to ask: what is it, what do you see, what do you make of us, as if strangers could tell at a glance, somehow discern this thing hidden to her: coupleness, a long future, parenthood. Now there was another time of similar public assessment living in wait for them: the couple parted by war, every gesture solemnly misinterpreted by a sentimental public. She wanted him to go because he wanted it for himself, but his departure made her worried and restless. It should be a moment of truth, but it could not be because of Edmund, because of one mistake, one night, ridiculous really. A part of her said: put it behind you, forget it, dismiss it all as a nonsense, but the other bit of her, larger and altogether irrational, fell apart at the thought of seeing him, touching. He had what she had seen vulgarly described in an American paper Nina had given her as a magnetic personality. Edmund did.

Pamela's hat announced her. A rather peculiar object made out of red silk and shaped like a flower-pot sat on the hall chair. In the drawing-room she was bent over a show-case admiring the miniatures. 'They used to take them on campaign,' she said, looking round. 'Rather sweet, don't you think? Photography's done for that, of course. I should prefer it myself.'

'Which?'

'Oh, the painting. The idealized version. One's best expression, sweetest smile, hair just so. You should have had one done for Gerard.'

'Petersen wanted to paint me,' Alice said. 'Did he tell you?'

'You could hardly fit one of his in a rucksack, my love.'

'I think he was joking.'

'No, no. He wasn't. Petersen is incapable of joking. He has no sense of humour whatsoever.'

'You must find that rather trying.'

'I do. Madly. I think I'm going to have to get rid of him, in fact.'

'Can't you keep him until he's done me?'

'I might,' said Pamela. 'It depends.' She sat down on the arm of a chair and lit a cigarette. 'Tell me everything. It's years since we had a talk. How was Scotland?'

'The same but different,' said Alice mysteriously.

'How are William and ghastly Nina?'

'William is very pleased with himself,' said Alice. 'In a

way I'm glad for him – to be rich, I mean – but Nina is a trial. She's so –'

'She's a bitch,' interrupted Pamela, 'a rich and beautiful one. Good luck to William, I say, but he's probably dim enough to stay the course. Sorry, darling, but you know I've always thought that.'

Alice gave her a look. 'I like the thought of Leith being done up,' she said. 'One has to be grateful for that.'

'Even if she is jam?'

'What?'

'Oh, you know, Aunt Hat's euphemism for trade. Ask her about anyone whose money comes from unorthodox sources, and she'll say: "Jam, dear, jam." You must know that.'

'I didn't.' Alice giggled. She went and sat next to Pamela on the sofa. 'Can you keep a secret?'

'Don't tell me, you're in pig.'

'Pamela, that is a most disgusting expression.'

'But apt.' She looked round for an ashtray. 'Are you?'

'No. That's something else I want to talk to you about. No, it's not that.'

'What then? Don't tell me, you've fallen in love with Gerard's best friend.'

'Yes.'

'Oh God, it was a joke. You haven't really, have you?'

'I suppose it's love,' said Alice, looking away. 'It's certainly something.'

'How did it happen?'

Alice told her.

'This is very serious,' said Pamela. 'Can I have a drink?'

After it had arrived on a tray, they started again. 'You need a mother,' Pamela said, 'not someone like me. I'm a bad influence, the black ewe. I know Aunt Bundock thinks so. I suppose you thought I would approve? I must say, I never imagined you would do a thing like that.'

'Is it so very terrible? Other people do it, I know.'

'You're not other people, darling. Other people don't have your sensitive constitution, and, besides, other people have their heads screwed on more firmly than you do. They wait until they've had some children, preferably sons, then what's one more or less, even if it does look like Uncle David or Cousin Jack or the Foreign Seccy, although that's a fate worse than death.'

'I told you, I'm not.'

'What's the point of it all, anyway? Gerard would never divorce you, especially not now.'

'I hadn't thought of it all having to have a point,' Alice said. 'Something happened. I live with the consequences, whatever they might be.'

'Whatever they might be?' Pamela mimicked. 'Listen to me, Alice,' she said. 'It's playing with fire. I don't think you quite realize what you're doing. People like you never get away with things like this. You need to be callous and calculating to have an affair with someone, you need to be able to be cruel. You're none of those things. I know Gerard's been difficult, impossible, if you like, but you say he's changed in some way, then you must give him the benefit of the doubt. How is he going to feel if he finds out, as it seems he's bound to at some point? How would you feel if he found out then went off and was killed? You'd never get over it. God knows,' she said, 'I've never got on with him in the past and I know he doesn't care much for me, but I think there is a capacity in Gerard for change. Very difficult people are often more capable of it than you or I.'

'You say all this and I know it's true,' Alice said, sitting back, twisting her hands in her lap, 'but there's a part of me no longer susceptible to reason. I can't be wholehearted with him at the moment. I suppose I feel I should have some fun, too.'

'You look perfectly miserable to me, but then that's only to be expected. I'm not unsympathetic, darling.' She reached out and put a hand on Alice's arm. 'I can see you think I'm being unfeeling and rather cruel, but believe me, I remember the ghastly agonies of toppling for the first time. You think you'll never get over it; worse at your age, too, when you're grown up enough to see faults but not experienced enough to admit it. I bet he's not awfully nice to you, is he?'

'Sometimes you ask too many questions.' Alice folded her arms and looked down at her lap with a rather rueful expression on her face.

Hopeless, thought Pamela. Hopeless, hopeless. The road to ruin and she hasn't the vestige of an idea. This romantic vacuum we're nurtured in makes of us the most easy victims. In a way she's so like Archie: makes up her mind to something and abandons herself to it, not allowing the possibility of changing her mind.

'What was the other thing? You said there was something else.'

'It's my insides,' Alice said. 'Apparently they don't work properly. I went to see this awful man in Harley Street called Mr James.' She looked up, caught Pamela's eye and began, mercifully, to laugh. 'He said I've got a displaced, or was it misplaced womb.'

'How very careless of you, my sweet. Where had you left it?'

'Do you know what he said to me?' Alice gasped. 'He said legs up afterwards...' Her voice rose to a shriek.

'Did he give you a demonstration?' Pamela was in the grip of the most paralysing giggles.

'Excuse me, my lady ... ' It was Bessie announcing lunch. Things were reduced since the butler had gone to be brave.

'Yes, thank you.' Alice waited until the door was shut again. 'He said it would be difficult to have a child – '

'But not impossible.' Pamela turned from the glass.

'Not in so many words.'

'I should mind very much if someone said that to me, whether or not I was married and wanting. Do you, as a matter of fact, want?' She lit another cigarette.

124

'I hadn't thought there was a choice. Marriage meant children, always.'

'It doesn't have to. But I know you don't mean that. You mind and it makes you feel reckless, doesn't it? You think – '

'I think anything goes,' said Alice. 'That's how I feel: blighted. We're all for it, one way or another: death or barrenness, what difference does it make?'

'There's a sickness about,' Pamela said, 'certainly. But you worry me. Pessimism of your kind is a form of vanity really, a delusion of fatality and humbleness that is only a disguise for doing what one likes. It applies to all of us,' she said, 'not just you.'

'You're very hard on me,' said Alice, getting up and waiting. 'No little warm corners of self-deception left.'

'I don't mean to be hard.' Pamela followed her to the door. 'But I can't leave you trotting towards the abyss. I'm too fond of you for that.' She paused. 'Have you told Gerard this?'

'I haven't seen him since,' Alice said. 'But I don't think I will. He wants it very much, you see, and I shouldn't like to deprive him of that.'

'He's got to find out sometime.' Pamela looked at her. 'What do you mean, exactly? It sounds as if you don't think he'll come back.'

'Doesn't everyone think that in the back of their minds?' asked Alice evasively.

'I suppose so. You've got to stop him being too horribly brave, darling. That's your task. Even if that's all you do, it'll be enough for now. Tell him to keep his head down and not worry about fostering the family tradition. I think extreme bravery is always founded either on stupidity or some fluke. Gerard is far from stupid but he'll have to be stopped from looking for opportunities. I do so hate the idea of all this wasted self-sacrifice.'

'Do come and eat,' said Alice, wishing she would shut up. She had had about as much as she could take in one morning. And she thought of Gerard and the journey he was probably planning at this moment, putting their whole drama into motion; as if invisible strings were pulling them across England to a town, a hotel, a room together, a shared bed: six feet of space in which to act out a parting, find the right words, sleep.

While the ship sidled in under cover of darkness, out of the perilous roads, past the lighthouse, the mole.

'You'll have to let me meet him,' said Pamela, eating late raspberries. 'After this, I feel it's my duty to run my chaperon's eye over him.'

'I can't think of anything I'm less inclined to,' Alice replied. 'You'll have him on toast. He'll be so off-put I'll never see him again.'

'If I promise to behave well?'

'I don't think it's a good idea,' said Alice firmly.

'Where will you meet, then? It can't be here, under Gerard's nose, so to speak.'

'He has a house in Hyde Park.'

'Just the teeniest little peep?'

'We'll see,' Alice said. Secretly, she quite liked the idea of showing Edmund off. 'But if we do come, *if* . . . you'll have to get Petersen out of the way. I really can't risk him subjecting Edmund, who is, after all, a dyed-in-the-wool soldier, to his rather lunatic views on the nature and causes of war.'

'Oh my God, you had the Just War lecture, did you?' Pamela put down her fork. 'You should have told me. The thing is, I agree with him, broadly speaking, but he's so very intense that he puts people off; does more harm than good. I really shall have to get rid of him. He's hopeless in bed, too.'

'Oh?'

'Don't look so horrified.' Pamela eyed her. 'All that celibacy did him no good at all. Years of monkish scruple, dither, dither, dither over having a spoon of jam at breakfast, made him quite hopeless when faced with real pleasures. Flesh tempts him wildly yet repels him at the

126

same time. He can't get it into his mind that women are ordinary, that the act itself is natural, animal. All women are goddesses to Petersen, from afar, and when he comes too close he finds their breath smells, or their feet are too big or something. It is all very trying.'

'Perhaps he will have to return to the cloister,' said Alice, who had begun to laugh.

'Or I might pack him off to the RAMC.' Pamela blew a perfect smoke ring. 'Otherwise, when they bring conscription in, as they will, I shall have to trail across London every day to Wormwood Scrubs with gruel and viper soup.'

'Couldn't you go once a week?'

'Oh no. I know myself too well. It would be every day, cursing and grumbling. Guilty if you do, guilty if you don't.'

'Rather like me,' said Alice.

'How is sweet Alice?' Petersen asked. He had been asleep on the sofa. The curtains were half drawn; several full ashtrays perfumed the room; the flowers that had been so wonderful last week were dead, dropping petals the colour of old parchment. Outside it was raining, that peculiarly English kind of rain that Pamela always thought of as drivel. Driven drizzle.

'Don't talk to me,' said Pamela. 'I'm not in a very good mood.'

'Has something happened?'

'No.' She sat down on a chair, still in her coat. 'Yes.'

'What then?'

'I don't want to talk about it.' And she began to cry. 'Couldn't you have cleared up a bit?' she said, sniffing.

'This is not like you.' Petersen stood in the middle of the room, bewildered.

'Yes it is. I like order. I hate mess. I can't work when it's like this.'

'You cannot be crying over a little disorder. Something has happened, you must tell me.'

'I'm crying for the whole world,' said Pamela, putting her hands on the seat of her chair. 'Can't you tell?' She looked at him. 'Or perhaps not. I never did make a good tragic figure, much too healthy-looking. I shall look like this in my coffin,' and she pinched her cheeks very hard with both hands so that they hurt.

CHAPTER
ELEVEN

Lyndhurst, an inoffensive address in Hampshire where he had gone after Woodbridge, was cold and uncomfortable but temporary. Gerard's hut leaked and shook in the wind. Its creakings kept him awake the couple of nights he was there, when he would come to as often as not to find he had been thinking of the past. Curiously, it was of Edmund he dreamt the most; sometimes his parents intruded, occasionally Alice, Alex came on and off stage – very insubstantial – but mostly it was Edmund; and not as he had last seen him either, so splendid and debonair and somehow treacherous. The Edmund of his dreams was the boy he had known and the young man, the companion of those interminable train journeys, the person he had known so well that it had been hard to distinguish what his own thoughts were and what received opinion. Edmund. Edmund.

They had not written to one another. Sometimes Lady Baillie mentioned Edmund in her letters, so that Gerard knew he was still up north but coming south soon, having been passed fit. Edmund's regiment was in the thick of it now, and Gerard wondered how Edmund was feeling, whether he too was possessed by this extraordinary feeling that hovered between dread and curiosity, the feeling of uncertainty, the chance of being killed. The distant past seemed more real to him than this odd, disjointed present: the hut with the wind buffeting it as if someone were brandishing a large feather-filled pillow outside. Again, he found it hard to believe he had reached this crucial moment with his life in pieces about him, so ill prepared.

Alice had sent him a wire about the hotel; it was the one facing the sea where they had stayed on their way to honeymoon in France. Odd how he had felt a honeymoon could not start until they were properly abroad; odd, too, how the sensation had continued once they were abroad. 'Honeymoon' as an idea was synonymous with mirage, or so it had seemed, a horrid state conjured by hoteliers to encourage trade. He had longed to measure up to what he felt was expected of him, to make gestures: flowers and champagne every night, staring into the beloved's eyes, but he had to admit it, the beloved had been rather bored by the G. Baillie version of the Continent: the cathedrals, the quiet hotels, but mostly the cathedrals.

His piety had been at rather a peak during that trip. He had thirsted for the surroundings and trappings of sanctity, that feeling of being on the right side of the tracks for a change. He had been so new at being a Catholic then that he had wanted to feast on the riches, to savour his knowledge of the club rules: trailing a hand in the stoup of holy water on entering, the genuflecting – it had taken him ages to discover how to curtsey without being nancy – the ritual of candles, the Stations of the Cross.

Alice had never asked why he took so long in each place, and would wait for him by the postcard stall or the main door. From the things she said he gathered she had thought he was doing the carvings, and a kind of coyness had prevented him from enlightening her. Twice a day on some occasions did seem a bit much to drag oneself across town from the Garden of Olives and up the hill to Golgotha; he had no wish to explain to anyone, least of all Alice, that religious love had burned in him then like a fever.

How different it was now, he thought, going past the docks in a cab, not only the place itself – the troop ships, the men in uniform – but his own sentiments at being there on business; no time for guide-books, pilgrimages, lingering over the architecture, dreams of holiness, where he was going. That other world seemed not foreign to him any more or strange or glitteringly exotic; instead it was a place he had journeyed through and would not return to, a stage in the apprenticeship he had sensed ending at Kildour. His concept of his own importance in the scale of things had changed: the old, sentimental ideas of God as a kind of personal supervisor had melted away, although quite what had taken their place was hard to say. He believed as strongly as ever, but it was a belief tinged with ruefulness and humour. He no longer took himself so seriously, and this allowed him a clearer, perhaps less attractive but certainly truer idea of his own nature; oddly, it was very much more comfortable like this. Again, it was hard to put into words that somehow he felt he was nearer the truth, whatever it was, than he had been then, involved as he was in an ecstatic observance of religious niceties to the exclusion of everything else, including his wife.

He paid the driver and heaved his things indoors, making two trips, jammed in the most awkward way possible into a segment of swing door. In the old days, there had been a doorman to see to all this; now a half-witted boy took charge of his things inside, accompanying him to the desk where he had to wait in a queue, drumming his fingers in irritation on the counter.

No sign of Alice.

Every time the door swung he looked over his shoulder expectantly. The fifth or so time he did this he realized he was *nervous*, as if he were still wooing her, lover-like, anxious: their relationship had gone into reverse in a way. All this was what had not happened before.

When at last he signed the register and was given the key, he had to wipe his hand on his trouser leg. Again, the gesture surprised him as if he had not imagined he could feel these flutterings and nervous plunges in his chest in connection with Alice. Nina, yes. There had

been all that, all the embarrassing physical manifesta-
tions of love: sweaty palms, the odd voices that sounded
like someone else speaking, the painful erections he got
just looking at the back of her neck, a hand fiddling with
the clasp of her necklace, let alone dancing with her.
Those rare opportunities had always entailed a trip to the
gents afterwards. Now it was the thought of Alice making him short of breath and feeble. Squashed into the box
of a lift with the boy he resisted the urge to wipe his
forehead. The lift stopped and then started again, throwing Gerard against his companion and knocking the
boy's hat off. 'So sorry.' He bent to retrieve it, resisting
the urge to wipe his hand again. The brim had been
greasy inside and his fingers stank of cheap hair oil.

'Thirty-four,' said the ghastly creature, struggling off
with Gerard's luggage.

'Thanks.' Sometimes loving one's neighbour seemed
so difficult.

Alone, Gerard realized that by some odd chance this
was the set of rooms they had had last time. A bedroom
with two enormous single beds, watercolours, not bad
ones either, of what had been the harbour and was now
the docks. A sea view not represented on the walls.
There was a kind of ante-room off, with a sofa in it, a
desk, some tired-looking mezzotints; beyond this,
through a lobby that had once been a housemaid's resting place, was a bathroom, advertised, he seemed to
remember, by a frightful Gallicism, *en suite*; hardly, he
thought to himself going in, hardly... Just a crafty man-
agement making hay out of a transatlantic public's love
of luxury. The bathroom contained, apart from the bath,
two vast basins and two mirrors. He looked at himself in
one, then the other; even in the rather bad light he
looked spectral, worn out, hardly the handsome bride-
groom. He ran some water and washed his face and
hands. The coldness made his skin ache; with one wet
hand he smoothed back his hair, wondering if it was
thinning or whether it was just the light. Baldness was a

family failing he thought he might have escaped; now he wasn't sure. For the first time he minded: had it gone back a bit or was it his imagination?

He went back into the bedroom and walked about restlessly, unable to begin on anything. Hurry Alice, he thought, please hurry. Time is so short now. I'm in love, he said to himself, going to the window. Or is it just the hour, the imminence of departure, that makes her seem so sweet, the fact she might bear my child? He stared out at the sea turned sheet steel in the late afternoon light. The brilliance made his eyes water and he turned away as the door opened, wiping his cheek with the back of his hand.

The creature entered, shambling, followed by Alice. She made a face at him as he fumbled for change, but said nothing until they were alone.

'Hallo,' he came back from the door and put a hand on her shoulder. 'How are you?'

'Well.' She turned her head aside offering a cheek but he put both hands to her face and kissed her closed mouth. 'And you?' There were callouses on his hands and she noticed a tear had settled at the corner of his eye. 'What is it?' She took one of his hands away and put a finger up to wipe away the tear; the skin there felt surprisingly fine and soft. 'You look tired,' she said. The tear had made her wonder, made her feel sorry for him. 'Have they worn you out already?'

'Pretty nearly.' He put his hand back on top of hers, bowing his head.

'It took an age to get here,' she said, disentangling herself, wanting the moment to pass, not wanting to feel this ... compassion for him, this wanting to protect him from something. What? Danger, the unknown? Or herself, perhaps; the power she could sense bestowed on her by him, by the set of his head, power to hurt, to make something more of that tear.

She wanted to be normal, prosaic, pretend this was any other occasion but the one it was, so she took her hat off and laid it on the bed nearest the door. Behind her, she heard him move to the window again, the slight click of the clasp of his cigarette case. Turning, she saw he had the cigarette in his mouth, was watching her over the flame. He snapped the lighter shut and put it back in his pocket without taking his eyes off her.

Alice went along to the bathroom and put on the light. In one of the mirrors she examined her face with desperate concentration. Gerard came in behind her and sat down on the edge of the bath. Every now and again he moved forward and flicked his ash down the lavatory.

'That's a filthy habit,' she said, going back into the bedroom to fetch a comb out of her bag. Coming in again she heard the hiss as the butt subsided under water.

'There isn't an ashtray,' he said apologetically, putting his hands on his thighs. 'Do you remember, we had these rooms last time?'

'Are you sure?' Alice spoke through a mouthful of pins: put it up and twist, pin here, so ... and another there. Damn. So easy when Mavis showed her, so difficult to do oneself.

'Positive.' He got up and went behind her. 'Have you really forgotten?' Their eyes met in the glass.

'I have. But it's not important, is it?'

'Yes. Everything is important now. It pains me that you pretend to forget. Why do you wish me pain? No,' he said, 'of course not. Don't bother with that.' He took both her hands from the crown of her head and pressed them to her sides, holding her very close.

She could feel his erection just above her coccyx. Of course she had known he would want her; why then this feeling of outrage, that he was asking for more than his due, all mixed up in a curious way with wanting him herself, wanting to wreak some havoc on him: biting, scratching, tearing? In the glass she saw his hands massaging her shoulders, rubbing shadows and planes into the velvet of her coat. The action excited and repelled her, something akin to the beastly hen and the chalk line.

He began to undress her rather deftly from behind, throwing her clothes onto the floor and into the bath. And all the while she watched, unable to believe the sight of herself: the naked stranger in the mirror.

He picked her up and carried her into the bedroom, putting her down on one of the beds.

'My hat,' she said feebly, feeling felt and feather under the back of one thigh.

'Damn the hat,' he said, looking down at her. 'Don't you know how beautiful you are? Don't you know how I love you?' He touched a shoulder and then ran a finger down her arm to the wrist.

'It's cold,' Alice said, turning her head abruptly. 'Hurry.' She closed her eyes, listening to the noise of him undressing: the sucking sound as he pulled his boots off, something jingling. Was he wearing spurs? She hadn't thought to notice.

Afterwards he leant over her, pinning her between his elbows.

'Open your eyes.'

She could feel his heart still beating like anything against her breast, the hairs on his chest.

'What is it?' His face was very close, the hair fallen forwards over his cheek. He looked dishevelled and boyish and terribly handsome.

'I want to say again, about the summer, how awful I was to you. I'm sorry.'

'Please,' she said, 'you mustn't keep on – '

'Listen to me.' He put a hand on her mouth gently, then removed it. 'I've had so much time to think lately, in spite of having so much to do. I behaved appallingly to you at Kildour. I want you to be able to forgive me that.'

'But I – '

'Shut up.' He pressed her sides with his elbows. 'At Woodbridge I used to leave the others after dinner and go upstairs to attack the paperwork. When I'd knocked off as much of it as I could, I used to think about you sitting in the drawing-room, or in your bed reading, and

I would long for you to be there with me. I wrote so many letters trying to tell you that . . .' she watched his Adam's apple moving up and down in the pause '. . . that I loved you.' Suddenly, mercifully, he rolled off her and lay on his back looking up at the ceiling.

How . . . she wondered, what . . . ? There is no reply to that. Even between real lovers when the love is equal you can't say, I love you too, without it sounding false or grateful or somehow bolstering.

'. . . It was never right in the letters,' he was saying. 'The phrases seemed wrong or hackneyed, so I left it. I didn't want to leave it any longer in case I don't come back.' He turned his head and looked at her. More unanswerables. 'We've got to have a child,' he said. 'It haunts me to go without.'

Mr James was suddenly in the room with them. 'Legs in the air,' he said, and vanished. Gerard would think she was insane.

'We will,' she said. 'Don't let it haunt you; we will.'

'It's probably my fault,' he said, taking her hand. 'I didn't tell you . . . didn't want to, never thought it could have any effect –'

'What on earth are you about to confess, Gerard?' Alice asked, sitting up slightly so that she could see him properly. 'Syphilis, or what?'

'Good God, no!' Gerard began to laugh hopelessly. 'No, not that. That's what Darnley had, going round in a mask like a Swiss cheese and gloves. No, no . . . ' He choked back the dreadful laughter. 'Just clap.' He coughed and sniffed.

'Clap?'

'Venereal disease.'

'You never told me that.'

'Are you angry with me?' Gerard turned on his side, watching her. 'Nobody ever said anything about its having any connection with one's fertility.'

'No,' she said, and she wasn't really. Just surprised.

'I just prayed that it might work somehow before I went off.'

136

'That is unfathomable,' she said, picking at the mono-gram on the sheet. 'These things take time, you know.' Mr James was back again talking about ova and the corpus luteum. All men had these adventures. All men. Edmund. Particularly Edmund. Clap: unpleasant little word. Clip, clap, clop. She was shaky about Darnley; for some reason she thought he had had leprosy. Thinking about it, it did seem a little unlikely. Going to bed in gauntlets with frisky Mary by his side must have been uncomfortable. Now she too began to laugh.

'What is it?' Gerard asked. He had been watching her with some consternation.

'I don't know.' She wiped her eyes with the sheet.

'You see I had to mention it?'

'I think it's very honest of you, very ... frank,' she said, beginning to fiddle with the sheet again. In fact it was quite irrelevant, but of course she could not tell him that. She began to see how it was possible to be utterly mistaken about human nature. She had thought he would have been far too busy in Woodbridge for think-ing about his marriage, about them. To her, lately, the distance between them had been as real mentally as it was physically; in her own thoughts she had withdrawn from him, pulling up those little roots of togetherness, substituting 'I' for 'we', making a new and separate existence for herself. She should have known he would be dreaming her up into some new shape, something to match his own extraordinary renewal, or change, what-ever it was that had happened to him. Now she was to be the mother of his child, the beloved wife, the very incar-nation of wifely perfection, when in all their previous life together it had been he who had withdrawn into his religion, his interest in architecture, his endless other pursuits in which she was not included. She should have known, but how could she? Everything he did now seemed distressingly unpredictable, a guessing game. It made her fear his acuity, this new sharpness.

'Are you cross with me, shocked?'

She had almost forgotten he was there. 'No. Why?'

137

'Hearing one's husband had a dose isn't something most wives would welcome.' He had an elbow crooked behind his head; her gaze travelled along the line of his arm to the wrist: white skin, veins blue and delicate-looking.

'Oh, that.'

'You are, aren't you?'

'What, Gerard?' This tedious persistence.

'Shocked.'

'No ...' She looked away again. 'It happened before I met you. How could I be shocked at it?' She imagined him as Edmund, herself cool and jealous. Hating.

'Some people would be.' On and on like a gramophone record. She could feel him looking at her, wanting ... what?

'You make too much of it all,' she said, dismissively. If he was Edmund she would be angry and hurt, underground rage, sulks. 'Everyone's done things they might not be proud of, only not everyone feels about it as you do.'

'Not you,' he said, touching her bare back. 'What could you have done? You haven't had much opportunity for a life of crime.'

'Oh, do stop,' she said crossly, loathing his levity. It was patronizingly indulgent to suppose nobody else had murderous thoughts or adulterous leanings. How could he know what went on in her heart?

'I was only joking,' he said, holding out his arms.

'I'm sorry. It will happen,' she said, making it up to him. 'I'm sure it will.' She could feel his heart beating, slow, slow.

'I hope so.' He put his chin on top of her head. 'It seems churlish when there's Alex if I should go under, only it's not the same. I love him dearly, you know that; he could be my brother, but he's not my son. I find it's not at all the same.'

'No,' gently. 'But at least there's someone.'

'There would always be someone,' Gerard said. 'Every

family has a someone somewhere. A distant Australian cousin, like your family, as William has, or a Canadian lumberjack or some dismal creature from another God-forsaken spot – '

'Alex isn't dismal,' she said. 'But do let's stop this; I find it quite hateful.'

'I've been brooding about it,' he said, lying down. 'Wrong to brood, isn't it? Not done. Introspection is unhealthy, Ma used to say, selfish . . .' He yawned.

In a minute he was asleep with his mouth just open. There was a catch in his breath each time he breathed in. Alice would have liked to sleep too, but couldn't; the small, regular sound maddened her but she didn't want to risk waking him by pushing him onto his side. She counted twenty then got out of bed and went away into the bathroom. She took the clothes out of the bath and put the whole lot together on a chair. Bath. Run taps. Wash the good body and make it clean again. Indiscriminate, pleasure-seeking body, with its arcane inward processes, the womb that was not where it should be. Perhaps she should try with the legs now, or crab-like with the hips, or was it too late? She lay down on the bath mat in the steam, propping the backs of her ankles against the basin.

'Dear God, Alice, are you all right?'

Gerard in the doorway, naked, pop-eyed, ridiculous. *She* was ridiculous. 'I'm . . .' Upside-down genitals, hairy thighs, fine knees, aristocratic knees, calf-muscles well developed from so much riding. Feet. Ugh. Always to be hidden. '. . . just doing my calisthenics.'

'Since when have you been doing calisthenics?'

'Recently,' she said, unwinding herself and getting to her feet. 'Someone Pamela knows.'

'How is Pamela?'

'Very well, thank you.' She turned off the taps and climbed in quickly.

'What was the party like?'

'Rather hellish.'

139

'Nothing changes,' he said, going out again. 'Don't be too long.'

Alice lay in her bath and tried to think, which she found very difficult. There was a kind of fog in her brain that prevented her from making any sense out of her situation. There was Gerard and Edmund and Edmund and Gerard. If Gerard was killed there was Edmund, if Edmund was killed – she would never, ever, not in a thousand years get over it – there was Gerard. I am the point in the triangle, she said to herself. If they are both killed I shall be alone with my memories (that at least sounded suitably melodramatic), if they both survive, then I am in the most serious trouble imaginable. Serious. Serious trouble. She began to doze, coming awake every now and again to turn on the hot tap with her toe, a discovery it pleased her to make. No maid to chivvy her along or fuss about the hair getting wet.

'Nearly ready?'

'Do hurry a little, darling.'

'Please get out now, I must telephone.'

Gerard came on and off stage several times before she found herself at the dressing-table, wrapped in a towel.

'I have to telephone,' he said, coming back in his dressing-gown. 'Promised I would. Then we could walk a bit before dinner, if that's all right with you.'

'Fine.' Alice fiddled with an earring. 'I'm nearly ready.' She took the stopper out of a bottle of scent. Looking in the glass she saw he was still there. 'Aren't we in a hurry?'

'Yes.' He moved out of range and began to dress. He couldn't get over her, how she looked. The smallest actions performed by her seemed sensual, exciting. He began to wonder if he was ill to feel like this. What on earth had she been doing in the bathroom? What was it she wouldn't tell him? She had become all secrets suddenly, Alice. Not so much furtive as maddeningly enclosed, guarding herself. Keeping something back. He sighed.

In the hall she sat on an enormous sofa pretending to read a newspaper somebody had left. Russian victory near Augustow. Where on earth was that? Mines being sown in the North Sea. Germans did it first, no comment from neutral powers, we are therefore obliged –

'Alice!' Somebody tapped her on the shoulder.

Johnny MacDonald, not seen since the grouse a million years ago.

'What on earth are you doing here?' She cast her newspaper away in bits and stood up to kiss.

'Going to make mincemeat of our friends over the water. Absolute carnage going on apparently.'

He was so cheerful she could have killed him, all health and ardour, but also a Fusil Jock. She would flatter him into telling her things. 'How is Edmund?'

'South tomorrow, I think.' He half turned from her, dropping pearls of information oh so casually: 'Got through his boards, although he told me he didn't think his head was quite right yet. Nothing the doctor chappies can do though, is there?'

'No. I am glad to hear that.' She looked round frantically for Gerard, who could ask for more without its seeming queer.

'Gerard here? Stupid question.' He smiled. 'Suppose he must be. You wouldn't be here for your health, would you?'

'There he is now.'

'The MacDonalds are coming,' said Gerard reaching them, smiling. 'When do you go?'

'In the morning. Boatloads of odds and sods. My Mama's been ill which is why I'm going a different way.' He waved at someone by the door. 'Must go. So long.'

'Hang on.' Gerard put a hand on his arm. 'How's Edmund?'

'I was telling Alice.' The blank blue eyes rested on her a second. 'He comes any day. Head not quite right, but good enough. See you there.' He moved away.

'Man talks in shorthand,' Gerard said. 'I think all the

141

excitement has gone to his head. Did he tell you anything much about E.?'

'No. He was in too much of a hurry.' Alice looked down at her shoes, walking for the use of, made by a little man in Soho. Having wanted to know about Edmund, she now wanted to cry at the smallness of her entitlement. He seemed more and more distant, the property of the army and those who would soldier with him like Johnny, casual friends who knew more about his movements and whereabouts than she did. But she would have to get used to it. All this was just a beginning, a foretaste of how things would be in the future when the uninformative banalities of the field postcard would be the only indication of his existence, a whole world of mud and blood underwriting a phrase such as 'I am quite well.' She sighed.

'Why?' asked Gerard, taking her arm.

'Why what?' The sky was on the edge of darkness: huge clouds shot with impossible colours.

'That sigh, darling. Don't be so sad. I'll be all right.'

'Will you?' She thought of Alex and his particular calamity. Did it mean Gerard? She supposed, reluctantly, that it must. Only it was absurd to believe in those kind of things. Every family had its Cassandra, probably. There would be a rash of them now there was a war.

They walked to the docks and peered. There were people about doing the same, watching the fascinating mechanics of it all. A horse swinging high in a net on the end of a crane whinnied in fright. A child shouted in excitement, somebody laughed.

'My horse won't like that,' said Gerard. 'Poor beast, so undignified, but it's too far to swim.' He squeezed her arm in excitement, walking her away round the edge of the crowd, pointing things out.

'Can we go back?'

She wanted to run and hide, bury her head in the sand, anything but to be here in the sight of the troop ships, the former pleasure-steamers and cattle-boats,

142

now a uniform grey. Anything but the slap of the water, salt smells, gulls circling like vultures. Anything but this hideous, hideous reality: a destroyer escort outlined against the empty horizon, its presence making her wonder what lay beyond or beneath where the submarines nosed their grey snouts along.

Standing beside Gerard in silence, sometimes looking at his profile, and sometimes at the view, Alice knew for the first time the agonizing grip of reality, the moment when fact bites. It was no longer a game or an idea, something to be read about and misunderstood in a newspaper. She had had a picture of herself at farewell standing on a cliff waving a handkerchief. Those armies she had read about in the paper marching about in Galicia or Silesia had meant and still did mean nothing to her. The Tsar was in the field, it said, that she could just imagine; only without knowing it until now she had imagined him as a kind of Tolstoyan hero – Prince Bolkonsky at Borodino or Vronsky in his best: a white uniform, a flowing *pelisse*, plumes and spurs, not a meek little man in a greatcoat. Those armies of millions, what did they mean? She was not entirely sure where Silesia was. But this, the grey sky and the sea, the grey ships awaiting their human cargo, this meant something.

'Cold, are you?'

'A little.'

'We'll go then. I should have brought my overcoat.'

'It's not far. I'll be all right.'

She removed her arm from his, hating herself for her coldness to him, but his tender concern made her unbearably aware of her own treachery. She had never expected to have to act out the lie on this level; at Kildour and before there had been justification in that she had felt he did not love her. If he had done so, she thought, unquestionably she would have loved him back. More often than not love is like that. We love those who love us, never mind who loved more or first; it usually comes about into a kind of equality, the finer points of which are

143

known only to those involved; from the outside there is a unity, visible to others who complete it by their approbation. Edmund, specialist in this kind of knowledge, must have known instinctively and at once that her relation with Gerard lacked this quality of wholeness. Clever Edmund.

'Penny for them?' said Gerard lightly, suppressing a desire to admire himself for his tact. He had not known Alice quite so tricky, withdrawn. A nasty little voice at the back of his mind was busy telling him that women were always like this, given their head. As soon as you begin to worship them they run away with the idea they can do anything, behave any old how. Nina was like that. Perhaps it was something latent in all women, even Alice, whom he had come to imagine was somehow different, a worthier object.

'I was thinking,' Alice said, after a pause, 'how I should feel if it was me. Going, I mean. Off at dawn, the unknown. You seem very cheerful,' she said, trying to think of neutral ways to bolster his self-esteem.

'Do I?' This was better, some interest at least. 'I don't know what I am, really. Waiting is like being in limbo. I can imagine myself as far towards France or Belgium as the horizon, then my powers fail me completely. I can't think of a battlefield as anything but a set piece – too many history lessons well learnt, I suppose – a sense of dignity and comportment about the whole thing, politely waiting for the off. No amount of training really dislodges that, I think, only experience.'

'I should feel fear,' Alice said, waiting and rubbing her arms while Gerard lit a cigarette, 'and excitement. I should think it was all very unknown, what you say – you don't even know where you're going, do you?'

'No idea,' said Gerard. 'Not Maubeuge, now Antwerp's going or gone; one of the Channel ports, Le Havre, Boulogne, perhaps, somewhere in Holland? Lord knows.'

'A nice cathedral town,' said Alice as they reached the

hotel. 'Like the ones we did on our honeymoon, do you remember?'

'Chartres, Rheims. Yes. How could I forget? Go on.' He sent her on ahead, unable to say more. The names made his throat ache suddenly. What would become of those places now? All that endeavour, all that hope?

Through the glass Alice watched Gerard throw his cigarette in a wide arc into the road. For a moment he turned towards the sea, as if looking for something. She saw his elbow move, hand to forehead and breast, twice on the collarbone. Would it help?

She hoped so for his sake, for all their sakes.

CHAPTER
TWELVE

Later, when she was properly awake, his going seemed like some dream-sequence. The luggage had gone down late the night before and he had left his clothes in the bathroom so as not to disturb her. She seemed to remember a knock on the door and Gerard getting up at once as if he had been lying there waiting. Low voices, a door closing, then the sound of running water and the clatter as he dropped his razor on the floor. After that nothing. Some indefinable time later he had bent over her, all creaking leather, straps, buttons, kissing her face, pushing her hair back off her forehead, saying something like: 'Goodbye, I'll write.' She thought she might have tried to sit up but that he had pushed her back. 'Take care.' Had she said that?

The room was empty of him, yet he was still there. In the bathroom a smell of limes, a smear of shaving soap on the shelf above one of the basins, bristles inside the rim not all washed away. He would be at the docks now, mucking about with horses and guns and men, no thought of her in his head: Captain Baillie, interpreter with the 7th Infantry Division, attached to the 22nd Royal Artillery Brigade, the property of the BEF, beyond her control.

She dressed and did her hair, went on impulse to the window to draw the curtains. In the road below, a truck went by packed with men; an elderly man with a stick, walking a small brindled dog, stopped to watch, raising the stick in greeting while the dog jumped at his elbow.

Beyond all this, the sea, grey-green, quite calm, and the sky, patched with autumn cloud, giving a dull light. Turning away she saw an envelope addressed to her on the dressing-table: Gerard's unmistakable handwriting. Inside, a piece of hotel writing-paper folded in half, written in pencil. How oddly random and careless of him to have left it where she might not have noticed it. It said: *'Au revoir – G.'*

Au revoir ... my God. She sat down on the stool and looked at it again. Pages and pages of loving protestations could not have had the effect upon her those two words did.

Her hands were cold and she saw that she had broken a nail. *Au revoir.* She began to cry.

She reached London towards noon, scarcely aware of the processes of travel: the train late and packed and dirty, going in through the tawdry underskirts of London, the houses backed upon one another, the people undernourished, the dirt and grime. The station was full of soldiers making their way to the horizon she had abandoned, to the boats which would swallow them up, in pursuit of glory. Khaki-clad avenging angels, weighed down like pack-horses under enormous packs. Somewhere a band played a tune she had known once but could not now remember. Everything had become so noisy since they had gone to war, so out of control; people shouting and pushing, wearing their hearts on their sleeves, weeping openly and kissing, cheering at the drop of a hat. In the cab she saw the base of Nelson's Column was covered with recruiting posters, peeled and torn. Someone sat astride one of the lions; she watched a policeman striding through the pigeons.

Home was the opposite, nearly too quiet. Gerard had been forgotten here, had been away too long. Even his desk was hers now, where she sat efficient among her box files and folders. He had been glad for all she had done, particularly for the books, delighted with the fur-lined bag, amazed and amused at the ear protectors.

The telephone rang very loudly.

'Alice?' It was Edmund, crackled and scratched. 'Alice, is that you?'

'Yes.'

'It's a terrible line, I'm shouting nearly. Can you hear me?'

'Where are you?'

'My club. I've just arrived. Will you have lunch with me?'

'When?'

'Now, you goose. Half an hour. Just hang on.'

I can't, she thought. I just simply can't. I'm too worn out with it all, with Gerard, with saying one thing and feeling another. It was better when she hadn't known, when she could do anything with him in her imagination. Now it would have to move forwards, she supposed, she would have to learn things about him and be disappointed. She would have to be beautiful. Her face was not in one of its obedient moods today. It hadn't mattered in Southampton, there was nobody to see, nobody to care, but his coming obliged her to go upstairs and wrestle with it.

Whatever she did made it worse. Powder went on and off, rouge made her look like a Dutch dolly, more scent was too overpowering. Sober clothes made her look as if she wasn't making an effort, brighter, better ones made the lily – the rather washed-out lily – look over-gilded. Her hair wasn't dirty enough to stay up properly. Again she thought of cutting it like Pamela, so much easier really. In the end she went downstairs, unhappy with herself, to wait. For the first time in her life she poured herself some of Gerard's brandy and drank it quickly, hating the taste but loving the sensation.

Ah, courage. Yes. She had another.

There was the knocker now, loud and confident. Voices in the basement, feet on the kitchen stairs. She ran to

148

the door and called down that she would go. The foot-steps ceased but did not return downwards. Cook, with Bessie at her shoulder, waited, betrayed by their silence. She closed the baize door firmly, took a deep breath, one, two, feeling the brandy burning its way through her insides like a lighted fuse, went to the door and opened it.

It was Petersen.

She was so thunderstruck she could think of nothing to say.

'Forgive me,' he said, sweeping off his hat with old-world courtesy, 'I was passing. I wanted to make an arrangement with you about your sittings – Are you well?' he broke off to ask. She was shaking her head at him and making pushing gestures with her hands. Behind him a cab had come to a halt at the foot of the steps. Out of it stepped Edmund, a band-box, tin soldier. Quite beautiful.

'Ah, I see. The husband returns for a last farewell. I must not intrude on a scene of such tender magnitude. If I may, I will telephone you.' He turned and went slowly down the steps, waiting for a word with Edmund.

'. . . must be captured . . .' she heard him say. 'As her husband, it is almost your duty to have her painted.'

'I beg your pardon?' said Edmund politely, turning from the cab. He looked up at Alice and then again at Petersen.

'Your wife has not told you that I wish to paint her?'

'An excellent idea,' said Edmund holding out his hand. 'Goodbye.'

'Who the hell was that?' he asked cheerfully as they went inside. 'Looked like the phantom of the opera. Is he another of your admirers?'

'They are not legion, you know.'

'No, of course not,' he said, pressing his hat to his bosom. 'Well, here I am.'

'Yes.'

'Are we going to stand here all day?' he asked, looking

around him, 'or are you going to ask me into the drawing-room?'

'I'm sorry,' she said, leading the way. 'I don't know what's come over me. I was expecting you and then it turned out to be Petersen. Rather put me off my stroke.'

'Who is he?' Edmund closed the door and put his hat down.

'A friend of my cousin Pamela's, a painter. He wants to do me.'

'Lucky man,' Edmund said, coming and kissing her with what he thought of as his specialist's kiss; women closed their eyes when he did this, always.

'Where were you earlier?' he asked, not letting go of her. 'I telephoned but was told you were not here.'

'Seeing Gerard off. He went at the crack of dawn.'

'Lucky blighter.' He paused. 'I'm sorry. You mind, probably.'

'It was rather cheerless,' she said, moving back a step, suddenly hating him for saying that. It was not part of the plan for him to think of them as a couple, to make allowances for their private sorrows, to make himself a polite third party. She wanted him to say, 'I'm glad he's gone,' and then do something thoroughly reprehensible and highly exciting like making love to her on the floor. As it was, she felt strung between them: Gerard's wife, Edmund's convenience; a little, social love-affair whose manoeuvrings were ordained and tacitly condoned by the polite, brittle society whose darling Edmund was. She had wanted more, much more than that.

'I brought some fizz with me,' he said, looking round for the bag. 'Get some glasses, will you, like a good girl.' When she came back with them, he was poised. 'Hold it out,' he said. 'There isn't anything quite like it, is there?'

'No, nothing.'

'Alice,' he said, looking at her, 'I'm not making you happy, am I?'

But she did not know how to answer this.

'Come,' he said, putting his arm round her. 'Let's sit down and talk. Don't cry,' he added, seeing she was about to. 'It makes me unreasonable and then I won't be able to say what I mean. I only want what is best for you,' he said, thinking how extraordinarily pompous he sounded. 'I do not think,' he continued, seating her beside him, 'that it is good for you to continue with me. I'm a most frightful bad influence.' He crossed his legs and patted her arm at the same time, nannying her.

'I always distrust people who say that sort of thing,' Alice answered. She fiddled with her wedding ring. 'Why do you want to wriggle out of it now?' she said, not looking at him. 'You began it. I would never have done that, not in a thousand years.'

'*Mea culpa*,' said Edmund, striking yet another false note, he could tell from her expression. 'I can't resist pretty girls, you see; a bad habit I seem to have grown up with. You're too nice. I don't want you falling in love with me. I'm not worth it.'

'Then don't resist me,' said Alice desperately. 'I'll try not to be more in love with you than I already am.'

'Brave words, sweet one. No don't, please don't.' He put his glass down, disposed of hers onto a polished table where it would leave a white circle for Bessie to tut over, and began doing the worst possible thing in the circumstances.

'You're so lovely,' he said, coming up for air. 'Why do you want to make yourself more unhappy?'

'You know the answer to that. Let's be reckless,' she said, knowing at once it was the right thing to say. 'Let's take today and forget tomorrow.'

'Perhaps you're not so nice after all,' he said. 'Perhaps you're more like me. Can you do it, do you think?'

'I can do anything,' she replied, so excited she could scarcely speak.

They drank all the rest of the champagne and went off to lunch tipsy and reckless. Edmund, who had fully intended this meeting with Alice to be his last, found he was irresistibly drawn to this unexpected and dramatic part of her nature. Weeks away had given him the opportunity to review his own behaviour: in any terms he had behaved badly, stringing her along, seducing her, blowing hot and cold, one minute the handsome, kindly mentor, the next in bed with her, the third undecided, vacillating, slightly cruel. Very cruel. But he had felt obliged to contact her, the old coercion of upbringing making him want to thank and to tidy up ends; this had meant a meeting: an utterly delicious and tempting day of frivolity. In a way he felt it was his due, although this thought was not articulated precisely: myth demanded a last draining of the cup to the dregs and dangerous, illicit company. Who knew what lay beyond the dawn?

'Quails' eggs,' said Alice, coming out from behind a menu. 'Poached brill. It ought to be swan and syllabub, really, oughtn't it?'

'Fearfully indigestible.' Edmund looked round for a waiter, no simple task now the German ones had been swept away and interned. The Italian replacements were slack and emotional, thin on the ground too. Over to his right (they were in, of all places, the Café Royal) he saw Nina with a party.

'Alice,' he said, 'have you seen who's here?'

'No. Who?'

'Nina.'

'How did we manage not to see her when we came in?'

'God knows. The place is seething. She may have come after us.'

'How many of them?'

Edmund looked. 'About ten. She's with that chump Evelyn Proctor. Where's William, by the way?'

'Destination unknown. I think we just go on, don't you?' she said, after a pause. 'If she sees us, we're not really doing anything so awful, are we?'

'Let's have some more drink,' said Edmund. 'Best

anaesthetic known to man. Gerard'll probably walk in next. It seems to be one of those days, don't you think?'

Alice began to giggle. In her present state Gerard was a figure of cardboard, an abstraction. She could not realize him at all.

'Isn't that Alice Baillie over there?' asked Lord Proctor, putting his hand on Nina's arm. 'Your little sister-in-law?'

'Where?'

'In the corner, trying, it would appear, not to be seen.'

'But how exciting, Eve dear, show me.'

'By the mirror. Who is that ridiculously handsome man? He looks vaguely familiar.'

'Edmund Kerr,' said Nina. 'The Harry Cust of the Colonies. One of Gerry's oldest friends. Do you think he's seducing her or just being nice?' They put their heads together. 'I had my suspicions in Scotland, but he's clever, Edmund, used to disguising his tracks.'

'They could just be having luncheon,' said Evelyn, 'but somehow one doesn't think so.'

'Even I am faintly shocked by that,' said Nina, striking a pose. 'I do think it should be hands off the wives of your closer friends, don't you?' This was a specially-designed Proctor-tease. William and Eve had been in the same house at Eton; he had also been an usher at their wedding at St George's.

'Madame de Lafayette knew better,' he said, looking at her appreciatively, smiling slightly. 'Friendship for a husband has never prevented anyone from falling in love with a wife.'

'How clever,' said Nina. 'I love your little bookish verifications, darling. Shall we leave them or shall we stir it up a little?'

'Oh, leave them. We'll say our hallos later. Look, they've seen us.'

Nina stood up and waved. 'Let's send them a bottle,' she said. 'Not that they look as if they need it.'

153

'How on earth can you tell?'

'I know that look at a thousand yards,' said Nina. 'I should be a sharp-shooter, really. I'm wasted knitting helmets.'

'Do you really, or do you just pretend and get your maid to do it?'

'Oh, I'm a demon at it. Helena is always dropping stitches and needing help. I'm as deft as anything,' she said, putting her beautiful hands on the table covered in beautiful, recovered Carnegie jewels.

'Whoops.' Boldly Edmund returned the wave. 'Spotted,' he said. 'If you did the same, it might make it all seem more above-board.'

Alice obliged. 'Eve has asthma,' she said for no reason in particular, sitting down again gratefully.

'Dear girl.' Edmund looked at her. 'Perhaps we ought to eat up and go.'

'Where to?'

'I must go shopping,' Edmund said. 'You must lie down.'

'I don't want to go home.'

'Let me leave you somewhere while I do my errands. It's my only chance, it has to be this afternoon. There are other things I should much rather be doing,' he said vulgarly.

'I'll go to Pamela,' Alice said. 'Pick me up there. She wanted to meet you.' Drink had made her forget her previous scruples about Edmund and Pamela.

Edmund made the waiter give him the next bottle without opening it.

'We'll take it with us,' he said. 'Waste not, want not.'

Nina came to speak to them as they rose to go. 'Won't you join us?'

'More pressing matters,' Edmund said, adding, 'shopping,' before Nina could misinterpret him. 'Thanks for the fizz.'

'Thank Eve for that,' she said. 'I'm sorry you won't stay.'

'Time's winged chariot and all that,' Edmund said, kissing her. 'Wish me luck, Nina.'

'When, then?'

'Tomorrow.'

'Good luck.' She gave him a rather wicked look.

'Gerry all right?' she said to Alice.

'Yes, I hope so.'

'When I have news of William I'll telephone. Daddy won't help me any more now. Says I can't keep secrets, so I have to wait for official channels. Don't forget Helena tomorrow, Alice. Your country needs you,' she said, turning away.

'Will you come for me, or will you vanish?' Alice asked as she climbed out.

'No fear,' said Edmund. 'I'll get you at six and take you to my palace on the park.' But he did not wave.

CHAPTER
THIRTEEN

'Pamela gave me a lecture about getting you tight,' Edmund said in the cab, taking her hand.

'Oh no! I expressly told her not to do that.'

'I rather liked her for it, actually. She's attractive in an odd way, rather bizarre; wild, I should think.'

'She can be,' said Alice, primly. She was cross and didn't know how to hide it.

'No sign of what'shisname.'

'No.' Petersen had not been seen all day.

'She paints very nicely. She showed me while you were still zizzing. I liked the seaside ones. You're angry with me,' he said.

'No.' With an effort she turned to him and smiled. Kitty again. A real heart-stopper. Funny how it came and went in her face. He felt the original tenderness for her stirring and stretching.

'Here we are,' he said.

A house like a slice of wedding cake, grand and blank, with a view, only it was getting dark and there was no time to imagine the stately trees, sweeps and vistas. Blinds were drawn upstairs and down; a suggestion of shutters and heavy, elaborate curtains. Lady Kerr's curtains. A house she might have passed a thousand times and not known it was his.

'I could ring,' Edmund said, 'but I won't. Don't want Mrs Flack getting too good a look at you.'

'Who's Mrs Flack?' Alice asked.

'An aged vulture who lives below stairs,' he replied,

156

doing deft things with a key. 'I left instructions for a fire,' he said over his shoulder. 'Food I've dealt with myself. I thought we had better eat in after our little lunch-time encounter and I don't think Mrs F.'s repertoire extends much beyond tripe and onions.'

'Why does she stay then?' asked Alice rather timidly, as if she half expected Mrs Flack to swoop from a pelmet or jump out at her from behind one of the many doors which led off the hall.

'Keeping the wheels turning or whatever the expression is,' Edmund answered, going across the hall and opening a door into some mighty abandoned room. A cold draught brought with it the smell of dust and gilt. He turned on a lamp adapted from a Chinese vase.

'Is there a Mr Flack?' Alice looked from the doorway into a room cluttered with the improbable shapes furniture assumes when dressed in Holland covers; chandeliers hung motionless in muslin swathes. A grand, chilly room with family on the walls posing sadly in the shadows. Grand and forgotten.

'Yes, there is, only he's old now and a bit gaga. She must have thought I meant Aunt's sitting-room,' he said, backing out and closing the door.

'Don't they ever come here?'

'Not often,' he answered, leading the way to the back of the house. 'I'm not a girl, you see. No need to be launched.'

'Why do they keep it then?'

'Because they have always had it.' As he spoke, Edmund opened the door of a room in which a fire burned up brightly. 'They like to know it's here, I suppose. Change is an unknown word at Kincraig.'

'How cosy,' said Alice, looking about her. Mrs Flack had misinterpreted Edmund beautifully. His aunt's room contained a small grand piano, a sofa and armchairs covered in some chintzy, hybrid flowers of yellow and cream. The piano was littered with photographs and an assortment of pretty and useless objects: bon-bon boxes and Bilston shepherdesses forever Arcadian on the lids of little pots, cut-glass scent bottles in chased, silver holders ... but it was the photographs to which Alice was drawn.

'Sleeping Beauty's castle,' said Edmund, holding his hands to the fire. 'You, of course, are Beauty. But what am I, Alice, the Beast or the Prince?'

When she did not answer he looked round and found her peering at the rows of faces on the piano.

'Tell me who they all are,' she said.

'What?' He came over to her. 'Oh those ...'

Masses of them: women in court dress, feathered, impassive, men in uniform; a large house somewhere with the party seated outside on chairs, clustered round a Very Important Person.

'The Norfolk cousins,' said Edmund over her shoulder. 'Still in hock from those parties. He', Edmund touched Tum-Tum's face lightly with one finger, 'had a fancy for my cousin Kitty. They couldn't keep him away for a bit.'

'Which one is Kitty?' asked Alice curiously, remembering sitting on that stout royal knee herself. The fat hands like bunches of carrots, the cigar breath.

'In the wings. She was only young,' he said, picking up the photograph and rubbing it. 'There. You remind me of her sometimes.'

'Where is she now?' Alice peered jealously at a young girl in white with a tiny waist.

'Fell off her horse and died,' said Edmund sadly. 'Nobody could understand it. She was as tough as anything.'

'And you loved her?'

'I think so,' he said, 'only one forgets the feeling. The fact of it is left, the little moraine of bitterness and dissatisfaction at something unfinished, a scar really. You are like her. Aunt Maud noticed it too. She told me before I even met you.'

'Was that why?' A connection. Something falling into place. A not unflattering something.

'It might have been,' he said, not looking at her. 'It might have been.' And he thought but did not say that she was too good for him, too altogether decent and straightforward, too trusting. She expected motive where there was only expediency, looked for a pattern, a philosophy, where there was only scavenging, a kind of hand-to-mouth emotional life that thrived on difficulties, mock-coldnesses, tiffs. If he was capable of love he would have loved Alice.

'My mother,' he said to break the silence, picking up another. 'A beauty by all accounts.'

'They were always beauties by all accounts, weren't they?' she said. 'If you die young you become beautiful in people's minds. It was the same with my mother.' She looked at the photograph in front of her: a ravishing female equivalent of Edmund with the elaborate hair that had been fashionable thirty years ago, strong brows, large eyes, sensuous mouth, the extraordinary luminous and beautiful skin tone of those late-Victorian women. She put it back and took up his father. 'A younger version of Uncle John.' Her interest touched him. He felt he had done little to deserve it.

'Play something while I do some drinks,' he said, turning from her. 'There's music in the stool.' He felt sad and heavy and regretful, unwieldy and awkward in a way he was not used to, as if the embers of some long-dead fire were being raked over and found lively still.

Alice found some Chopin she had laboured over as a child in the schoolroom at Leith, but the piano was out of tune and the notes sounded squashy and almost soft, not by any means the enamelled perfection the composer had intended. Every now and again she raised her eyes to the Norfolk cousins and thought of Kitty. Pretty Kitty, dead Kitty. Kitty who had gone out like a light on the hunting field in the heyday of her generation and who would not know this war. Kitty, whose descendant she was, last in the endless line of women who had loved Edmund and wanted to know his secrets. Perhaps Kitty had known them, perhaps it was her death that had soured Edmund and made him empty hearted; this vacuum in him, this lack, that was skinned over by charm and ease and looks. Any sensible girl, she thought, would have gone home by now. Any sensible girl would probably not have come here in the first place. But I will stay, she said to herself, because I know and he knows I know, that there will be one moment, one split-second when it will have been worth it, one moment when he will have wanted only me, one moment when I shall possess him utterly.

'There.' He came and put down a glass and took her hands off the keys. 'We're going to have a pik-nik in front of the fire. The dining-room is so cold we'd never survive. Go over and sit in front of it while I get candles and food.'

She sat on a corner of the sofa holding her hands to the flames, listening to Edmund's firm tread crossing the hall and vanishing into a room beyond. He did not come back immediately and she fell to wondering about Gerard, seeing once more in her mind's eye that scene at the docks – was it really only the night before? – the horse being swung high over the water, the pitiful whinnyings. Gerard, too, was the other side of the divide now, perhaps riding on Hitchy Koo down one of those interminable pavé roads bordered by poplars that seemed somehow the essence of abroad, riding into the war. But, try as she would, she could only see him alone: a solitary rider vanishing down a straight road into an empty horizon; guns, limbers, the foot-slogging infantry, supply wagons, the songs – soldiers always sang, didn't they? – were a reality talked of by the newspapers but unimaginable, somehow inhabiting a different dimension. Perhaps this was because (she got up and put her hands nearer the fire, turning them this way and that, thinking it through) because she had gained the idea that this war, however vast its dimensions, was to him something personal, almost a crusade, in which he would find redemption: Jerusalem shifted northwards to the flat

160

boredom of the Franco-Belgian countryside, Eternal City in the midst of slagheaps and coalmines, all the ugly smugness of industrialization. Jerusalem the Golden? Hardly.

Edmund came back with candles dripping wax and smoking wildly. 'Damn!' He looked at his hand and shook it. 'Food next. All very primitive, I'm afraid. You don't mind?'

She shook her head. 'No. But can't I help?'

'It's all right. I'm enjoying myself, really.' He went away and came back again with a hamper. 'You are to pretend this is Ascot,' he said, putting it down on the sofa and kneeling to undo the straps. 'Somewhere in the shadows lingers your entire acquaintance, in their best, of course.'

'Of course.'

The lid squeaked as he pushed it up. 'The King and Queen are hiding under the piano for fear of suffragettes and . . .'

'. . . the horses . . .' Alice took a plate and a glass.

'. . . are in the hall, lined up at the foot of the stairs, awaiting the fearless Flacks.'

'Edmund.'

'Yes?' He looked up, leaving his hands in the shavings.

'Promise me something.'

'What, sweet one? You're all serious again.'

'To remember this. Nothing more . . . but properly.'

He got up and came to her. 'Shall I take you away afterwards? We'll do a Vronsky and Anna, go into exile somewhere. Kenya. Somewhere hot: apricot skies, lions. I'll become a white hunter.' He touched her cheek. 'I won't forget you.'

She could not speak.

'We would have made a fine pair, once, wouldn't we?' he said, holding her hand and twisting her rings round and round. 'But you're not made for a life of crime. Go back to Gerard and love him. He's worth twenty of me.

I've wronged him a great deal ... and you too,' he said. 'I was born amoral, I think. Not "im" but "am". "Am" is worse because it's a permanent state, a life sentence...'

Alice put her head on his shoulder, holding back the tears, concentrating, forcing the moment to a halt. Somewhere out of time she would always be here with him in this forgotten room hearing the echo of their words, those words that would continue reverberating even after they had climbed the stairs to Edmund's cold bedroom and made sad and passionate love between the damp, unaired sheets. Even after she had gone home alone in a taxi cab procured by Edmund to her own bedroom in Gerard's house to await the telegrams and cards and letters that would shape the rest of her life, she would still be there in that room with him in the white house near the park – Edmund's blinded, shuttered palace – on a dark night at the beginning of the Great War. *Mort pour l'amour, la patrie, la verité...*

CHAPTER
FOURTEEN

Gerard lay on deck wrapped in his cloak, looking up at the stars. There was a half moon and a dead-calm sea; perfect conditions for submarines. The boat, once used for ferrying cattle between Canada and Liverpool, was part of a fleet of troop ships moving towards an unknown destination with all lights out. Raising his head slightly he could see the outline of their destroyer escort.

It had been a hell of a two days. They had embarked at nine o'clock the previous morning and spent the whole day going round in circles, calling at Ventnor, then making in the direction of Bordeaux, before turning back to England again. After dark they had come opposite the lights of a large town and were informed by an Admiralty tug that it was Dover. Dover, for God's sake! Cheering news had whispered its way on board that there were several German submarines in the neighbourhood.

All day they had waited and wondered, unable to communicate with the shore; now they were on their way again. Under his back he could feel every vibration of the engine; the deck was hard and it was extremely cold. He stretched flat, tucking his cloak round him. Strangely, he found he was quite calm after all the tensions and excitement; a kind of stillness had taken possession of him into which he relaxed utterly. Looking up at the stars reminded him of doing the same thing as a boy: the same sense of awe, the awareness of a numinosity, an otherness.

I am the same man still, he thought, turning on his side, the same who had persecuted his wife, who always seemed to want what he had not got, who argued with his father, who allowed petty differences to cloud relations with family and friends, the same and yet different; change had entered in through suffering and reflection. It had been there before he was aware of it, nestling in his unconscious mind. Loving Alice, this new love he felt for her, was a part of it, a wanting to make not just amends but newness itself, regeneration. He could pray now, the block, the difficulties and distractions were gone. Infinity, the other side of the universe, was here beside him in the great silence of the night. He put out his hand and touched the deck, encountering the edge of his new friend Mahoney's cloak. Mahoney shifted, muttered something, threw out a hand. Above their heads stars danced.

Dawn. A low-lying coast.

'Where are we?' Gerard sat up. Mahoney was on his feet leaning over the rail.

'Zeebrugge,' he said, turning slightly to look at Gerard. 'Belgian–Dutch frontier. There's a huge mole, about half a mile long. Come and look.'

Gerard came to join him. They lay fourth in a row of five transports. Everything was grey: sea, boats, sky. On shore some figures scurried to and fro, gulls circled and shrieked above their heads. There was the usual pause in which nothing at all seemed to be happening. Gerard turned from the rail and lit a cigarette, cupping his hand over the metal lighter. What had he expected? Trumpets?

'Fed up?' Mahoney puffed on his own cigarette, stuffing a lighter back into his pocket.

'Not exactly.'

'It's the hanging about that gets me,' Mahoney said. 'You wouldn't know there's a war on with this lot; and there they are in England jumping up and down, telling us what brave chaps we are, all blood and thunder. I bet you anything the Belge won't know who we are, where we've come from or where we're to go to.' He turned back to the dour coast, flicking his ash into the wind.

All day they marched. A warmish autumn in Belgium: cultivated fields, neat, ugly villages. Life was going on as usual here; it was not so much, thought Gerard, that the peasant mentality was impervious to war, rather that – certainly in this part of the world – they had grown used to soldiers coming out of nowhere, a part of folk memory that cropped up occasionally and regularly like an eclipse of the sun or an extra-hot summer, usually without benefit. Armed men had been coming out of the mists here since time immemorial. In the hamlets people stared and waved, shouting greetings and incomprehensible encouragements in Flemish, a language like Dutch, Gerard decided, which one appeared to need a cleft palate in order to speak properly. In the fields women suspended in the act of picking or plucking looked at them under their arms, nudging each other and straightening for a proper stare. Colonel Fasson beckoned Gerard alongside.

'They think we're Germans,' he said, waving at a group of women who stood the other side of the ditch, digging each other in the ribs. 'English,' he called, smiling.

One of the women detached herself from the group, came across the ditch on an old plank and into the road. Trotting alongside, she fumbled under her apron and produced an enormous red apple which she pushed into the Colonel's hand.

'For God's sake, tell me what she's saying.' The Colonel continued to nod and smile as if he was in a box at the opera.

'A gift from her own garden for the brave soldier?' Gerard improvised. 'I don't speak Flemish, you know.' He watched the woman fall back.

'Agricultural gifts not covered in Deshumbert?'

'No. I'm afraid not.'

'You'll have to do the best you can until we get to a place where you can speak the lingo. Most of them do have French, don't they?'

'Most of them, yes.'

Gerard turned and rode back down the column. It was stupid, so stupid, not to have been prepared for this, a first test failed. Why had he not thought of it? Just a few words would have helped, ten minutes' homework before he left: 'Hallo', 'Goodbye', 'How much?', 'Where to?' It was no good saying, Oh well, they took me on for my French and German. A good officer would have looked at the map, made some sensible predictions, known what to expect ... and yet, and yet, so what? He could make mistakes and, admittedly, it was a very small error of judgement. It was no good taking everything as a personal challenge; in a way the challenge was in adapting, in making the best of things, in shrugging them off and starting again. There might come a time, he thought, looking out over the flat countryside, there just might come a time when the different parts of his nature were so much in harmony that this peculiar pain and difficulty he felt when things went wrong, when he seemed not to have acquitted himself properly, would pass unnoticed; he had a quick intimation that the loss of personal vanity restored the world to one in a new and quite different way; was not, as he had feared, a withdrawal to a place where things mattered so little that one was indifferent to them. Rather the opposite.

They had a rendezvous, a small village called Oostcamp, five or so miles south of Bruges. But news of their coming spread mysteriously faster than the brigade's progress, so that by the time they reached Blankenberg and then Bruges they were heroes, not because of anything they had done but simply on account of being Englishmen.

If the country-people were cautious and then rather

charmingly enthusiastic, the townsmen mobbed them. In Blankenberg the column was decked out in flags and Belgian colours, cigars and yet more apples were stuffed into pockets; the gunners gave away their badges, horses wore garlands. They became not part of an army but instead a bank-holiday crowd on their way to a little roistering elsewhere. It was the same at Bruges although it was beginning to grow dark and everyone was tired. Outside the town Gerard was sent ahead with a small party to find the village.

Headquarters was a large château belonging to a Count someone or other who had fled to Paris, but the family was still in residence in the shape of the vanished nobleman's brother-in-law and his wife who had themselves fled Liège.

'It was like musical chairs,' the Countess said, as she took him upstairs to his room. 'We looked out of our windows and saw the Germans coming, so we went quick as anything, helter-skelter, down the stairs and into the cars. Luckily we were packed.'

Gerard looked at her sideways. She was tall and smart and dark; quite unruffled. 'What about furniture, paintings and so forth?'

'We had to leave all that, of course. There is only a limited amount you can pack into a motor car.' She went ahead of him into a bedroom. 'We hear since that the Germans looted and burnt everything. But we are safe. We have sanctuary here, temporary perhaps, I don't know. In these times we give thanks for the smallest of mercies.' She gestured at the room. 'If there is anything you need, please tell me.'

He could have come for the shooting, Gerard thought, as he thanked her and closed the door. The bedroom reminded him of a thousand similar rooms he had inhabited for the inside of a week in large houses like this one.

Tomorrow they would go down in their shooting things to breakfast; the Count would be wearing good tweeds so as to appear very English, but would spoil the effect out of doors by wearing one of those curious pork-pie hats with a feather in, the kind that continental sportsmen seemed so fond of. He would have a very smart, new-fangled gun from Purdey's, Gerard decided, as he went to the window; couldn't give the man too much of an advantage. Light from a downstairs window allowed him to see the dim outlines of a formal garden with yew hedges and gravel pathways. There was some elaborate topiary whose shapes he couldn't make out. Somewhere the peacocks would be roosting. And in the village at the end of the long drive were the men and guns and horses. It was not a game, although it was hard to take it seriously so far. These people took it lightly enough or so it seemed.

He tried to think if Kildour were smashed and burnt by the enemy whether he would behave with such dignity, such almost light-heartedness. His house was integral to him, the visible outward sign of who he was, what his family had been and still, thank God, was; such a large statement, in fact, that it was never spoken of in those terms and only ever obliquely referred to by himself or his friends as a good place, or a decent shoot. But without it, what would he be without it? Insufferable, probably. One of those people always on the look-out to impress in some way or other by demonstrating their good breeding or their impeccable connections. A bore with a tremendous chip on his shoulder. It was a terrifying thought, and yet the Countess carried it off with enormous dignity, as Alice had carried it off when it seemed that through her father's insane stupidity and selfishness she would be in the same situation. He had known that about her, yet had not felt it. For the first time he realized what social death meant. Anything would be preferable, almost anything.

A thump on the door distracted him. It was the Adjutant, Massingham.

'Colonel wants a word before dinner. The library.'

'A minute,' Gerard called.

'Right-o. Door across the hall from the foot of the stairs. Don't be long. Dinner smells too good to wait.'

It was, too. If there were shortages or things difficult to obtain, this was not apparent. Again, Gerard was overcome by the feeling that it was a game, a dream, that there was no enemy, only the pheasants limbering up in the dark woods outside. Candles and chit-chat and excellent wine. Paris was substituted for London, Joffre for French, the King was Albert not beaky George. Once the Colonel left the table in response to a message but came back again and sat down, saying nothing. A minute or two later he was discussing Longchamps with the Countess in such a way that Gerard quite expected to hear him say he would be off there tomorrow on a whim.

Once or twice he had a glimpse of Mahoney's face grown darker and more florid with drink; there was something about Mahoney he found immensely attractive, a dark humour, an ease, a scepticism about his religion that both scandalized Gerard and made him laugh, rather against his will. He was a Catholic, but always referred to himself as a Roman Candle, who fiddled the system with all the practised deftness and lack of scruple of a black marketeer. Beside him, Gerard felt naïve and, frankly, envious.

'Lip service,' Mahoney had said on the boat. 'Take what you want and leave the rest. I do. We all do. Converts are in the most difficult position of all, forced to do everything by the book, reducing the intellect to the status of a puppet. Infallability is regarded by most of us as one of the quirks of kingship, a natural conclusion to the Syllabus of Errors. Once you have something like "Ineffabilis Deus" you can expect any nonsense you like from Rome. It won't wash, you'll find. Make up your own mind and don't for God's sake feel guilty about it.'

Gerard had become friends with Mahoney swiftly; the unusual circumstances in which they met allowed something to develop which might have taken years in other surroundings. There was a response each found in the

169

other which allowed them to speak freely, yet their conversations were not peppered with landmarks: by some tacit but unspoken agreement background was kept in the background.

Mahoney was from the south of Ireland, Gerard knew. He occasionally referred to the place: Gerard had an impression of something Palladian, a white house with pillars and doves, too many sisters, declining funds, a brother who was a monk; all hopes resting on this scion, this character with black hair that appeared to defy gravity and grow upwards in extraordinary spirals, boot-button eyes and the pink cheeks of a cherub. There was nothing remotely 'pi' or cherubic about Mahoney, yet he gave off the impression of an abounding kind of decency, a wholesomeness.

'Stay,' he had said to Gerard after dinner, indicating a fire, a bottle, a book-lined snug.

'I've had it,' Gerard answered, 'really. Enjoy yourself.'

'I will,' said Mahoney, raising a hand and, at the same moment, beginning to talk his execrable French to the Count.

On his way to bed, Gerard met a small boy in striped pyjamas coming down the corridor.

'Hallo.' The only indication of the child's foreignness was the exaggerated perfection of his vowel sounds.

'Hallo.'

'Are you here to kill the Germans? Mama wouldn't let me stay up.'

'Yes, I suppose I am.'

The boy looked him up and down. He didn't seem very sleepy. 'Mama says,' he went on in his unsexed aristocratic voice, 'the English always say things like "suppose" or "possibly". Hedging their bets, she calls it. I should like to kill lots of Germans,' he added. 'I should like to wipe them out.'

And I should like to wring your neck, thought Gerard. 'Oughtn't you to be in bed?'

'I *suppose* I should.'

'Goodnight then.'

'G'night.' The child went on his way, bare feet going slip-slap on the carpet.

Lessons, thought Gerard: I am being taught something. He closed his bedroom door gently, trying not to disturb this delicate train of thought. There was something he had caught a glimpse of, the faintest outline of a pattern, a feeling that events were not so random as they might appear. What, he wondered, lifting a curtain back with one hand, what would God have of him? What was the plan for his life?

All of a sudden he was possessed by a most distinct feeling that he had reached one of those moments he had read about in the lives of the saints, one of those turning-points in life ignored at peril. The tentative and uncertain steps he had taken towards loving his wife, towards listening and learning from others were but the beginning: one small step towards transfiguration. Much would be required of him here. For the first time he felt this knowledge as a physical reality, a kind of pain. His heart raced in his chest, there was sweat on his forehead.

At once it was a certainty to him that he would die here somewhere out in the flat fields, amongst the pheasant covers, woods, the prim villages, and not, as he had always imagined he would, in his bed at Kildour, full of years and honours, surrounded by his descendants. It would not be that, but alone in the dirt, unsung. His old life seemed to recede from him, lovely and safe, leaving darkness in its wake ... darkness but not bleakness. There were tears in his eyes. A voice in his head said: 'Made Whole Again'. Nothing else, just those three words. No flashes of light, no angels with carved immaculate faces, no trumpets. At this he smiled a little; trumpets, or the lack of them, seemed so far the theme of his war.

There was a writing-table and a chair against one wall.

Gerard sat down and fished about for his notebook and his cigarette case, swearing quietly under his breath when he could find neither. He was not surprised to find himself irritated and cursing because of it; in a way it made what he had experienced the more true: the new man was everything the old one was. He found his pen and wrote: 'I do not think I shall come back from this war.' He looked at the words and wondered if he should go on. There was no answering call from within his soul to them, only a mild kind of embarrassment at their melodrama. It seemed it was not possible to communicate intuition of his kind without sounding absurd, without looking as if he were clutching at a martyr's crown. What would his father make of such words, his mother, Alice? Alex? Alex ... The more he thought about it the more he began to see an invisible link between Alex's experience at Kildour and his own; without being in any way able to say why or explain, he knew there was a connection. The boy had known, all along he had known it. Even to suspect this placed an intolerable burden on Gerard's every action from now on. It would be like sitting an exam and knowing all the answers. But then wasn't it the same for everyone? Every life came willy-nilly to the same conclusion; in his case it was only a question of shortening, of knowing the distance to the finishing post was truncated.

He got up and began to walk about. The only answer was to go on, to drift with the tide of war, to do his best. There was nothing new in these aims. In this light a withdrawal to the cloister would be like cheating, removing oneself from the sphere of difficulties. Everything rested with him now: he would have to make a tremendous war.

Step one: sleep before exertion. If God was a reader of novels, he thought, climbing into bed, then it would have been a moment for a terrific dream or a reassuring vision of some kind. As it was, he dreamt of nothing but himself interviewing a German prisoner, mysteriously

172

clad in chain mail leggings and a tunic top, asking one question over and over again: 'Has your Regiment lost many horses? Has your lost Regiment many horses? Many horses your lost Regiment has . . . ?' War broke into his sleep in the shape of Massingham, the Adjutant, who came into his room at four o'clock in the morning, telling him that they were to retire at once to Ostend. There was no explanation for this.

As Gerard dressed in haste and collected up his few possessions, he found he was immensely excited to be on the move. He would not forget this place, this quiet château with its formal garden and its park, the odd collection of inhabitants, but to go in haste seemed somehow fitting; nothing now could be planned or legislated for, thought of in advance. The testing-time was begun.

He looked back, once, at the uncertain outline of the building behind him, a blackish shadow in the thinning light of dawn, feeling a strange attachment to the house where he had spent so few but such important hours, feeling very alone too. It was as if he was saying goodbye to a whole way of life, an affectionate farewell to sets of values that would (he hoped) remain, but that were no longer enough. We are all of us alone at the end, he thought sadly. No amount of children, of possessions, of alliances whether political or social, could obscure this single and singular truth or make the slightest difference. The Kingdom lies within, he said to himself, repeating it several times, as if saying the words over and over again would somehow secure a response from the part of him fallen so strangely silent.

CHAPTER
FIFTEEN

The next few days were almost indescribable chaos. In keeping up with their movements in his diary, Gerard could only think it was like playing box and cox with the enemy; but the delays and hesitations, the toing and froing, the frustrations, he found he somehow managed to take in his stride.

At Ostend the brigade had to entrain from the main station in the middle of the town. The station-master had produced a train for guns and wagons with a flourish, expecting to be congratulated on his cleverness, but had neglected the most important item of all: ramps. Gerard found a company of Belgian Engineers and explained to them in French that ramps were vital in order to run the equipment onto the train from the end. After some time had passed, in which there were many consultations, two baulks of wood were produced, both extremely long and mighty enough to bear a legion of elephants. So far, so good, although Gerard found himself wondering how the pyramids had been built, coming to the inescapable conclusion that Egyptian slaves must have been more attuned to the wishes of their masters than their latter-day Belgian equivalent. After a further delay and many difficulties a magnificent ramp was constructed at the end of the platform, leaving a space of about a yard between the last truck and the end of the ramp. The train was then backed up to close the gap, giving the gentlest of taps to the end of the ramp ... which promptly collapsed with a crash that resounded through the station.

Gerard began to laugh. Hours afterwards he had only to catch a glimpse of Mahoney's face in order to be overcome again. He didn't think he had seen anything so funny in all his life. The Colonel, of course, was of another opinion.

After this the Belgians were sacked from the station and the British took charge of matters themselves. The endless journey was resumed once more. Back to Bruges, on to Ghent, detrain in the direction of Melle. For the first time gunfire. The days were beginning to run into one another, old distinctions between day and night lost in a new pattern ruled by railway timetables, and information concerning the whereabouts of the enemy which seemed scanty at best. London, Gerard reckoned, knew more about the war than they did themselves.

Another billet in a deserted château, another dinner. Gerard was just lifting his cigar to his lips when terrific rifle fire broke out from the positions directly in front of the house. A silence round the table. Faces too much taken by surprise to hide their expressions of fear, shock. Gerard felt his bowels contract. The match burnt all the way down to his fingers before he dropped it with an exclamation and a curse. The spell was broken.

In a rush, food baskets were packed up, horses saddled and the brigade stood to arms. They slept outside in the dark, dozing through the long reaches of a cold but exceptionally fine night. Gerard lay with his arm through his horse's bridle, and would wake every now and again in the dead starlight whose meaning or unmeaning he no longer puzzled over or tried to fathom, and thought of Alice asleep in London or his parents in their separate bedrooms at home, at Kildour. Once, without any kind of rancour, he thought of Nina and her perfect beauty. She would be out somewhere, he supposed, now that William had come to the war, dancing or drinking, beating life up into a frenzy in her inimitable way, always in pursuit of the next moment and the next, the thrill or spill round the corner, the unattainable.

He would rather be here, like this, in this almost parody of a boyhood dream of heroism. So often as a child he had thought of himself as one of Alexander's men, or with Hannibal guiding the elephants over the impossible Alps, or on the plain at Troy. And he thought of the firing he had heard and how it had appeared to roll up and down the lines, sometimes dying to a solitary shot, at other moments a continuous roar; and of how it frightened him, although he guessed this was not extraordinary. He did not fear fear itself, the recall of the blood to the anxious heart, the nerve-ends contracting, but what did frighten him was the thought of losing his grip on the slender thread of his own nobility of purpose, the silver vein of courage that made his every action accountable. That he feared most of all ... if thou be willing, remove this cup from me ... He remembered the padre and '*Deus le volt*'. If those were the most dangerous words in history, then Christ's continuation, 'nevertheless not my will, but thine, be done', were the most courageous, containing within their perfect simplicity the full flowering of the Crucifixion; it was all over then, really, bar the dying.

All the next day they remained in their positions, waiting. Rumours flew about concerning the numbers of Germans in front of them, ranging from a few battalions of German advance guard to several army corps. Gerard and Mahoney between them cooked up the idea that there was no enemy at all, until three prisoners of the Landwehr were brought in to give substance to the idea that out there, somewhere in the lurking places of the villages, there was a German or two.

The captured soldiers belonged to a division which had just arrived from Antwerp and had got lost in a wood during the previous night attack. They were, Gerard found, flexing his linguistic muscles properly for the first time, pathetically eager to tell all, an all which amounted to very little. He had a hand-written list of questions supplied by the Chief Interpreter of the Division, mostly to do with food or the lack of it, searching questions about the amount of ammunition and horses, enquiries over sickness and whether the water was brackish or not. He had no need of the list of admonitions the grand panjandrum had included: 'Will you pay attention to me!' 'You may speak confidentially as no one will know it was you who gave me this information', 'There can be no object in your concealing this from me.' To have them written down seemed almost an insult to the decent fellows in front of him.

Later that day, there was another retreat. The 7th Division followed the Belgians and the French marines back through Ghent. The townspeople were pathetically anxious to understand why their saviours of the day before were now going in the opposite direction. Gerard was repeatedly questioned about the likelihood of the Germans arriving; it was very difficult to know how to answer. He could not say there was no danger, nor could he say the truth, which was that the Germans would occupy the town within an hour of the British force leaving. Panic would have caused the population to flee, blocking the roads and preventing the retreating troops from being of any use. As it turned out, the Germans entered the east side of Ghent as the British left the west.

The war was truly closing on them now. The night march was a forced one and it felt like it too. The carnival feeling of the very beginning, the bank-holiday riotousness had long since evaporated. The men had been in the trenches all day and had stood to arms the night before; now they were marched without halting – except for five minutes at a time – from seven in the evening until seven the next morning, in a column of seemingly interminable length, led by a staff officer in a motor. There was no smoking and no talking and certainly no singing. The Germans were known to be north, east and south of the division, in control of countryside extending from Ghent to Lille; an advance from the direction of Courtrai or Roulers would have pushed the British right back to the sea and on into it or over the Dutch frontier. With a sense of oppression, almost of impending doom, the column followed the motor which could only go at walking pace and made enough noise to be heard at least ten miles off. As so often happened with the army, one thing was seen to be quite obviously and in direct contradiction of another.

On his horse Gerard fell into a kind of stupor, neither asleep nor truly awake, aware of the rocking motion of the beast beneath him, the sound of many pairs of feet, wheels on pavé, the put-put of the ridiculous motor. The time passed, somehow . . .

At Aeltre, after five hours' rest at Hansbeke, which was crammed full of wretched *marins français* who had never fought on land before, Gerard met William, who was in charge of Scots Guards' transport.

'Surprise, surprise,' Gerard said, dismounting. 'How are you?'

'Gerard!' William separated himself from the people he was with and came over. He looked pleased with himself, cheerful, rudely happy.

'Things going well?' asked Gerard. 'I heard from Alice you were on your way.'

'I don't know if anything's going at all,' William said, accepting a cigarette. 'Talk has the Germans forcing the bridges at Nevele and Deyenze, but you know talk.' He looked at his brother-in-law with interest. There was something strange about him, a look of spirituality, a difference of some kind, profound, but not immediately visible to the casual observer. For a start he looked extraordinarily relaxed for a man who had been on the move for days without much rest: the way he stood holding the bridle of his horse with the beast plunging its nose up and down as if looking for something to eat; there was something in that stance, impossible to name, the way he would murmur to his horse every now and again.

Gerard did not, as he would have done in the old days, pounce upon any morsel of information and crown it with something better. In fact, he seemed hardly concerned at all to hear of the endangered flank. All very odd.

'Talk has it,' Gerard said, 'Thielt's a shambles. Market square jammed, that kind of thing.' He looked up at the sky as he spoke: two crows wheeled and then sank towards a tree-top.

'Nina tells me,' said William, prodding, also looking upwards at the ragged birds, 'that she met Alice lunching with Edmund at the Café Royal.' He did not add that Nina had made the most unseemly remarks about the purpose of that apparently innocent luncheon.

'May I borrow your wife?' Gerard placed the toe of his boot on his cigarette and ground it out.

'I beg your pardon?' William frowned.

'Joke,' Gerard said. 'I had a note from her recently, mentioning it.' Carnegie was hinting at something. He did not entirely care to imagine what. It was what being married to Nina had done for him, a kind of corruption. He owed the Almighty any number of *Te Deums* for that lucky escape. 'How well you look,' he said, by way of changing the subject. 'War seems to agree with you.'

'Haven't seen much of it yet,' William said, looking at his watch. 'I ought to go in a minute.'

'War is this.' Gerard looked him in the eye. 'Endless interstices of boredom, frustration and fatigue, punctuated by occasional high-spots of frantic, engrossing activity.'

'That's too high-faluting for me, dear fellow,' said William. 'War's war and that's that. Obey orders and get killed for your pains.' A temporary aberration prevented him from remembering his still-lively hopes of a staff job.

'And the rest.' Gerard climbed back onto his horse. 'Good luck. My love to Nina.'

'Goodbye.' William shaded his eyes with his hand, watching Gerard go. It would not have surprised him to see the damn horse sprouting wings.

CHAPTER
SIXTEEN

Their progress continued towards Ypres, via Thielt and Roulers. Thielt was a nightmare of slummy billets and confused troops, the 7th Division, the Belgians and the French all arriving at the same time. HQ was downgraded from a château to the back regions of a small tobacconist's shop where a planning session was conducted in a dark little formal parlour full of cheap relics and antimacassars. Every time Gerard looked up he found himself eye to eye with a plaster image of the Virgin, a part of whose chin had somehow been chipped away, giving her the distressingly lopsided look of a leper victim. Roulers was better. They bought chocolate and eggs and sat down to a decent dinner in comfortable billets. It had begun to rain very heavily.

At Ypres Gerard went on ahead with his trumpeter to look for yet more billets. During the course of this expedition he came across a distressing scene: two German officers, whose aeroplane had been brought down by British naval guns, had been escorted into town in a motor. Gerard found them in the Rue Jacob off the main square, a little cobbled street so jammed with guns, transport and troops that their car ground to a halt. In front of the vehicle stood a French corporal yelling with excitement and gesticulating like a marmoset; it would have been farcical had he not been armed: he had an automatic pistol with which he made repeated stabbing gestures in the air or aimed directly at the two prisoners. His finger was on the trigger and there was death in the air; Gerard felt it, the crowd felt it. A Belgian soldier came forwards and took hold of one of the officers in the car, shaking him like a rat. Gerard acted then, quick and incisive as a snake. The Belgian was in the gutter, the crowd going backwards, pressing on itself, murmuring, ashamed.

'I'm sorry,' Gerard said in German to the officer who had not been manhandled. 'Very, very sorry.'

'We confidently expected to be torn apart,' the man replied, not looking at his neighbour who had put his head in his hands. 'Thank you.' He made a movement with his lips that might have been an attempt at a smile but was horrible to behold. Leaning down from his horse Gerard smelt the sweat of fear, saw a treacherous tic beating in the delicate skin under one eye.

'It was nothing,' he replied, shocked. The man was pure affliction. It had frozen his face and made him an automaton. Gerard drew back, shouting for a passage to be made for the motor and its occupants, watching them make their halting way out of danger.

So much for the enemy, he thought, wiping his forehead. Close to, the man was in torment. Yet the incident disgusted Gerard and as he made his own way through the crowd he wondered why this should be so. To the mob they had been sub-humans, captured figureheads of a hated nation; something of this, perhaps, had rubbed off on him. He seemed to recollect the vestiges of an icy indifference, a kind of revulsion for them upon entering the street that had held him in thrall until it was almost too late.

Outside the cathedral he paused to read the time of the masses and it occurred to him there that Christ had probably felt as those two men did: abandoned and accursed, drawing the whole world's torment through himself. It made him want very much to go to mass. He felt defiled, debased, unclean. It was the old argument that if hatred of others is a sword then it cannot reach them until it has first passed through one's own body;

simply to have been there, in that crowd, was ample demonstration of that.

Gerard found billets with a prosperous bourgeois family who could not do enough to make the officers comfortable. He had a hot bath, the first since Southampton, and read his post, which had miraculously caught up with him again. He found Alice's letter curiously unsatisfactory: she had not been feeling very well, was going to a hotel in Brighton for a couple of days; Cook was being difficult and making threatening noises about leaving for factory work and better pay. Alice wanted to give their motor as an ambulance and would he mind? It would be amusing, she said, if he saw it coming and going out here. He had already seen London buses toiling to and fro still covered in posters and playbills, so, yes. Why not?

He looked at the letter again. Nothing about *her*, what she was really thinking, the inmost self quite disengaged. She said politely that she missed him, was looking forward to his first leave ... It made him wonder what he thought was missing. Or perhaps he was just tired and expecting too much from a letter. That was it, probably.

His mother, however, was everything he had expected she would be. She had a *Daily Mail* map installed in her boudoir, and wished to chart his progress with coloured flags. He wondered what she would make of his march from the extreme north to the south of Belgium – to say nothing of the various circlings in the middle – should he have been able to tell her, which of course he was not. A parcel was following, she said, if there was anything else he needed ... His father's leg, abnormally dormant for the short period immediately preceding the shoot, was troubling him again, but he sent his regards. Gerard vowed to write a separate letter to his father shortly in order to induce the noble lord to write an independent reply. He could think of no other way of forcing his hand from a distance.

He put his mother's letter on the cork seat of the chair next to the bath and lay back with warm water up to his chin. Kildour in October: the trees would have finished turning, the battle of leaves would have begun again, the roses, though . . . they would still be blooming; Macindoe would be tidying up the great border for winter, hindered by arguments with Lady Baillie over arrangements for next year. The bracken by the monument to his grandfather on the back hill would have turned russet. Everything the same; only he was changed. Alex was well, he said, busy. Glad of distractions in order to help him take his mind off his Thurlby grandfather who had died two weeks before, a man whose grandfather had been with Wolfe at the Heights of Abraham and who had held Wolfe in his arms at the moment of death, the moment Canada was born. Another link severed, gone for good. Gerard fell into a half-doze, imagining the scene, hearing the cry:

'They run! They run!'

'Who?'

'The French, sir . . .'

Sometime later he got out of the bath, shaved and dressed, then went to bang on Mahoney's door.

'Four o'clock mass,' he called. 'Are you coming?'

'Save us,' Mahoney flung the door open. 'Yes, I'll come. Just let me shave. We'll have to spout first, or at least I will. I know you're as pure as the driven snow.' He turned back to a glass propped against a jug of hot water. '*I saw a pretty maid*,' he sang, rolling his eyes.

'Where?' Gerard was amused.

'Tittuping along in front of the Cloth Hall – not that you'd be interested.'

'How do you know?'

'There is a Mrs Baillie, isn't there?'

'Yes.'

'Or, I beg your pardon, Lady Baillie.'

'Lady Alice Baillie, if you're going to split hairs.'

'Begging her ladyship's pardon . . .' Mahoney turned

and flicked some lather at Gerard. 'Besides, you have a look about you, m'boy. Seen it before.'

'What look?' Gerard took his cigarette out of his mouth without lighting it.

'Oh, you know, the wise eye, priestly. I've seen it before.'

Gerard stared.

'Don't be embarrassed. Nothing wrong with a bit of holiness. Besides, you're a sport. Must be to put up with me.'

'You need your head examining,' said Gerard, turning away.

He had not been entirely honest with the priest. Something had warned him to keep his premonition to himself. What had happened to him seemed so far beyond the confines of the rule book that he felt it almost an unfit subject for the bat and ball of ordinary penance, so he settled upon a good chiding of the venial and left the rest to God. To be a convert, he reflected, backing awkwardly out of the confessional, was to be almost too aware of how the Church carved up her territory: such and such for the laity, such and such for priests, the cream for those who did the most work, the contemplatives. To try and break that pattern would be the equivalent of the street sweeper in Victoria Street walking into the chamber of the House and taking a seat. He had no wish to cause ructions, so he kept his peace.

In a side chapel dedicated to the Virgin he went and knelt, looking towards the bank of candles that illuminated the carved marvels of the Mother of God. The child sat easily in her arms. Occasionally, in the swaying light, a particular feature would be picked out: a lock of hair that strayed from under the improbable crown, the side of a nostril or the baby's fat hands held up in pleasure. He looked so long that the statue appeared to swim under his fixed gaze, only turning away towards the altar when the shape of a head and a pair of military shoulders broke up his field of vision.

184

'The altar is quite properly regarded as a tomb,' he could hear Father Kinahan's voice saying, 'tremendous and yet simple Immolation.' The quiet, unbloody sacrifice under the creatures of bread and wine . . . Creatures, he thought: marvellous, really.

He found himself staring at the Virgin again and then at the shape of the head and familiar set of the shoulders of the man who had obscured his view. He rubbed his eyes and looked again, realizing that he was staring at the back of Edmund's head.

His heart turned round in his chest for pleasure; it was as if some immense but unconscious prayer had been answered.

Gerard got up and went awkwardly towards his friend, knocking into a chair on the way. Edmund did not look round. He sat with his hands in his lap and seemed to be staring past the statue at the dull glow of the sanctuary light. On a seat beside him lay his cap.

'Edmund!' Gerard touched him on the shoulder from behind.

'You!' Edmund stood and clasped Gerard's hand in both his, an almost womanish gesture of affection. 'It's too extraordinary,' he said, 'I was thinking of you just now.'

'When did you get here?' Gerard asked him as they made their way out.

'A minute ago,' Edmund caught his eye and then looked away. 'There's some nonsense going on about billets. Personally, I think we'll be lucky if we see a pillow and a blanket in a dug-out. The wind's definitely getting up now. I rather think we're all for it, somehow.' He fished in his pocket and blew his nose on an enormous khaki handkerchief.

'Never thought I'd find you in a place like this,' said Gerard, grinning.

'It's free and quiet,' Edmund replied, strangely resenting the insinuation. He was at a low ebb. The interminable journey across West Flanders had worn him out before he had even been in a show. The thought of Alice

185

was gnawing at him too; he was beginning to wonder if he might not have met his Waterloo there; it would bloody have to be like that. She was sweet and charming and graceful and giving and self-sacrificing and definitely not for him and he thought he might be falling in love with her in so far as he was capable of falling in love with anybody. Typical bad timing.

And now here was Gerry all holy and curious and strangely jolly looking, grown somehow inexplicably titanic and splendid in the weeks they had been parted.

'I'm glad you lunched with Alice,' Gerard said, without irony. 'She enjoyed it very much.'

'She did? Good.' Edmund looked around him rather wildly.

'I must go to mass now,' Gerard looked at his watch. 'Will you wait?'

'How long?'

'Half an hour.'

'Can't you skip it?' asked Edmund, not knowing whether he wanted to stay or go.

'No.'

'Forgive me,' Edmund said, 'that was tactless.'

'It doesn't matter.' Gerard put his arm around Edmund's shoulders and walked a little way towards the great door with him. 'That's all past now, gone, done with. You must have found me very odd in the summer,' he said. 'I was going through a kind of trial which is finished now.'

'You speak with finality, Gerry.' Edmund found he couldn't stop himself from saying things that led the conversation into deep water. 'Has something happened?'

'Yes . . . and no.' Gerard took his arm away and turned to him.

'Tell me . . . what?'

'I know I'm going to buy one here.'

'That can't be true . . .' Oh God, what next! He started to feel sick with emotion. Feelings he didn't know he had

186

began to rise within, bursting like bubbles into conscious thought: guilt and betrayal, blighted fruit of an early training so long and conveniently put aside.

'It doesn't matter,' said Gerard, to whom, suddenly and inexplicably, nothing did any more. He looked past Edmund through the gateway in the carved screen towards the altar where a priest moved to and fro with a beautiful formality. An unseen choir had begun upon the antiphon.

'How can you say that?' asked Edmund angrily, wiping the back of his hand across his eyes. 'How can you say it doesn't matter, haven't you thought of Alice, of your parents, of me ... bloody hell, Gerry, how can –'

'You don't understand. Don't go on.'

Edmund looked at Gerard and nearly feared him. He was as remote and serene as the carved figure of a medieval bishop he had admired earlier, peacefully asleep on his stone bier, foot firmly on the serpent's head.

'I'll wait,' he said.

He watched as Gerard went through the screen and took a place next to a dark-haired man whom he appeared to know, watched as the clouds of incense flew upwards, watched as the Host was raised over the bones of the martyr, watched Gerard go in a line towards the altar and saw him come back again unknowing and humble, gone from him into some mysterious place where he could not hope to follow, made clean again by a pellet of handmade wafer over which incantations had been pronounced. And yet ...

Some two weeks after this Alice went away. Brighton had been hell. Autumn had turned as sour and as vicious as the news from the Front. On the couple of occasions she had ventured onto the pier, the wind, chill and bitter, had turned her back again.

Sitting alone in her room or in the downstairs sitting-room provided for residents, she could not think why she had come. It was a kind of masochism to pass the days in this bleak but smug place surrounded by ersatz reminders of Prinny's vanity and vulgarity: the ballroom known as 'The Prince Regent Room', the grander bedrooms called after members of his family or hangers-on (she, herself, was in Princess Charlotte), the ghastly mock-Chinese wallpaper in the dining-room; even the salt- and pepper-pots were Sheffield-plated pineapples. If Alice hadn't been feeling so ill and so utterly alone it might have been a wonderful, continuing joke. As it was she found herself eating less and less as the days went by: roast beef, wine: all the dark, bloody things made her almost faint with nausea. Coffee was insupportable. She longed, at all the wrong times, for bouillon, salt biscuits, and had a strange craving for beer, but the genteel atmosphere of the hotel made this an impossible request. But she stayed on, as if remaining would achieve something. She was not sure quite what.

She had known at once she was pregnant, long before any doctor worth his salt would have anything to do with her. It was the traitor body turned sentinel; she felt as if she had changed gear and was moving now at a slower pace, battening down the hatches, turning her thoughts inward. For five or so days she had felt like this and wondered what was the matter with her, then the sickness started and she had known for sure, yet it was so early, so impossibly early.

There was nobody she could tell yet, not even Pamela. To Pamela it would all be too easy, doubts and hesitations would be waved aside, objections silenced and, above all, she wanted time to think, time to look at the pieces of her life and put them back together again in some different pattern. The advent of the child demanded reformation, but she wanted it to be right, to be able to examine her soul at any given time and find the same answer sitting there, unassailable.

Edmund had slammed doors in her face, so many doors that she came to believe him, almost. It was hopeless with him about the child, she knew, but in an odd way it wasn't really the child that made matters hang in the balance, although it had undoubtedly precipitated a decision – the father could be either man, its paternity a subject of a most tremendous doubt – no, it wasn't so much that as her own choice in deciding between the two men. Whichever one she chose would be the repository of all her confidence, all her hope; the decision seemed to her to bring with it an almost mythic resonance: an Oedipal drama or a happy home, but which? To the world there was no doubt. The world's choice would of course be Gerard; his was undoubtedly the senior claim. In law, the infant was his; but if she chose Edmund, even if he abandoned her, she would somehow hang onto her decision and let the world collapse around her ears. It was a choice between passion and duty. The outcome would mould her finally in one direction or another for ever. And so it was to Brighton she had gone to contemplate the abyss. Sometimes she thought she was deceiving herself by this rather elaborate and expensive means. At others, she felt it was the last time left to her when her own wishes would carry any real weight.

On or about the fifth night, she awoke at two in the morning and knew it would be Gerard. Loneliness had brought her round to him, and want: want for the child to have the best, the better father; it was exactly for this purpose the enforced solitude had been made to continue. Something can be made of it all, she said to herself. Something could be made of Edmund, too, her other self said, some tremendous patchwork of passion and reverse, doldrums and high-points. 'Consistently inconstant,' she said to the empty room; in spite of knowing, as at bottom she did know, that he had a special feeling for her (always the moment when he turned child in the dark), in spite of all that, it was a nonsense, a phantasm. How could she have deceived herself otherwise? Her father had smashed the mould of himself in a moment of violence and semi-insanity. She knew that she could not entertain any such a feeble giving way.

In spirit she would have to return to Gerard and give him what he wanted most, furthermore give it to him in love and truth. Then that too seemed beyond the bounds of possibility. Such perfection simply did not exist; nobody else would even have imagined it could. She would return and make the best of it, discover the person he had now become, this new being she had shied away from for so many weeks. He was all uncharted territory now.

She tried to feel good or glad and found either impossible. Virtue's reward was not piety or smugness but a love of virtue itself, a combination of subject and object that made distinctions impossible. Perhaps it would come.

She sat up in bed and turned on the light, wondering about them both. Last letters from Gerard had been about a week ago. Edmund had not written at all. Tomorrow was the first of November. From the newspapers she knew a terrible battle was raging near a place with a name that stuck in the throat – Ypres, to rhyme with Pepys, Gerard said. At this moment they could both be dead, she said, frightening herself, and then all my sordid little deliberations would seem exactly what they are: vanity.

She lay down again, trying unsuccessfully to imagine them; somewhere they lived, probably not dead or valiant at all, but chatting to friends or lighting cigarettes, having a drink, nursing men and guns; doing all the prosaic and normal things, but in spite of all that, absence made them heroes, absence made them men who might have to be remembered always as they were last seen. This distant ennobling was a kind of insurance, really, just a practice run, in case... Her thoughts turned to Alex and his grandfather, whose funeral she had attended last week. Dear old Sir Ben, who really had led a noble and a good life, a happy remembering, none of the cracks papered over. In the middle of the service she had wondered if this was the calamity that Alex had had a notion of; and yet it could not be. There was nothing calamitous in dying quietly at the end of your life, laid to rest in your own churchyard by family and friends. But Alex himself had seemed, if anything, excessively normal. Just a boy up from school. He did not mention it and neither did she. It was all guesswork, uncertain, another phantasm perhaps?

Alice reached London to find it all, in any case, decided.

A telegram, freshly delivered, lay in wait for her, a little, unexploded paper bomb from the War Office.

CHAPTER
SEVENTEEN

Afterwards, Gerard knew he should not have told
Edmund that he knew he was going to go under; but
they had been three and it had been impossible to talk
privately. Edmund seemed anguished and despondent,
burdened; it was all he could do to be civil to Mahoney,
so they had parted quickly and unsatisfactorily.

'An old friend?' Mahoney had asked, as they made
their way back.

'The oldest. We're neighbours at home.'

'Something's eating him; bad state to be in here. He's
not usually like that, I imagine?'

'No. Rather the opposite,' said Gerard heavily. He had
an odd feeling that Edmund's gloom was to do with
some other matter as well. Something had been weighing him down before their talk. However flippant he
might appear to be about being found in a church, it
would take an almighty upheaval to get him into one.
Even impending action would not be enough of a spur;
he knew Edmund well enough to know he would relish
that sort of thing and be good at it. It was definitely
another matter altogether. He would very much like to
have known what.

'A spot of activity will ginger him up,' said Mahoney.
'Best palliative known to man for curing personal life.'

'Unless it cures you altogether by killing you.'

'There is that, of course,' answered Mahoney, and
laughed.

*

192

They continued their retreat the next morning to a field a mile south of Ypres station. More waiting, more hanging about, but with a certain outcome: Ypres, it seemed, was to be defended at all costs. In the evening they marched back through the town and into billets in an abandoned tobacco factory, about a mile north-east of the town. Sometime towards midnight orders were received that a little village called Zonnebeke was to be taken by assault before dawn.

'We're really for it now, aren't we?' Mahoney said in a low voice to Gerard when the briefing was over.

'Seems like it.' Gerard shifted on the rickety chair. He didn't really want to talk, nor did he want to seem windy. He pushed his cigarette case at Mahoney, which was a mistake for it meant he then had to offer him a light.

'Steady ... ' Mahoney took Gerard's wrist in a firm grip. The shaking flame made his face ghastly, nightmarish. He took the cigarette from his own lips and handed it back to Gerard.

'Thanks.'

'*De rien*, old fellow. Sooner we're out of this tip the better, if you ask me. Pity they couldn't have left some of the goods behind.' They were sitting in what must once have been the manager's room, a suffocating little cubicle with a bare board floor and one window over which a piece of sackcloth had hastily been nailed. A table and some ancient chairs had been procured from somewhere. The only light came from the Colonel's Orylux which had been pulled down the far end of the table in order that the other battery commanders might have a better look at the map spread out in front of them.

'What does "beke" mean?' Bolster called. 'The place is littered with them: Zonnebeke, Zillebeke, Hansbeke, Hollebeke ...'

'River, or rather stream, I think.' Gerard got up and went round to where Bolster sat. God, what a country it was for names! In the bad light to have a map full of such names seemed almost like a bad joke on the part of General Staff: his eye picked out one or two of the worst: Passchendaele – perhaps that wasn't so bad, Passion Dale; an Oxford English accent could make a joke out of almost anything: Strooiboomhoek, Gheluwe, Becelaere. I don't want to die here, he thought, in this land of ugly unpronounceable names. He tightened his grip on the back of Bolster's chair.

'Look out,' somebody said, 'you're dropping ash on the map.'

'Sorry.' Gerard withdrew into the shadows. 'Losing your nerve, already?' a voice inside his head asked. It's the limbering up I dread, not the actual moment, he said to himself desperately, making his way back to his seat next to Mahoney.

'It's like trying to jump a fence without a horse,' Mahoney whispered in his ear. 'Once we're on the go it's all quite easy, you'll see.'

'I'm sorry you can tell – ' Gerard began.

'Don't be sorry.' Mahoney bent forward and placed the remains of his cigarette under the toe of his boot. 'It's the same for all of us,' he said, without looking round. 'Why should you be the only one?'

Three am parade, dead silence, no smoking, no talking. After a mile they passed the barricades that had been their advanced post the evening before: two poplar trees felled and lying across the road forming a sharp S-shape. In the pitch black the voice of a military policeman could be heard, warning the column picking its way through to beware of the ditch.

With dawn the news came down the column that Zonnebeke had been occupied without opposition. German spies, always excellent, had warned the Uhlans of the impending attack, allowing the village to the British. A decision was taken to entrench a position covering Zonnebeke and Gheluvelt. Everyone, except the inhabitants of Zonnebeke it seemed, knew the great wave was about to break over their heads. On being billeted in the village the following night, Gerard was astonished to see shops open and life going on in the ordinary way.

Twenty-four hours later, after a beautifully thought out and very elaborate plan for the capture of Menin made by General Staff had been foiled by the untimely intervention of the enemy, Gerard saw these same people flying for their lives with shells bursting round them; and a horrible, shocking, sorrowful sight it was too. There were farmers with their carts containing not only women and children but all their movable goods as well, including dogs, cats, hens. There were people on bicycles, cattle being driven along the road, horses, donkeys, carts drawn by dogs (a detail that could have been borrowed from Bosch), and even an old woman of eighty being trundled along in a wheelbarrow by her husband of the same age. The guns which had gone forward returned through Zonnebeke and took up a position a mile or so on the Ypres side. HQ remained in Zonnebeke. The next day the guns moved forward again to positions immediately in the rear of the infantry, who occupied the trenches dug providentially two days ago.

The Battle of Ypres had begun.

Two miles or so away to the south-west, Edmund's company was in reserve, waiting out their time in the grounds of a charming château. It was a pretty place, not large, but laid out in a pleasant way that reminded him rather of Kincraig. Looking through the trees he could just see the glint of water from a lake, a little lake made for pleasure and picnics, surrounded by trees, some of them quite rare and unusual (Aunt Maud had given him a good gardening education). Behind them was the house itself, a perfect, pocket château, a seventeenth-century gem with a greenish, mansard roof, elaborate, ornate balconies, a terrace like the one at Kildour containing some mossed statuary and enormous brimming stone pots overflowing with plants. Summer had lost its grip here, but only just.

Out of sight, the stable clock chimed the hour. It would not have surprised him to find the Baron out for a walk with his dogs. His train of thought was interrupted by the sound of gunfire from the direction of D Company in the hollow and the distant whine and crump of shells. Puffs of white smoke rose into the air like cotton-wool balls towards Zonnebeke.

Gerard was out there somewhere. Edmund wondered if praying was this: this sudden extra keenness to things, or was it just adrenalin feeding the flighty heart, duping it into omniscience? More gunfire. A runner came into sight, dodging in and out amongst the trees in the park. Time was running out; it was both exciting and slightly nightmarish to know they were about to go forward into action at last, like a dream almost ... the ancient trees in the park, the lake, gunfire, and the man running towards them, the perfect house behind with its blinds demurely drawn as if somehow that would keep everything at bay, and the runner coming towards them...

'Trouble,' said Thompson, shading his eyes with his hand.

'Yes, seems so.'

Keep him, me, safe, please ... anything. I'll stop thinking of her; it couldn't have gone on anyway, not after seeing him like that ...

The man tripped and fell, then got up again.

'Bloody rabbits,' said Thompson. 'Four-footed curse. What they need here is a good ...'

But Edmund wasn't listening.

Gerard had spent the morning with Mahoney in his dug-out immediately behind the infantry trenches which contained some men of the South Staffordshires. Intense excitement and curiosity had proved to be the spur Mahoney had spoken of. With his Zeiss glasses Gerard scanned the skyline. The countryside reminded him of Essex or Suffolk, flattish but enclosed. There were many hedges and small woods dotted about, the odd farm with outbuildings.

For the first time the enemy was visible, no longer the mysterious force they had heard so often and with whom they had played tag in and out of most of the villages and towns in Belgium, but there, trickling over the skyline in open order, their faces almost distinguishable. Rather shocking this: a face placed a man, made for an infinitesimal curious pause.

Up above, the sky was a chalky, innocent blue. Birds sang on, undeterred by the bombardment. The range was narrowing now: Gerard had his glasses fixed on a field, a very green field, divided by a fence of barbed wire. In the middle was a gate.

'Let me look,' said Mahoney, taking the glasses. 'They're bunching to get through that gate, you know. Next time we'll get them.' He handed the glasses back. 'You've got a better view than I have,' he said, looking up slightly at Gerard. 'Range the battery for me.'

'Of course.'

It was a life-long ambition this: to range a battery of guns in action. He began measuring off the angle with the graticules of his glasses between the place where the guns were then firing and the gate in the fence where he had seen the Germans. His heart seemed to have slowed almost to a standstill; he thought of nothing but the number of degrees necessary to make the switch. He ordered a round of gunfire. Two shells burst precisely where he had hoped they would in the gateway. At once, as if in slow motion, twenty or so Germans lay down. They're just taking cover, Gerard thought to himself. The fire stopped, but the Germans did not move. Through his glasses he counted them in a circle some twenty yards in diameter.

The German infantry were now in the hollow beneath, impossible for the guns to reach. Gerard saw their scouts emerge from a pheasant cover not two hundred yards away and went on watching as the British infantry opened fire and the Germans began to fall, taken by surprise, haphazardly, like ninepins. The sight numbed him. He could not understand how it seemed so simple, not only to get the angle of fire right, but also how easily and obediently the German soldiers lay down and died. Some vital connection seemed to be missing, as if he had thought of all deaths as crucifixions: the long, slow torment in the heat, and the flies; not this neat, clinical, apparently painless act in a green field under a well-behaved sky.

It was almost a relief to find himself properly frightened when the German field artillery discovered the position of their trenches and the shrapnel began to arrive. Every time he put his head out even a fraction half a dozen bullets smacked past his face, making a noise like enraged mosquitoes.

'When there's a lull,' he said to Mahoney, 'I'm off.'

'Yes? Thanks for your help.' Mahoney put a hand on Gerard's shoulder. 'Go now,' he said a minute later. 'It's quietening. I'll be seeing you.'

Gerard spent the afternoon on errands for the General, picking his way forward to the Colonel of the South Staffs in his trench and back again into Zonnebeke. The shrapnel bombardment had been stepped up; bullets from the shrapnel and pieces of shells flew about the streets of the town like hail. The shells seemed to come in bursts of about six at a time and the air was thick with flying lead, fragments of steel, slates from the roofs, glass and bricks. Rifle bullets whined down the main street, smacking into the walls of the houses with a sharp thud, throwing up little puffs of red dust. By tea-time the Germans had started to use high-explosive shells aiming for the spire of the church. Gerard watched a window of ancient stained glass smash and scatter into a cloud of coloured fragments. Beneath his feet the town rocked.

At HQ he met the medical officer. 'Mahoney's badly

wounded,' the doctor said. 'I've got to go and find an ambulance.'

'How badly?'

'Can't tell till I've found him.'

Gerard turned on his heel and went out again into hell. The news sat like a stone against his heart, chill, heavy. The plan had gone all wrong: he had assumed, without realizing he was doing so, that his friendship with Mahoney somehow afforded him protection. And now Mahoney lay wounded near the windmill. He must have gone forward into the infantry trenches to observe, and been hit there. Reaching the outskirts of the town where the houses were more spaced out, Gerard waited until the latest shell had burst before running like a hare between the gaps amongst the houses. Rifle bullets would have to take their chance. He could not legislate for everything.

At the windmill, he met a young officer of the Queen's with about twenty men.

'We're all that's left,' the man informed him, 'out of two hundred and fifty. The fellow you want has been dragged out of the trench and taken behind that cottage over there.' He pointed to a small house on the other side of the road.

'Thanks.' Gerard was off again, dodging and weaving his way across the road. 'I'll be seeing you,' Mahoney had said this morning. *I'll be seeing you.*

There was nobody in the scrubby garden behind the cottage. A path ran round behind a hedge which shielded the privy. An abandoned hen picked its way across a bed in which some flowers bloomed aimlessly. Outside the back door he noticed a bowl of water still half full.

They had him in the kitchen lying on some straw. The room was full of the noise of his breathing. The range was still neat and moderately clean but the tile floor was filthy. There was a smell of grass and blood. Somebody had been sick.

'Doc not here yet?'

'No.' A man kneeling beside Mahoney looked up. He had a flask in his hand which Gerard recognized.

'What's in that?' he asked, coming to kneel on Mahoney's other side.

'Brandy, I think. It's hopeless.'

'Go outside,' Gerard said, seeing the man would be sick again. 'I'll wait here.'

In between the sound of Mahoney's breathing and the sound of shells crashing in the town, there was the man being sick outside. He looked down at Mahoney and took his hand. His face was the colour of sea-water. There was a small hole in his head just above his ear where a bullet had passed clean into his brain, but hardly any blood. He looked at the cold hand in his. There was a heavy signet ring on the little finger, bloodstone and gold; the crest was a bird of some kind, a falcon perhaps? He would not live. There was no hope. What could the significance of a heraldic device matter now?

'Bloody silly ... ' Mahoney's eyes had opened. He spoke out of the back of his throat as if fighting some hidden spring of fluid which threatened to well up.

'It was meant to be me,' Gerard said. He put his other hand over Mahoney's to restrain himself from tidying back the lock of hair that had fallen forward over his forehead. If there was any hope, then the lightest of touches might blind him or edge the bullet deeper into his head. 'You should have been more careful.'

'Too late ... now.' Mahoney shut his eyes and then opened them again. 'The psalm,' he said, pulling his voice out of the waters. 'Say the psalm ...'

Gerard swallowed and then began to speak. Words he had not known he knew came into his mouth: 'Thou shalt purge me with hyssop and I shall be clean; thou ...'

'... shalt wash me and I shall be whiter than snow ...'

The last light was going out of his eyes. He sighed like a child rising up towards consciousness from a deep sleep; some dark blood came out of his nostrils. A little crimson ribbon fell down his chin, then it was done.

Per ipsum, et cum ipso, et in ipso . . . it was a prayer for the rising soul.

Aeons passed.

'I see I'm too late.' The medical officer came bustling in, already tired enough to wish he hadn't bothered. 'We'll have to get him onto a stretcher and take him into Ypres. Give us a hand, Baillie, will you?'

'Of course.'

'Bloody hell,' said the doctor, puffing, as they heaved the body onto a stretcher. 'I'm surprised he survived even a moment with that. Poor fellow. Was it awful for him?'

'You couldn't have done anything,' Gerard answered. 'He was much too far gone.'

He performed the last rite of passage himself, pulling the blanket gently over the sad head.

CHAPTER
EIGHTEEN

Four days after Alice's bombshell, Edmund hitched a lift in a converted Daimler into Ypres. His battalion had gone out of the line for a few days; the losses had been staggering, but for those left hanging about it was almost worse to be doing nothing. The first couple of days had been all right: that was when life re-formed itself and the littlest things, being able to have a bath and a shave or a decent meal with a bottle of wine, seemed sources of extraordinary pleasure. For forty-eight hours he had thought of nothing but physical indulgences. After that, his mind began to take over again, reasserting its claims, sifting, thinking, remembering.

It had been nearly a game to him, apart from odd moments like the one at the château when he had seen the man running in an eternity of slowness towards them, because it was exceptional to have time to think in the thick of things: action was instinctive, leading onto something else and something else. Only last week, going forward to the village across the turnip field, with the ruined farm on their right in the trees and being sniped at by one of the bastards left behind in the village; falling with his sergeant into the ruts, bullets smacking into the earth that had, in the rain, taken on the texture of Vaseline ... nearly a game, nearly.

A strangeness was beginning in him now, a feeling that could have been something like defeat if he had wanted to examine it closely, which he did not. Danger, lived with too long, soon stopped being funny or a lark, becoming, instead, just a monotony of stretched nerves and sleeplessness. He had had to write a letter to the sergeant's wife too: 'Dear Mrs Watkins, your husband died like a hero in a field of turnips ... The poor b. got a bullet in the neck, plunging eagerly into the carotid. Died at once.'

Edmund gripped the dash of the motor so hard it hurt. He had not been angry before; now he could not get rid of it. He took his hand away and put it in his pocket, feeling the stiff edges of Alice's envelope, running his finger over the crest on the flap. Now this.

They had entered the outskirts of Ypres; every other house had a shell through it, but the shops were open and there were people on the streets. He saw a girl look round and wave as they went past. She was quite a pretty thing, there was a nice figure beneath the frightful dress, but he did not respond. In a way it sickened him to see the inhabitants going on as if nothing were happening out there, charging over the odds for everything, putting in huge bills for compensation. Having a lovely war.

'Do you know where it is?' the driver asked, as they came off the Menin Road into the main square.

'No, but put me out here. I'll soon find it.'

He was on his way to the Rue de Lille, to the British hospital, where, according to Alice, Gerard lay with a bullet through his leg.

'In haste,' her note had said, written quickly in pencil. 'This comes tonight with Hughie Eldon. Gerard is wounded, to be found in a hospital in the Rue de Lille, Ypres. A bullet in his leg, and worse. Go and see him. I am afraid. A.'

Secretly, he hoped Gerard would have left. He feared to see him after their last meeting. What did she mean 'and worse'? Was he demented or something? He tried not to think about Alice. It seemed so pointless; now, particularly. Now, when Gerard would be needing her.

'Rue de Lille?' he asked a crone behind a stall selling

goat's cheese. She said something incomprehensible, holding up a cheese as if to tempt him, sniffing at it herself with exaggerated pleasure. She had a moustache the Brigadier would have been proud of.

Edmund shrugged his shoulders and went on through the market place into the labyrinth of streets to the right of the Cloth Hall. He stopped to light a cigarette, throwing the match onto the cobbles. It was not as if he wanted to give her up, but it was foolishness, lunacy. Now, when Gerard would be needing her. Particularly now. Oh God! He stopped walking a minute wondering if *he* was losing his grip. His thoughts had stuck in a groove and went on repeating themselves monotonous, insistent, never going forwards or backwards. Just the same old thing over and over again. He felt hamstrung, utterly, utterly feeble; there was none of the old agreeable glow of other dalliance; it was this that made him think it might be love. Like good medicine it had to taste unpleasant to work. He got no pleasure from it, just a sort of nagging ache, a want. He began to walk again, turning a corner and coming face to face with a Red Cross flag tacked to the railings. Here it was: the Catholic school that was now the British Hospital in the Rue de Lille.

After some enquiries, he found Gerard in the officers' ward. He hesitated in the doorway, looking into what had once been a classroom. A blackboard remained on one wall at the far end over a raised platform. Facing the blackboard on the wall to his left was a large, wooden crucifix. The room was very crowded. Two of the beds had screens round them.

'Baillie?' he asked an orderly, not seeing Gerard.

'Over there in the corner, right by the daïs.'

'Thanks.' Edmund went slowly down the row of beds, holding his cap in front of him with both hands like a mourner. He found himself unable to look into the faces of the men in beds. Sun poured through the uncurtained windows making the room warm. Outside, the bloody birds were singing their hearts out; beyond that, further away and so familiar now that he no longer registered it, was the sound of guns.

Gerard was asleep. There was a cage over his left leg, a small hillock under the blanket. In his hands, pressed face down on the sheet, was a small calf-bound book. Edmund looked down at Gerard's sleeping face. Against the pale skin, his eyebrows and eyelashes seemed very dark. There was stubble on his chin and a cut on the side of his neck as if he had been hit by some flying object. He took the book out of Gerard's hands and looked at it. It was *The Imitation of Christ*. He turned it over and read a passage marked in pencil: 'You must still be proved in this life and many trials await you. Consolation will sometimes be granted you, but not in its fullness. So be strong and courageous, both in doing and enduring what by nature is repugnant to you. It is necessary for you to become a new man, and to be changed into another person.'

'He writes well, doesn't he?' said Gerard.

'You're awake!' Edmund closed the book with a snap. 'I've lost your place,' he said, handing it back.

'It doesn't matter. I open it anywhere and just read.' It was an obvious lie. 'There aren't any chairs,' he said, seeing Edmund looking round. 'It's not like a normal hospital.'

'I didn't expect to find you,' Edmund said. 'Why haven't you been moved? They must be tight for space. There were chaps in the courtyard as I came in.'

'Administrative error, I don't know. I'm going tomorrow.' He paused. 'How did you know I was here?'

'I had a note from Alice.'

'Ah ... Alice.'

Their eyes met.

'She is afraid for you,' Edmund went on. 'Hughie Eldon brought me a –'

'I shot a man through the heart,' said Gerard, giving no indication he had heard the last part, 'in Zonnebeke, where I got this.' He put a hand out to the hump under the sheet. 'House to house search. My provo-sergeant was killed too.' He closed his eyes. The thought of his own death was not a torment to him, not any more; but the dead ground, the testing-ground in between – that was the agony, the long afternoon in the heat. It was no longer the dying that counted but what went before: 'doing and enduring what by nature is repugnant to you'. He had taken the cup and was gone away up the hill to Golgotha.

'Shooting the enemy through the heart,' he said, opening his eyes, 'is that a sacramental action?'

'Gerry, I . . .' Edmund felt demented. It was like talking to someone who was not properly there.

'Don't.' Gerard held out his hands. 'Go,' he said. 'Leave me.'

Nobody could understand it, nobody. Could not see the distinction which persecuted him. The priest had been worse than useless, well-meaning, hopeless. 'My son,' he had said, 'God will forgive you. He knows what was in your heart. There is nothing escapes his notice,' and he had quoted sparrows at Gerard who had stopped listening. There seemed no point. He had had murder in his heart, and had wanted to kill the German spy in plain clothes who had come towards them with a rifle after they had battered the door down. What can I say? thought Gerard, avoiding the priest's decent, eager gaze. God knows too that moment of blackness when I heard nothing but the blood rushing in my head, saw the man's lips moving; only afterwards, afterwards, like the gap in time-keeping in a large room containing people singing, only afterwards, that half-heard cry, the echo . . . *'Ich ergebe mich* . . . I surrender.' He had broken every rule, sacred rule, military rule. Killing was sin. He did not see how he could be forgiven that. How did men live with this sort of thing? All that nonsense about Just War; there was no such thing. There was only one man killing another in corroboration of the aims of statesmen, kings, cardinals, who did not do these things themselves but invented justifications for them in the shape of causes and so-called violations.

'God has forgotten me,' he had said to the priest.

'It is always dark towards the foot of the cross.'

'I am not at the foot,' Gerard said. 'Does it shock you if I say I feel as if I am hanging on the accursed tree too?'

'I shall have the sacrament brought to you,' said the priest, absolving him.

'It won't take,' Gerard had said to him. 'Stony ground. I'm like the withered tare. It's no good to me...'

'Gerry?' He was still here. Edmund. Still here.

'What?'

'Is it your leg, the pain ... ?'

'I don't notice it,' Gerard said, putting the palms of his hands against his cheeks. 'They give me morphine. I have huge dreams, vivid, in colour.' He spread his arms out on either side of the bed like a sacrificial victim.

'Oh,' Edmund said, stupidly. He did not know what he had expected, but it had not been this. 'Nice ones, I hope,' he added. He could not think whether to go or stay.

'Not very. I ...' Gerard stopped. It had come back to him suddenly as dreams do. He had been with Mahoney again on the morning of the day he was killed, watching the dead Germans through his glasses as they began to rise from the circle in which they lay, only the one he was looking at in particular had Mahoney's face. And he felt an insupportable guilt and sense of shock when he realized it was Mahoney, his own friend, whom he had killed.

Edmund waited.

'When I'm gone,' said Gerard, 'you will look after Alice, won't you?'

'You mustn't talk like that.' Oh stop him, dear God, someone, stop him, this ... awfulness. 'You'll go home and heal up and be well again.'

'Promise me,' Gerard insisted. He would give Alice up to Edmund in atonement, seeing suddenly she would be happy with him. They would have children and be pillars of society. He had a need to persecute himself. 'Call one of your sons after me,' he said.

'Stop it,' Edmund shouted. An orderly looked round and frowned. The man in the next bed woke with a start and called out.

'I'm sorry,' Gerard closed his eyes once more. 'You shouldn't have come.'

'I had to come. Get better, Gerry, please.' Edmund leant down and took his hand, pressing it.

'I'll have Christmas at home anyway,' Gerard said, looking up, making a huge effort to respond to the plea in Edmund's voice, 'and perhaps you'll have some leave and we can meet. Just like the old days,' he added.

Edmund passed the back of his hand across his eyes. He had never hated himself more than he did in that moment.

'Be seeing you then,' he said, turning away and walking down the ward.

CHAPTER NINETEEN

Alice telephoned Lady Baillie. It was a trunk call, unspeakably extravagant, that would have caused the trustees to splutter and bluster.

'Gerard is coming home,' she shouted into the mouthpiece, after waiting ten minutes for her to be found. There was only one telephone at Kildour, not in the hall or anywhere convenient, but in a musty cubby-hole outside the still room.

'Thank God.' There was an odd gasping sound which could have been emotion or some interference to do with the wires, or however it was telephones worked. It was, after all, a very long way from London to Kildour. About the same distance in time it was to Ypres.

'I must come at once,' said Lady Baillie, panicking.

'No. Don't.'

'What was that?'

'I mean not yet. Don't come yet.'

'But I must – '

'I need two days,' Alice said. 'Come on Monday.'

A pause. 'Monday then. Will you deal with Lennox Gardens?'

'Is Lord Baillie going to come?'

'I think so.' Another pause. 'Yes. He will be coming. Is he getting better?' She meant Gerard.

'He must be,' Alice said. 'They'd never make him do the journey otherwise.'

'Of course not. Thank you, darling, for telephoning. We're very grateful.'

She thinks I'm being selfish, Alice said to herself. My wifeship looked upon as an interregnum when something serious happens. But I must have him to myself for two days to see how the land lies, to hear about it all, to tell him about the infant. She supposed Edmund had been to see him, although he had not acknowledged her note. His silence made her wonder, made her nervous, as if there was something sinister in it; but now was hardly the time to be thinking of Edmund. All that had to stop. She would have to learn virtue again, so difficult once one had misplaced it.

The day after Edmund's visit, Gerard left the hospital at Ypres and went in a motor ambulance to the station. He felt ill enough (in spite of what he had said to Edmund) to be indifferent to the idea of going home although he very much wanted to see his wife. He knew he was suffering from a spiritual malaise which the wound only disguised; he had an idea of himself now as a carrier of infection, as if his short experience of war had put him apart from others. He knew the nightmare he had seen at the back of other men's eyes was a part of it as they were, had contributed to it as they had. It was the mark of Cain. Men who had killed men. You never got over it. There were chaps, he knew, who lived healthy pagan wars – Edmund was one – who could go on and on relishing the challenge; chaps upon whose shoulders the yoke of duty sat light as gossamer, but he was not one of them, nor could he allow his conscience to slide out from under by placing the onus on the state as, probably, others did.

His departure bothered him in another way as well: it was too easy to go out of the war on a train to the coast, too easy to catch a boat to England, too easy to be a hero. It was the artificiality of the thing, as if brutishness could be solely contained within the shifting boundaries of some emerging salient, ceasing to exist in neat England, safe England, England which sent men in the sacred cause of justice to murder their brothers. War, to a man at the cutting edge of it, was something total, a piece of baggage to be carried throughout life, growing, as in his case, heavier every day. He had no idea how to adapt the rules to the figure of himself: the figure of himself was a soldier shadowed backwards for generations by men in uniform, men of military stock; he could not separate himself from his family's expectations of him. Or he could, but had not the courage and, in a way, the selfishness to do so, so that when he asked himself what he intended to do, he had no answer. Grow better, he supposed, go back, do it again and again until he was killed himself. Sometimes in hospital he had prayed for a quick death, an ending, anything – gangrene, pneumonia, some infection, swift and rapacious and painful. Instead, the bullet had shifted, almost, it seemed, offering itself up to the forceps, as if some mysterious, motivating force within him had taken charge, some *vis medicatrix naturae*, and was controlling him in defiance of his wishes.

He lay all day on a stretcher in the waiting-room with his fellow patients, amongst whom were several Germans. The train did not come and did not come. Next to him lay a German boy of about seventeen, shockingly wounded. There was a bandage around his head and a thick pad of dressing over one eye, as well as a sort of cummerbund around his middle. Even so, the undamaged side of his face visible to Gerard from where he lay seemed horrifyingly youthful, the curve of cheek only a very few steps removed from that of a child; the view a mother might have on a nightly checking. Seventeen: Alex's contemporary.

Once, they talked.

'Where are you from?' asked Gerard in German.

'Mainz.' The boy turned his head slightly, shifting the seven ages of man in that smallest inclination. 'I was called to the colours', he said, 'at the beginning of August.' He spoke slowly and showed no surprise at being addressed in his native tongue.

'Were you at Antwerp, then?' Against his will, the conversation was assuming the shape of an interrogation.

'Yes.' The boy put a hand to his eye and then took it away again. 'We marched here in six days,' he said politely, as if he was being catechised.

'What did you do before?' asked Gerard gently. 'You must have been at school, surely?'

'No. I finished last year. I help my father with the farm. I've lost an eye,' he added. 'Better than an arm or a leg. At least when it's over I can go back to doing what I did before.'

'Yes.' Gerard fell silent.

'It is like hell,' the boy said suddenly, 'pure hell. I am glad to be going to England. We were told to expect a quick victory, but they lied to us. It is all lies.'

Gerard did not reply.

The train journey to Boulogne took fourteen hours. The train dawdled its way to the coast at five miles an hour, stopping in the darkness at every station along the way. Dozing, Gerard would come to and see men in uniform going to and fro under the dim lights. Once he saw straight into a station bar where people on stools drank *marc* or cups of powerful coffee. Somewhere else there was a longer halt still, while someone very important indeed was put onto the train in a closed compartment.

'Staff with gout,' Gerard heard someone say. It was probably true.

At Boulogne the trainload of injured men was transferred to a large hospital ship, seething with doctors and nurses. The voyage was rough and Gerard was extremely sick. There was talk on board of a Belgian refugee ship that had been blown up some hours earlier by a German submarine just off Boulogne, but Gerard could have told anyone who cared to ask that simply by his presence on board they were guaranteed safe passage. He was not to be allowed to die yet. Another train

212

at the other end took him to London and Mrs Colin Ward's nursing home in Grosvenor Street. He had a room to himself (arranged by Alice) and it was here he heard the news of his child.

'Are you sure?' He looked at her in disbelief. It was too large a piece of news for him to be anything but sceptical.

'I am now.'

'When will it be born?'

'July sometime, or August. I hope you're glad,' she added rather anxiously. His reaction was not at all what she had expected, although admittedly, it was difficult to be ecstatically joyful about anything when you were in bed with a leg up.

'Of course I'm glad.' He looked at her. 'But it takes time to adjust to this kind of thing. Fatherhood.' He shook his head slightly as if there were water in his ears. 'And you, Alice. Are you glad?'

'It's something tremendous,' she said, colouring.

'Do my parents know yet?' The heir, he thought, wondering why he felt nothing, no dynastic stirrings at all, just a blank, a rather tired blank.

'I thought we could tell them both on Monday.'

'Both?'

'Your father is coming too,' she said, suddenly wanting his happiness. He looked so ill and sad, in spite of the doctor's good report. 'Does that please you?'

'He never writes to me,' Gerard said, looking past Alice to the window. In a tree outside a bird sang sharp.

'He leaves it to your mother.' She stopped, thinking he was not listening.

'And?'

'It's not uncommon, you know, for women to do all that sort of thing.'

'Is it uncommon to be pained by it, do you think?'

'Are you?'

'It seems necessary now,' he said, speaking slowly, 'to make things good.'

'Because of the child?'

213

'Because of everything.' He made a face and sighed, not wanting to explain, having made up his mind to keep his premonition from her; in any case, he had had the most severe doubts about it lately. Sometimes he wondered if he knew anything any more.

'Tell me,' she said rashly, but unable to wait, 'did Edmund come and see you in Ypres?'

'Yes.'

'Was it all right . . . ? I mean, it must have been nice for you to see him – wasn't it?' Even to her own ears it sounded miserably lame.

'We didn't have a very satisfactory talk, I'm afraid. I wasn't feeling my best.'

'But he came?'

'Oh yes. I didn't quite know why you had sent for him,' he said, deliberately making it difficult for her.

'To see you,' she said, looking away.

'To see or to oversee? I don't awfully like the idea of your corresponding with Edmund.' It had come back to him afterwards, this. He had worried about it on and off over the last few days. It made him unexpectedly angry to think of them conspiring even in a friendly way. His other faculties, dulled by the major shock, were slowly coming back to life. She should not have written to Edmund. There was something wrong in it.

'I wouldn't have done it, if I'd known you would mind.' She made herself look at him. Do not panic, Alice. *Do not panic.*

'Did he write back and tell you?'

'Yes . . . no.' She looked down, shamefaced. 'No, he didn't.'

'Then it would appear to have been an exercise with very little point, wouldn't it, Alice? Wouldn't it?'

'Why are you persecuting me? I was terribly anxious. The telegram was not explicit. You might have been dying, for all I knew.'

For a long minute she watched him consider the justness of this.

214

'I apologize,' he said, but he looked grim. 'I'm in a state. Everything seems such a shambles. All the things I set out to do seem to have fallen in ruins about me.'

'Your diary, do you mean?' she asked, longing to strike the right chord.

'Oh, that . . .' He shook his head wearily. 'I have some notes, more jottings, really. I wasn't there long enough to make much headway in that direction. It's more a sense of failure, a feeling that I haven't measured up.' She had sent Edmund to see him and had then lied about her reasons. Why?

'You couldn't help being wounded.'

'I don't mean that,' he said vehemently, hating her for not understanding, hating her for weaving these skeins of intrigue about him, hating his own wrecked past purpose. 'I wanted a good war,' he went on. 'I wanted a war that would make you all proud of me, I wanted –'

'You can go back,' she interrupted. 'You will go back, the doctor assured me you –'

'Nobody understands,' he said, crushing a handful of sheet. 'I can't endure the killing, the pointlessness.'

'Is it pointless?'

He looked at her in silence.

'What about duty? You have a duty to fight, don't you?'

'Duty,' he said bitterly. 'No man was ever more conscious of his duty than I.'

'I thought you would enjoy the primitive manners of it all,' she said. He was making her quite desperate with his suspicion and his bitterness.

'Look,' he said, taking a breath, letting go of the sheet. 'You're confusing two things . . .' After all, how could she understand? There was so much he could not tell her. 'I do enjoy what you call the "primitive manners" of it all, the roughing it, the companionship. I made a friend,' he added, 'who was killed. I was with him when he died. In a few short weeks I grew to love Mahoney as if I'd known him all my life.' Deliberately, he refrained from

215

drawing a comparison with Edmund. 'In that way, war has infinite compensations. It tears the outer casing off life in a way unmatched by anything else, lets you to the heart of things in half the time. You live at a mighty pitch in war. Everything that chokes up the avenues of the soul is cleared out, leaving one stripped down, able to make friendships of the kind I made with Mahoney.' He sniffed.

'He must have been splendid,' Alice said gently, conscious of the inadequacy of words. 'Go on.'

'I don't know why I'm telling you this.' Suddenly, he was grateful to her.

'Because you must.'

'Must I?'

'Yes.' The conversation was veering at last. She would have to cancel out his guesswork over Edmund by making him need her.

'I want to tell you about Zonnebeke,' he said. 'Will you let me without interrupting?'

'Of course I will.' From his look she wondered what was coming. In the beginning she had sensed a secret, guessing Edmund. But perhaps it was not, perhaps there was something worse.

'In Zonnebeke,' he said, 'the General asked me to go with the provo-sergeant and search the houses for spies. When the Germans leave a place they have a trick of leaving men too, usually concealed in the cellars of houses with telephones waiting to relay information. We'd had a lot of harassment of this kind and it was decided something should be done.' He stopped talking and lit a cigarette. 'All the doors were locked before the owners left the town, so we found an enormous bar in the forge, so large it needed two men to carry it, and we began battering doors down, checking. The sergeant and I would take up our positions, revolver in hand, on each side of the door, whilst the two men charged across the street with the iron bar. They would collapse on the pavement and we would rush in. It became a bit of a

216

competition between the sergeant and me as to who would get through the doorway first. He was a good deal older than me and in a way I think he felt protective – Am I boring you?' he asked.

'No. How could you be? I always look vapid when I'm concentrating.'

He smiled for the first time, just a little and very quickly. But it seemed a triumph to her.

'We'd grown a shade careless by this point,' he went on. 'Secretly, none of us believed we'd find anything. We bashed the door down. The man was waiting. He moved more quickly than anyone I've ever seen in my whole life. He shot the sergeant and got me in the leg before I had a chance; losing Perkins, who was just in front, made me falter ...' He put his face in his hands, seeing it again. The wide hallway and the staircase curving; not feeling the pain in his leg at all, not even noticing until afterwards. A perfect bit of shooting. Everything taken into account. Only the man's lips moving, the cry, the call. What had it been? He was not sure, not sure of anything any more.

'Gerard,' Alice said anxiously. 'Go on. You must finish.'

'He had a rifle but he wasn't in uniform. I saw red, it actually happens ... I shouted something, he did too ... I think he wanted to surrender. But I killed him anyway. I couldn't have stopped myself.'

'A bit late,' Alice said, gathering herself, 'wasn't it? And highly unlikely, it seems to me. You had him like a rat in a trap; he would have fought to the last. Are you sure you heard that? There must have been so much other noise too. You mustn't torture yourself.'

'Everyone says that, but you're all wrong. You all miss the point which is that there is no point. The rules say that if he made that cry, I murdered him, if he didn't I didn't. But the whole thing's a sham, a horrible sham. The man is dead. You can't cover blood with words, say a death isn't a death but merely a casualty because the rule

217

book says so. The real point is that men should not be made to do these things to each other; it is a part of one that should always be leashed. Killing is high, heady stuff; life never more real than when you're dealing death. Every cell in my body fizzed with exhilaration. It disgusts me,' he said, 'it torments me.' He began to shake his hands together like somebody ancient, somebody senile.

'If you hadn't killed him,' Alice said, going to him and taking his poor hands, 'he would have killed you.'

'I'd rather be dead,' he said, staring past her. The shudder seemed to have gone into his shoulders and down his spine. 'I cannot forgive myself. I am answerable for this; if not now, then in some other place at some other time.'

'No,' she said, 'no. That's not right.' She pressed his face into the collar of her dress, hating herself for the revulsion she felt towards him. Hating the torment in him that could not be touched or soothed or dealt with in any normal way. Again, as always, he seemed to have set himself apart from her.

After a minute, he said, 'Lie next to me. I want to hold you.'

'Is that wise?'

'Help me, Alice.' His voice was raw. 'Don't leave me now. Please.'

'I won't,' she said, suddenly unbearably moved. 'I won't.'

CHAPTER TWENTY

Gerard lay in bed in St Luke's Terrace, unable to sleep. He had been in front of a medical board the day before and had been told he could go home. Tomorrow he would go north with Alice to Kildour. Home. He said the word quietly under his breath. This was one of his homes: number 1, St Luke's Terrace, but he felt a stranger here; it was as if the house had awaited a different person, another Gerard Baillie.

He looked about his room at the so-familiar things – Uncle Banjo's watercolours, the small portrait of his grandfather in his masonic robes, the tallboy – but the sense of rootlessness, of unattachment persisted. He could no longer connect himself with these things which once had seemed to contain, in a small way, the essence of him. He wondered if it would be the same at Kildour. Turning his head slightly he saw the Tacitus was still on his bedside table; his own hand had laid the book down there months ago. Picking it up he saw how careless he had been with it: some of the pages were squashed and there was a glass mark on the cover. Beyond the half-open door and the dressing-room in between, Alice slept. So much had happened since they had last lain here in their separate rooms, since they had last shared a vestige of normal life together. So much. But now. You couldn't go back. It was no use to go along the same path another time; lying here in the lamplight, waiting for it to be morning.

He had liked his room in the nursing home at Grosvenor Street; the tree outside, the wretched but companionable bird that always sang, the way the sun came round at mid-morning. Alice had come every afternoon to talk or read things out of the newspaper to him, an indulgence he allowed himself on account of the pleasure it gave him to watch her face as she read, so that the news of the great battle at Ypres faltering and dying away, the appalling casualties (the 7th Division had been withdrawn to 're-fit') had had the edge taken off it by the association in his mind of that news and the sound of Alice's voice; the way she would look up at him from time to time to see if he was listening, her hands turning the pages.

So then, Alice. He was not impervious to hints, to the slight sense of innuendo Nina had brought with her, like the faintest trace of some much stronger scent when she had come to visit him at Grosvenor Street, William's shiftiness at Aeltre, Edmund's anxiety on both occasions that was not entirely to do with compassion. He wondered if it was illness, the way he had become his own exclusive object, or all the other things that had happened to him that had made him so sharp, so highly aware of the smallest nuance in a tone of voice.

So then. Edmund and Alice. What? A small flirtation, she lonely, he unable to resist? He never had been able to leave well alone, Edmund. A small flirtation or the whole hog? They hadn't had much opportunity ... but Alice's anxiety over their meeting, her hopeless and transparent attempts at lying, that look in her eye – he was feeling his way forward now towards something – the way she had wanted to know what had been said between them which implied such intimate knowledge of Edmund that it made him shiver slightly. Writing to him like that. Edmund, who always, in the end, wanted to be in everyone's good books, Edmund, who might have confessed. Guilt. He heard his voice shouting at him again in the hospital at Ypres. The child. Gerard sighed and turned on his side, thinking of Alex who had come to see him last week. There had been things he wanted to say, but it hadn't been possible with Alice there. And the child. His mind would come back to that. Whose child? If it was Edmund's, then the monstrous unfairness to Alex was beyond endurance. But he had nothing to go on, only the pricking of his thumbs. It was becoming one of those situations where the worst, guessed at in self-mockery and bitterness, was met with an incriminating silence that spelt out the message as clearly as any written confession of guilt.

He looked at his clock and saw it was three in the morning. He had grown afraid of sleep. In the day, the war receded an infinite distance from him and there were times now when he found it hard to believe he had been there, but night drew him back into it, night joined him again to Mahoney. Sometimes he became the German spy, at others he was again one of the men in the circle in that field of green green grass. Once, puzzlingly, he had been the captured airman in the motor at Ypres whom he had spoken to and defended. Always he woke from these dreams shocked, guilty, sweating. But he knew he had to go back. Knew it without being told by Alice, by his father.

Sitting up in bed, he reached for his cigarette case and lighter. Filthy habit to smoke in bed, but the war had done that for him in the short time he had been there. He thought of his father and of the conversation they had had; of the unsatisfactoriness of it, and of how, before Lord Baillie had arrived, he had been in the grip of that so-spurious affection for his father that long absence invariably induced. But Lord Baillie had come at the conversation in his usual bullish way, starting on the offensive, just as he had always done, always, always.

'You seem sprightly enough,' he had said, eyeing his son sitting up in bed. 'Leg all right, then?'

'It's much better, thank you.'

'Pity the b. got you at all. At least you finished him off. Must have been satisfying, wasn't it?'

'Actually, no.'

'I see. Upset you, did it?'

'Rather.'

'The first time I killed a man,' Lord Baillie said, leaning forward, adopting a confidential, clubby, men-amongst-boys sort of tone that made Gerard admire him if for nothing else than his new subtlety in conversational tactics, 'the first time,' he continued, 'the blighter wouldn't lie down and die, kept twitching. Had to deliver the *coup de grâce* with the butt of my weapon, then I had to go and be sick under a thorn bush. Never forgotten it. Still see him sometimes, at night,' he added unnecessarily, as if Gerard might have thought he meant Boodle's or the H. of L. 'Not easy, the first kill. Still, it doesn't do to brood about it. You're not brooding, are you?'

'Must we discuss it, Dad? I find the whole thing extremely painful.'

'It's not your job to find it painful.' He sniffed a mighty, disapproving sniff. 'You're a soldier with a job to do,' he said. 'Leave it at that.'

'You obviously couldn't.'

'I don't brood about it,' his father answered, 'but then I'm not so concerned for my immortal soul,' he added, in a ghastly parody of a Scotch accent.

'Let's leave my immortal soul out of it, Dad.' Gerard wondered how long he could keep this up. 'What's the weather like in Lanarkshire?'

'What it's always like,' Lord Baillie replied in a long-suffering tone. 'Quite dismal. Rain, rain, rain. Pheasants will have foot-rot soon.'

'Did you get my letter?'

'Yes.'

'Why didn't you write then?'

'Completely stumped by the act of putting pen to paper,' Lord Baillie said, rubbing his moustache in embarrassment.

'This from a man thinking of writing his memoirs –'

'Writing me memoirs is fun, although I seem to get into a bit of a dead-end over Hardinge. Showed some to Butters who nearly went through the roof. Said it was libellous. I was rather proud of it, actually,' he added modestly.

'When I go back, will you try?'

'If you don't mind agricultural drivel.' Lord Baillie got up awkwardly, magnanimous in his escaping. 'Cows' stomachs, staggers. The diurnal round of disease and death,' he went on, gloomily. 'Slumping profits.'

'Rather like the news from the Front,' said Gerard. 'By the way, you've heard *our* news, haven't you?' In the end he had left it to Alice.

'Nice to have a boy round the place again,' Lord Baillie answered, hand on door-knob.

'What happens if it's a girl?'

'You'll just have to get busy, won't you? Glad you're home for Christmas,' he said, unexpectedly. 'Your mother's like a cat with seventeen tails.'

'Where is Ma?'

'Visiting Helena and her group of balaclava-knitters. Mentioned Alice.'

'Gives them something to do, doesn't it?' Gerard said, in a last attempt at camaraderie.

'Keeps them out of mischief and the A. & N. buying useless and expensive items for you. Your mother mentioned something at breakfast called an upside-down pipe.'

'Where am I supposed to use this article?'

'God knows. It's not as if you're a submariner,' his father answered cryptically. 'I'll be back in a few days.'

Gerard put out his cigarette and debated whether or not he should turn off the light. 'You're a soldier with a job to do, leave it at that.' If only it was so simple. If only he could use the props offered him, the props everyone else adopted in the end. But he could not.

Lying back on his pillows in the dark he could feel his wound throbbing. Wasn't that enough, wasn't that his badge of courage? In the eyes of the world everything boiled down to that in the end: the eyes of the world. He would go back and do his bit.

Half-sleeping it seemed as if he could hear Mahoney's voice in his thoughts: 'Don't take it all so seriously, my dear chap. In the end it all comes to the same thing. In the end nothing matters except . . . ' Except. There was a camaraderie in death: the dead don't die, they go on talking to us in our thoughts, shaping things, holding out hands across the divide. Once you had known and loved the unjustly dead, that youth, that death more beautiful than any Chatterton because it was so robust, so bullish, so splendidly unsentimental . . . once you had known that, a part of you went too. In a sense he was half-way there already. Mahoney was so sensible, sensible . . . Oh God, why? . . . Such a bloody good fellow. He couldn't be dead, it was his voice, know it anywhere. . .

CHAPTER
TWENTY-ONE

Edmund had sent his aunt and uncle a telegram from Folkestone. Leave had been so unexpected he could scarcely at first think what to do with such a precious commodity. He had five days, which meant London; it could have meant Paris – he had been quite tempted by the idea of Paris – and there were some people he might have stayed with, but it would have meant behaving and he did not want to behave. He wanted drink and noise and the hot darkness of raffish clubs below pavement level; and he wanted a woman who would not remember him afterwards, a woman who would ask nothing of him.

Since he had received Alice's letter he had been possessed by a kind of despair, something much, much more subtle than straight unhappiness, because it came and went unpredictably, overwhelming him when he least expected it, catching him out when he thought he had it under control.

My dearest Edmund (she had written),
Now Gerard is home, the time for truth has come, as you expected it might. You are right. My duty is to him and I must be with him now as wholeheartedly as I am able. This is not easy, but neither is it impossible.
There is a further reason for this decision. I am pregnant and the child will be born in July sometime. I do not know if the child is yours or Gerard's,

but in any case it would be impossible to make it yours. There is no choice but to say it is the Baillie heir, long expected and cause, as you may imagine, of much rejoicing at Kildour.

I am sorry if this letter sounds cold or stilted or both. It has taken me hours to write. I cannot seem to say what I want which is that the brief moments of happiness with you will never be forgotten.

A.

How she had kept her head! A child, indeed; his, as likely as not. It was not the first time. But it made him admire her, made him grateful, made him want her. Gerard would be pleased, too. He seemed to have come out of it all right: an heir, if he was lucky, marks for trying if he wasn't.

When he thought about his last two meetings with Gerard they seemed, in retrospect, aberrations, early falterings. He would get over it and have a good war and a wife and child to return to. He had grown too emotional, that was his trouble. Went about with his head in the clouds half the time. If he had any sense, he would let the war ground him, teach him to stop behaving like one of the chosen. Edmund was a little bitter about Gerry and his moral table-turning. Made a chap feel uncomfortable to be always at a loss, to be trailing miles behind in understanding. He had had a good wound, reduced his chances, statistically speaking, of being killed. Now he would have to get on with it, like the rest of them, taking the rough with the smooth, learning to cope.

Edmund arrived in London two days before Christmas and found it all very odd. The first day he slept, the second he drove around in a taxi cab looking into shop windows and at the crowds on the pavements. Once he made the man drive past number 1, St Luke's Terrace, but the house was shut up and gone away. He could tell. They would be at Kildour playing families and making plans. Gerry would be basking in the combined glow of parental and wifely approval. Alex would be there, the innocent sycophant, wanting to know what it was like, asking for more.

The night of the second day he found himself unbearably lonely. It was Christmas Eve but his aunt and uncle were not coming. His Aunt Maud had fallen on the hall floor, coming in from outside in her snow-boots, and had cracked her pelvis. He had had a plan (far divorced from the spirit of Christmas) for a club and a girl but although he was restless it suddenly seemed too much effort. After supper he had sat in front of the fire with *Punch* and a bottle of whisky, bored and unsettled. He would like to have gone to see someone bonafide, someone like Nina who would entertain him and make him laugh, possibly even bestow the ultimate upon him. But Nina was away. Everyone was away: either at the war or in the country.

He got up and began to pace the room, feeling sorry for himself, stopping at the piano and picking up the photograph that contained Kitty and the King-Emperor. If Kitty had lived he would have married her, would have had that sweet face and rows of small replicas to exclaim over – or would he? He put the picture down and leant both elbows on the piano top, sending his parents sprawling. Was that what he wanted? Would he have given up all the delight that had come between? Alice. He hated himself for all the tedium of these dreary unanswerables. I must go out after all, he thought, go out and see someone. It was intolerable to be here in this morgue-like atmosphere, surrounded by the past, these nagging shades.

She was called Letty, the girl. Short for Lettuce.

'All alone on Christmas?' she enquired with dreadful mock tenderness. 'What about a little dance to cheer you up?'

They took the floor, crowded and dark. There was a

smell of sweat and innuendo. Cheap scent, pores opening in the heat.

'Back for long, are you?'

'Not long.' Over her head, Edmund looked into the
shining faces of the negro band; glittering teeth and
eyeballs, locked up in their rhythm, swaying and obsess-
ive, bunnyhugging in their seats like sexual perverts.

The girl nestled against his front. 'Let's have a little
fizz,' she said, handling her consonants with care. 'After
all, it's Noël . . . Joyuze Nohelle. . .'

Edmund pushed her off and fled. Past the ugly crimi-
nal at the desk and up the steps. Running.

In Regent Street he stopped and thought, heart going
like a piston. The night air was cold and made his throat
hurt.

Pamela.

The name floated up out of the nearly abandoned
street, the rich, darkened shops. Perhaps he had known
all along he would go and see Pamela. Pamela, who
knew Alice so well. As he walked on and then stopped a
passing cab, he thought he could somehow feed on
Pamela. She would tell him things and give him drinks,
play music to him; let him take over, battening down the
hatches, locking doors, until the world only centred on a
cluttered sitting-room, a fire. He would stop time and
thought with Pamela, stop the pain in his heart. He did
not think about Petersen, or that she might be busy, or
out, or asleep, or not want to see him. There was a bottle
in his pocket, hastily shoved there on leaving his house
which, from time to time, he would press to his side as if
it were a weapon.

'I thought you might come back,' Pamela said, opening the door.

'Can I come in?'

'You're lucky Petersen's not here.' She took his coat
from him.

'Where is he?'

'I don't know.'

'There's a bottle in the pocket, hold on ...'

'What do you want, Edmund?'

'I need ... ' The words fell in emptiness; he smoothed his hair back with one hand, still looking at her. He did not mind her un-welcome. Anything was better than the tart's coy provocation.

'I suppose you want to talk about Alice.' She led the way down the long passage to the sitting-room. 'Sit,' she said, indicating the chairs, a small fire. 'Do you want a drink?'

'Very much.'

'Have you seen her?' He took the glass. Her whisky, not his.

'Once.' She sat down opposite, not inclined to help.

'How was she?'

'Calm. Deliberate. It was the right thing,' she added. 'Don't expect any sympathy.'

'You're very harsh.'

'Honest, perhaps?'

'Was she unhappy?'

'I should have said so, in a way.'

'In a way.' He echoed her words. It was not enough; he had wanted more than that. 'Is it my child?'

'Does it matter?'

This astounded him.

'It would only matter,' Pamela went on, 'if you decided to take a stand, reveal things. I should imagine that is highly unlikely.'

'I think I love her,' he said, putting down his glass.

'But not enough.'

He sighed.

'Why do you know all this?'

'Because I love her too. She is very vulnerable. You must leave her alone. She is expecting a child, Gerard is not well. I don't just mean his leg,' she added.

'He's demented,' said Edmund bitterly, 'and making everyone pay for it. He seemed almost lunatic when I went to see him, kept talking about a man he had shot, a spy. I think he had convinced himself it was murder, a personal thing, not war.'

'Is there a difference?'

'Of course there's a difference. You can't have an omelette without breaking eggs.'

'Presuming one is hungry in the first place.'

'You're very sharp,' he said, looking up angrily. 'There are men out there being blown to pieces for King and country, and you can sit in front of your fire and be clever about it all.'

'Someone has to be clever about it,' she said. 'It's no betrayal to question why such a thing should have come about. These things must be questioned. Haven't you asked yourself why it is we all crave violence so much? Don't you see that all the little betrayals, all the violations of friendship and trust combine, in the end, to this?' She put a cigarette in her holder and he saw that her hands were shaking.

'You're saying I'm personally responsible for this war?'

'We're none of us exempt, Edmund. We're all as corrupt as each other.'

'You're mad.'

'Probably.'

'Why didn't you say any of this last time we met?' he asked, getting to his feet. It seemed pointless to stay.

'What? About the war?'

'About Alice.'

'Where was the point? You'd got her tight; nothing I could have done would have prevented her from going with you. It's different now.'

'I'll go,' he said. 'Thank you for the drink.'

'I'm sorry.' Pamela put a hand over her face. 'I have been hard on you. I'm sorry if you do love her.'

'It's all right.' On impulse he went and knelt by her chair.

'What do you want, really?'

She looked into his face.

'Comfort,' he said. 'Will you comfort me?'

'It would be most terribly unwise,' she said. 'I don't know how you have the nerve to ask.'

CHAPTER
TWENTY-TWO

Gerard would have liked his home-coming to be a perfect ending; when he thought of the place, of Kildour, he thought of it as he had last seen it: an infinite sky, hills glazed with heat, the feeling good weather gives one of having all the time in the world. As it came about, they arrived late into a cold of the most violent kind, the dereliction of a climate whose regulating forces had vanished, or resigned, leaving only debt.

It was bitter, beastly, unpleasing. He imagined the woods full of dead birds and the stiff bodies of small animals; sub-zero would at least lend dignity to those pathetic carcasses, in the same way it might preserve a man left outside a day or two; stop decay anyway, the smell. Spring would not come here again.

Going home on the train to Scotland he had tried to imagine what it must be like for the men out there. Soldiers had ways of making themselves comfortable, he knew that. It wasn't all rats and doom and the scream of shells hurling overhead, but to be cold in this kind of weather was worse, to be inactive. Fear did at least send the blood rushing round the abandoned arteries. He wondered if the temperature made a difference to the pain of a wound – there was a reason why people cut their wrists in the bath: warm water, the skin softer and more malleable – whether it took longer to die in the winter; only a matter of minutes, probably...

They had a picnic lunch in their compartment somewhere near Crewe. He recognized the hamper from

Ascot or Goodwood, one of those days last summer, Gold Cup Day, perhaps, when there had been four queens present: Queen Mary in her emeralds and Sunny Lake winning; the searches in the Royal Enclosure ... What had the threat been then? Suffragettes! Absurd that a band of women could rattle the upper classes more than a war appeared to do ... Hats and bets, champagne, the idlest of idle talk.

He looked away from his reflection in the window and thought this might be his last journey: Crewe, Preston, Carlisle, how many times had he done this in his life? The familiar stations, the landmarks: cooling towers and factory chimneys, sad, shiftless towns of the Black Country. Crewe, where there was a train to everywhere: Preston, Lancaster, the North, Penrith, Kendal and Shap; climbing, climbing into Scotland – as a child he could never understand why it was always 'up' to London, when it was quite clearly downhill all the way from Kildour – then towards home. The different accent at the stations, the people nicer ... How odd that it might be the last time.

He wiped his chin with a table-napkin (nothing had been forgotten) and lit a cigarette, sitting back in his seat and closing his eyes: that our end presses on us through the smallest of physical details – the satisfaction of smoke, the crumbs in his lap, the wine, which, when he put out his hand for it, was the dregs. He expected to find it very cold in purgatory; it was one of the things that worried him on and off, not an item that could really be mentioned to a priest either: 'Tell me, dear Father so-and-so, what is the climate of the world beyond, the moral climate, that is? Is it heated upwards by the furnaces, the boiling lake, the pit (must be hot in there) or kept at a more reasonable level by the divine in-breathing of the celestial presences above? I should like to know what to pack: field glasses? waders? or my underwear?' Comforts for the damned were masses for the dead. Intercessions in November and any other time

233

you pleased. Cost you, though. He would prefer plum cake and whisky, a little light music: *Iolanthe*, perhaps, to remind him of what he was missing. It must be so crowded in purgatory as well, noisy too. All those Germans and everyone else marching on the spot awaiting promotion to better things, or the other ... the Glass House. Hell was undoubtedly a never-ending series of fatigues: trench-digging, maintenance work, stokers and stirrers...

'Why are you smiling?' Alice asked, folding her napkin.

'Difficult to explain.'

'It must have been amusing,' she said. 'You've been doing it on and off for five minutes.'

He looked at her then away out of the window again. It was growing dark outside, so early. She was too keen to share; guilt or relief, something, made her over-interested in him, as if she were trying to haul herself out of what he suspected was a truer measure of her feelings for him, really a kind of neutrality, as if it were truce between them. At other times she was watchful; he felt she might be trying to decide something, form some words, a declaration. He longed to be able to say, 'Don't,' put a finger to her lips and say, 'Enough, don't go into it, I know. And it doesn't matter because you'll have a clear field soon.' He was not exactly bitter, more bored, oh, and hurt; it was like being asked to leave a party in your own house. He hated them for it sometimes. Hated. It was new to know this, or had he always known it? He had lost everything: his self-respect, his wife, soon his house and his life, even God had performed his familiar vanishing trick in times of trouble, the sounds of doors slamming, bolts being drawn. Prayer was a joke, intercession the telephone wire which had been cut or had a bomb dropped on it. Forgiveness? Well no, not really. Not yet.

And Alice? He watched as she rose and went out into the corridor. Lavatory, again; the mysterious vicissitudes of pregnancy: aversion to certain foods and wine, *'quel horreur'* at smoke, sleeping like the dead. Alice. The wages of sin were to love and see vacillation in a face: that was a death, but a death of the heart, leaving just enough life so that one was aware of the ache, the beat, beat of a want. That would be forgiveness if only she ... And he remembered her lying in his arms on the bed at Grosvenor Street, knowing that she was not exactly pretending, it was more a delusion, really, somehow persuading herself that this was a new beginning; only there was so much that needed to be made good, so much between them that was not honest, but that would not respond to ordinary methods. He could only say the volition was not his; the impetus, whatever it was, that would carry Alice over the boundary into loving him, would contain within itself everything, this certainty of him. Love like this should be a mixture of knowledge and compassion, but he was quite unable to encourage or discourage her. He could only wait.

'All right?' She came in and smiled, then sat down, brushing imaginary crumbs off her skirt. There was a book beside her which she picked up.

'What are you reading?'

She mentioned a novel by Meredith which meant nothing to him. He watched her as if he might see in her face her reactions to the characters moving about on the page in front of her. No book could any longer exert even half enough pull to distract him from this pointless inquisition he was exercising upon himself. Lives of drama and passion, meaning, suffused with the idea that everything had a correspondence, was something weighty, important. Once he had felt like that too, but he had lost for good the vital sense of himself as a cog, as a man whose actions mattered or contributed anything to the sum. Looking aimlessly out of the window he suddenly felt overcome by an access of dreadful gaiety: he would go back to the war with a rose between his teeth and slaughter the Hun in droves. He would do well in the artillery (he was to ditch interpreting and be a proper gunner on his return) and get a Brigade. He would turn his back on God. If God wanted him, He could come and get him. He would lower himself once more to the level of ordinary mortals and not worry about killing Germans and the stains on his sanctity. He would learn to see them as the enemy and get rid of the inconvenient notion he had somehow cultivated of regarding them as individuals with families, wives and children, mothers, histories, roots.

The house came out of the dark at them; a figure in the doorway that could have been any one of two or three generations: his father, himself, his grandfather ... a ghost? He blinked and saw Alex waiting for them in the bad light. The car slowed to a halt, the chauffeur straightened his hat, got out, came round to open the door for them. Gerard was glad of the extra seconds; to be here was joy, yes. Why then the odd feeling he had had as they came up the drive of disappointment, abandonment almost, as if winter was here to stay?

'You made it!' Alex came down the steps two at a time. He took Alice's hands and kissed her, looking into her face. 'Are you well?'

'Very.' She put a hand on his shoulder and pressed down quite hard. 'Here's Gerard,' she said, hoping he would link gesture and remark as she had intended. To have been all day with Gerard was to be very conscious that things were not right with him. He spent so much time not even attempting to pick his book out of his lap, but just looking out of the window and sometimes smiling to himself as he had been doing after lunch; only they were not the kind of smiles that suggested happiness or serenity or even a joke. He had looked wry, rueful, the way he might if someone who knew him well had been teasing him too hard. Occasionally the colour had come and gone in his face as if he had embarrassed himself in his secret thoughts.

'G. Hallo.' Alex put his arm round Gerard's shoulder,

letting Alice go into the house. He wanted a moment to say something like thank God you're back in one piece, or I've missed you and it's not the same without you here, thank God you're solid and real and I've had a dream of your death and tell me it's wrong, but he couldn't find the words and it seemed a moment in which (as it had been in Grosvenor Street) it was required of him to be as ordinary as possible, or were all opportunities lost because of that kind of misapprehension?

'Nice of you to wait in the cold,' Gerard was saying, 'but really you shouldn't have bothered.'

'How's the leg?'

'Oh, all right. It walks well enough.'

Gerard stopped just inside the door, forgetting Alex. The otherness he had feared in London had taken possession of him at once. He looked at the rows of portraits and wondered at the connection between those august and rather good-looking people and himself. They all looked so sure of themselves, so certain in their life's work, so pleased with the alliances they had made, the money they had brought with them, the wars fought and won. Objects of awe, icons, none of the joins showing, no sign of the struggle coming through: the children lost in infancy, the reverses in campaigns, the debts. Putting on a good face, literally.

'I'll go and find aunt and uncle.' At a loss, Alex moved away, looking towards Alice for a sign, but she had gone to the fire still in her fur and was warming her hands.

'No need.' They were coming out of the saloon, stately and upholstered.

'Good to be home, is it?' asked his father.

'Oh, yes . . .' *Let go*, something said to him, *accept. There is so little that is any good, so few things that can be called innocent or complete*, and he looked about the enormous room and at his family and knew that he had come right back into himself, as a mountaineer might descend from the excitement and uncertainties of the heights to the cabin in the valley, glad of respite, of time to give thanks for the smallest things.

Alice was speaking to his mother, who had embraced her. His father went to the fire, rambling and grumbling. Gerard saw Alex laugh at something behind his hand. Just for once he would believe in it all, just for once. And he knew then, in that single moment of trust and unquestioning, love of the proper kind, that neither sought nor asked more than was given, and, believing, was complete.

CHAPTER
TWENTY-THREE

'The trouble with human nature,' wrote Gerard, sitting in the library the next morning after a late breakfast, 'is not its propensity for sin, but its tendency to flux.' He put down his pen and got up. What he had written seemed clever and pointless. It was the difficulty in believing in any thing, any stand, for more than five minutes at a time.

He had slept badly. Mahoney, with all the insistence of an importunate actor, had made another appearance last night, playing Edmund this time. It was all he could remember. What had been said or done was beyond his grasp, but he had woken unsettled, full of all his usual fears, misgivings and doubts, compounded by a sense of loss he couldn't at first fathom. He paced about the room a bit, distracting himself by reading the titles of the books, tapping chair seats to shock the worm, running his fingers (as his mother really ought to do) over the top of Cicero's head and finding, horrors, dust, dust, dust ... Reassurance. He looked out of the window across the frozen park, past the skeletons of the trees, the huddled, motionless cattle. And why did he want reassurance? This was not comfortable, he wanted to stop, but the little voice had got up a head of steam again; he wanted reassurance because he wanted to know how much longer he was to live in order to adjust the balance of his life accordingly. If he was to die, he would like to settle up his accounts, make things good with people who mattered, like Alice, so that he could present his papers to the recording angel with a clear conscience; this was all very well, commendable in its way, but the really shocking thing was to discover that if he was not to die immediately, he wished very much indeed to be quite brutal with Alice, as if he had gone nowhere since last summer, was not only unchanged but worse than he had been before. Wickedness was not muddling in the dark, wickedness was blinding light, glare almost, knowing there was a choice.

He would like to get Edmund by the scruff of the neck and say, 'Look here, what have you been up to with my wife, *old fellow*?' Then he would hit him, rough him up a bit, spoil that so-handsome face, stop him ruining anyone else's life. The more he thought about his own fist making contact with Edmund's jaw, the more disgusted and the more angry he became both with Edmund and himself. It was almost like sexual excitement, this dark, perverted rage, this longing to make himself felt. Perhaps that was the essence of the sexual act, not the longing to feel someone else, breasts and thighs and the curve of a neck or a back, but to feel that in contact with skin and hair and bone one was coming up against oneself, seeing oneself, being returned to oneself. It was all very confusing, very frustrating . . .

'Gerard?'

'What the – ?'

'Were you busy?' Alex looked round the room as if searching for evidence, then back at Gerard. 'You'd rather be alone, obviously.'

He began to go back round the door.

'No, don't go. Stay, please.' Gerard pressed the back of his hand against his eyes. 'Just give me a minute.'

He turned away, trying to compose himself. We carry hell about with us, he thought. This is hell, here and now, these sordid darknesses, these hatreds. The treadmill, the pit, St Teresa's hole in a burning wall are child's play compared with this. There is no need for anything after death when we can do it so efficiently for

240

ourselves. All at once he was possessed by a great longing for peace, for nothingness, an end to it.

'Gerard?'

'Yes.' He turned to face Alex. 'I'm sorry.' He tried to
speak briskly, as if he had been interrupted in the middle
of something that didn't matter.

'I wish there was something I could do.' Alex watched
and waited, not knowing for sure whether he was
wanted or not. Gerard was making him afraid.

'Stay with me,' Gerard said. 'Let's sit down and talk.
I need to hear about ordinary life again, school, what
you've been doing. I've been too much on the other side,
I think.'

'The other side? What do you mean?'

'Irregularities,' Gerard replied evasively. He sat down
like an old man in an armchair opposite Alex. 'We can all
have too much excitement, you know.'

'I wish . . . ' Alex took a breath. 'You're like my brother.
Can't you tell me what's wrong?' He blushed, hating
these awkwardnesses, these ridiculous stumblings,
longing for a way of saying what he felt. But they were
not a family who said such things to each other. He
began to babble about school.

Gerard pretended to listen. He was touched to the
heart by what he had heard and seen, but he had to be
careful, could not let himself be undammed by the boy's
obvious, if ill-expressed, sympathy. He realized from the
enormous longing that welled up inside him as Alex
spoke that he had a need for confession, but he knew
also that the person in question would have to be both
strong and neutral to him, as a good priest would be, or
as Mahoney might have been. He needed absolution too,
needed the sickness drawn out of him in a way no boy
could do, or should be asked to do. Alex was tempting
but impossible, although he would like to make an act
towards him, an act of love, a gesture that would in
some way counter the desolation that had invaded him,
a mark of appreciation, something symbolic but unmis-

takable that Alex could not doubt when it was all over.

He had reached bottom; nothing could be changed, the past remained unaltered whatever he did now, and the future? Acts of grace, he thought, a pattern reforming, one or two things left to him that might set his own world back on its axis. It was all he could do, a private re-dedication but which had to be performed with the taste of wormwood in the mouth, in the full knowledge of that choice he had regarded earlier.

He could ruin Alex's life by telling him that the child that might supplant him was a bastard or at least a creature whose parentage was in doubt; he could ruin Alice's life by threatening her with divorce and spoil his parents' dotage with law-suits and uncertainties, not to mention the decent upright pair at Kincraig; or he could begin again, change the course of things, with the smallest of acts of love.

'Come,' he said, interrupting. 'There's something we have to do.'

'Where are we going?' Alex put his legs, which had been hanging over the side of the chair, back on the floor. For some reason he felt the utmost reluctance to follow Gerard, a physical thing almost, as if some unseen but monumental force were pressing his spine to the back of the chair. With horror he recognized it: the dread and fear, the bound, unworking limbs.

'Just to the gun room.' Gerard had his back to him and his hands in his pockets. 'Come on.' He looked round quickly and then went to the door. Nothing, it seemed, was without pain. He knows, Gerard thought. It is as I suspected. He knows, and he has always known. My poor Alex. He bowed his head and waited for the sound of footsteps.

Slowly and in silence they made their way across the hall, through the baize door, down the long, cold passage beyond. They met nobody. It was as if the house had cleared a way for them or, in some way, the act were being performed in a different dimension; the dimension

242

in which an eighteenth-century Miss Baillie occasionally performed her sad little drama of elopement: footsteps on the stairs late at night, the swing door flapping to and fro, the sound of horses' hooves outside, and always winter.

Gerard went in first and switched on the light. The room was cold and smelt unpleasantly of the insides of rubber boots. The warmed, cordite, linseed smell of the summer had gone, the whiff of use and care. His gun cases lay on the bench in a corner under the window.

'I'm not coming back,' he said, facing Alex, looking into the face blind with sadness that was so like his own.

'I know.' Two words to end a life; that nothing would ever in any way be the same again. A rite of passage in a house that had sent so many sons away.

'I want you to have my guns.'

It was the act complete, like the power going out of him. 'Take care of them, won't you?' Turning away, he felt the presences in the house jostling him, tasted history in his tongue, was at once all of them: the First Lord with his horse moving under him, the Second writing the speech that would put him in the Tower, and the countless actions, greatnesses, betrayals, loves, that had come between. He was centuries old, yet made new again; himself and yet not himself.

'You knew, didn't you?' Gerard turned again and put a hand on Alex's shoulder, a shoulder so rigid and still it could have been carved from marble.

'In the summer ... I dreamed about you,' Alex said, looking up with wet eyes, feeling the hand on his shoulder, the press of the ring on the little finger. Good hand, strong hand, capable hand. All wasted. Out of a pure effort of will he brought up his own and placed it on top of Gerard's. The brothers' clasp which said everything.

'Don't go,' he said. 'Please don't go.'

'I must.' Gerard pulled his hand away very slowly and gently. 'I am obliged to.'

*

Before tea-time, and knowing that she would probably be asleep, Gerard went into Alice's room. The curtains were not drawn but it was rather dark. Outside, it was snowing again in a serious way, very silent, very bleak. He looked out of the window across the deserted lawns at the great blinded shapes of the yew trees, remembering the summer, remembering what had been done in this room. The sound of Alice weeping. Sounds. Was it sounds or smells that brought the past back? Mahoney's drowning voice, the first enfilade, the trench outside the château in Flanders raked with shot. The sound the child might make at birth, ushering the future in. Alice breathing.

'Why are you here?'

He turned from the window towards her voice and went to sit on her bed.

'To see you.'

'Oh.' She sat up slightly, awkwardly, not knowing how to behave to him or what he wanted of her.

'Does it move?' he asked, putting his hand on the part of the eiderdown that covered her stomach.

'Not yet.' She seemed rather surprised at the question. 'I wonder sometimes if it's there at all.'

'Except that you feel rather ill, don't you?' He took his hand from her middle and touched her face, pressing his fingers to the skin where it covered the jaw and then downwards to the neck. He could feel her swallowing.

'Sometimes, yes. Less and less often, in fact.' She took his wrist and pulled it to her mouth, running her lips along the back of his hand.

'I love you,' she said, knowing it was the greatest risk she had ever taken in her life.

'I know.' He put his head on her breast, felt her arms coming round him, her hands on his back.

After a minute, he sat up, taking both her hands in his.

'I've had a telegram,' he said, watching her. 'New Year's Day.'

'Oh no . . .' She wiped the corner of one eye.

244

'You knew it would be soon.'

'I suppose so.' In spite of herself, more tears. 'Gerard, I'm –'

'No. Don't.' He put a hand either side of her sad face and kissed her. 'Love me for nine days,' he said, 'with all your heart. Then there will be nothing left for me to want.'

CHAPTER TWENTY-FOUR

He stood on deck a long time watching England going away from him. Alice had come south with him the day before, New Year's Day, and then as far as Folkestone that morning. He had tried to persuade her out of it, knowing only too well the erratic nature of the train services to the coast.

The journey had begun happily enough and the train, a Pullman, had galloped into the chalk downlands and then stopped, inexplicably, for four hours, three miles from the town. At first the extra time seemed a bonus, and they managed a good lunch in the dining-car, but then, afterwards, the time began to hang and hang. They both tried to read but every now and again one or other of them would look up and attempt a smile, as if to say: This is quite ordinary. We are on a train which has stopped. Soon we shall begin again and reach the station and take a cab to the water's edge; it is nothing out of the way.

There are only a limited number of times you can say goodbye, Gerard thought, and certain things which must, for some reason, always be said at the final moment; as if partings only struck a nerve at the moment the kiss was over, the last pressure of a hand in a hand, the long, reluctant second in which one bent down for a valise and turned away.

She had been very brave, the only indication of her despair in the fierce way she had hugged him, not appearing to notice that her hat had fallen off. 'Always know . . .' she had said, as he bent to retrieve the hat and put it on her head again.

'Yes.' He put a hand under her chin, for a last, impossible look. 'Yes.' He bent and picked up his things. '*Au revoir*.'

'*Au rev*–' She made little jerky waves at him with her hand, as if to say, go quickly, please. No more of this.

At the top of the ramp, he turned to look down for her face in the crowd. She was there but she did not wave, as if in some way unable to.

It grew dark out at sea and very cold. Men in the bows and stern had been told to watch for submarines. Gerard listened to the noise of the engines and leant over the rail; the wake was white and rushing in the gloom. There was spray on his face and hands, wind in his ears. He put his hand in his pocket and felt the cigarette case and lighter, his rosary. In the other was a prayer book and a photograph of Alice in a leather folder with his name on it. So few things and yet all he needed. He turned and went inside. An officer in the artillery, who had swopped his interpreter's armband for command of a battery, returning to work near Ypres.

A week later he was killed near Zillebeke going between a couple of his positions. He heard the shell coming and flung himself off Hitchy Koo, knowing it was meant for him and hoping thereby, in an illogical way, to save the animal. He may have put up a hand in that first instant, as if warding off a blow.

Both horse and man were scattered in terrible fragments, leaving pitifully little to retrieve – a bunch of keys, the little, painted photograph of his wife in its leather folder, and the prayer book.

The day before had been a Sunday and Gerard had persuaded the priest, Father Brown, to come over and say mass in one of his gun pits. '. . . And it amused me', he had written to Alice on the morning of the day he was to die, 'to make the place churchy. We made an altar out of

247

the signallers' basket fixed across the trail of a gun, with two siege lamps and candlesticks! I teased him about it being the first time he had said mass on a loaded gun...'

He was buried, as he had asked to be, in the nearest Catholic cemetery, which happened to be at Zillebeke, laid to rest in the jagged shadow of the half-ruined church. A cross with a durable inscription was placed on his grave and the authorities notified. Later battles would destroy both his grave and the church under whose protection he rested, enabling his shattered remains to mingle with the thousands and tens of thousands of others who lay in that smashed and ghost-ridden salient.

Father Brown wrote a last letter to Alice: 'As far as his spiritual welfare is concerned, I have not the least fear, because he was indeed a good soul. I buried him last night, and the officers that could be spared came to the burial. This morning I arranged the grave and put some flowers on it, encircled with a little crown, for indeed he has well merited his crown, only a more glorious one.'

Epilogue 1920

'Go on,' Edmund said, seeing her hesitate, but avoiding her eyes. 'You go ahead.'

He watched her move forwards, skirting the shell craters, towards an undistinguished heap of stones that had once, so the kind woman in the hostel at Zonnebeke told them, been the church, the focal point of the village, here at Zillebeke. Wild flowers and all sorts of grasses grew out of the pits and dents in the battered earth. He watched a butterfly hover about a flower like an abandoned scrap of paper. Somewhere there were bees and crickets. The sun was very hot on his face. Gerard's death seemed long ago, in the ancient beginnings of the war. Perhaps he had been lucky, in a way.

Edmund put a hand over his eyes, shading the glare, watching his wife's back as she made her way towards what she had been told was the spot. He couldn't think what she would make of it. There had been so many deaths here. The whole place was a graveyard. Yet she had insisted on coming, perhaps to mourn the child too, the child born two months early in the Blue Room at Kildour, a little boy who had died without opening his eyes. Lungs, the doctor said. Some medical term he could not now remember.

Edmund sighed, and turned away.

Francesca Duranti

The House on Moon Lake

'An utterly original book and quite the most enjoyable I have read in a long time'

Listener

'It is not until the terrifying climax that we realise that Francesca Duranti's graceful and literary prize-winning novel is really a horror story of the kind Henry James might have thought of. I found it thoroughly scary'

Nina Bawden

'It is elegant and mysterious – a delicious book. It gave me great pleasure, and I think it is the finest European novel I have read this year'

Mary Flanagan

'*The House on Moon Lake* has won the Bagutta Prize, the Martina Franca Prize and the City of Milan Prize. I wish there were a prize we too could give it'

Independent

Flamingo

Lee Langley

Changes of Address

In CHANGES OF ADDRESS Lee Langley paints a fresh and intriguing portrait of India in the 1940s. She evokes the sights, sounds, smells of the bazaars, the bleached beauty of the landscape, the British in India, the outbursts of violence as the country struggled towards independence. Events are seen both through the eyes of the solitary child trying to keep her balance in the wake of her turbulent mother, and through the narrative of the adult she becomes, trying to understand the woman whose effect on her life was so devastating.

'Miss Langley has a fine comic touch, a vivid sense of place and tells her story with subtlety and spirit.' *Daily Telegraph*

Flamingo

Lewis Nkosi

Mating Birds

From his prison cell, where he awaits death by hanging, the young African recalls the events that brought him there: his upbringing and the advice given him by his Zulu father, his time at University where political dissension surrounded him, and finally his overpowering obsession with the 'English girl' he meets under the intense blazing sun of a racially segregated beach.

'Possibly the finest novel by a South African, black or white . . . passionate and perfectly controlled.'

Washington Post

'Here is an awesome passion handled by a writer who has the depth of feeling, the authority of experience and the skill to sustain it . . . Nkosi writes unforgettably.'

Nadine Gordimer

Flamingo

Eva Figes

The Seven Ages

'A bravely original book, a panorama of one thousand years of our history through a woman's eyes as uncannily moving as the birth and deaths that stud her poetic pages.
David Hughes, *Mail on Sunday*

'Bold and idiosyncratic . . . . written with evident passion.'
Penelope Lively, *Sunday Telegraph*

'Virginia Woolf would have so welcomed this book, representing as it does the direction she hoped literature would take. Here, at last, palpable, embodied, is that accumulation of centuries of unrecorded lives that she wished for. I read many of its pages in a daze of wonder.'
Tillie Olsen

Flamingo

Penelope Fitzgerald

Innocence

'I know of no one who expresses so deftly and entertainingly the way in which life seldom turns out as expected. A wonderful book.'　　John Jolliffe, *Spectator Books of the Year*

'This is by far the fullest and richest of Penelope Fitzgerald's novels, and also the most ambitious. Her writing, as ever, has a natural authority, is very funny, warm and gently ironic, and full of tenderness towards human beings and their bravery in living.'

Anne Duchene, *Times Literary Supplement*

'*Innocence* wields a curious fascination, replete with the sense of sleepy, slightly anxious fatalism that pervades much of the Italian cinema of the period. Its magic, and its message, are as oblique and inconclusive as the lives of its characters, but both have a lingering power, refreshingly fictive, deliciously un-English.'　　Jan Dalley, *Literary Review*

Flamingo

Flamingo

Flamingo is a quality imprint publishing both fiction and non-fiction. Below are some recent titles.

Fiction

- ☐ The Thirteenth House *Adam Zameenzad* £3.95
- ☐ Bright Lights, Big City *Jay McInerney* £2.95
- ☐ Human Voices *Penelope Fitzgerald* £3.95
- ☐ Offshore *Penelope Fitzgerald* £3.95
- ☐ Nelly's Vision *Eva Figes* £3.95
- ☐ The Joy's of Motherhood *Buchi Emecheta* £3.95
- ☐ Home Thoughts *Tim Parks* £3.95
- ☐ Sex and Sunsets *Tim Sandlin* £3.95

Non-fiction

- ☐ The Tao of Physics *Fritjof Capra* £4.95
- ☐ The Turning Point *Fritjof Capra* £5.95
- ☐ The First Three Minutes *Steven Weinberg* £3.95
- ☐ The Dancing Wu Li Masters *Gary Zukav* £3.50
- ☐ Before the Oil Ran Out *Ian Jack* £3.95
- ☐ Indian Country *Peter Matthiessen* £3.95
- ☐ Nine-Headed Dragon River *Peter Matthiessen* £3.95
- ☐ Chinese Characters *Sarah Lloyd* £3.95
- ☐ A Journey in Ladakh *Andrew Harvey* £3.95

You can buy Flamingo paperbacks at your local bookshop or newsagent. Or you can order them from Fontana Paperbacks, Cash Sales Department, Box 29, Douglas, Isle of Man. Please send a cheque, postal or money order (not currency) worth the purchase price plus 22p per book (or plus 22p per book if outside the UK).

NAME (Block letters) _____

ADDRESS_____

_____

_____